THE CARPET AT CANNES

by Duane Byrge

A Murder at the Movies Mystery

In Memory of
Bob Osborne

“A film festival is no place for a film critic.”

Vernon Young

Chapter 1

Day 1

The half-moon was smudgy white but ripening nicely for its star entrance at the Cannes Film Festival. Like a diva, it would not make its full appearance until the closing weekend of the twelve-day festival when it would bestow its gaze on the festival's glamorous awards ceremony. The fact that it was the Cannes Film Festival might make one think the burgeoning moon was some sort of special-effects rendition.

Ryan Hackbart savored the spectacle because the moon, the sea, the breeze, and a ticket to *The Ice Princess* party were all his. A sexy publicist from DeSimio & Associates had offered him $300 for his party ticket and when he declined she upped the ante to an X-rated proposition. Everyone was interested in the party. It had become a cause célèbre, a hot ticket.

Across the barricades, zooms of light flickered as paparazzi swarmed, hoping to get a walk-bite or photo of someone famous. There was talk that Robert Downey, Jr. would be attending, since he would be appearing at the closing night ceremonies for a festival tribute to director Gus Van Sant.

Ryan had just arrived for the Cannes Film Festival, after enduring a thirteen-hour trek from Los Angeles. He was the head film critic for The Hollywood New Times, the top Hollywood trade paper for the movie industry. Ryan stood just over six feet tall with wavy, light brown hair and a physique toned by daily afternoon runs at the UCLA track and regular Tae Kwon Do workouts at a dojo on Sunset, where he was a third-degree black belt. He dressed well but erratically, and when he won special praise for his "costume design" as he called it, he took it as an indicator he lacked style at other times.

Although it was Ryan's seventh trip to the festival, it still always overwhelmed him that he was at the celebrated Cannes Film Festival, where the likes of Cary Grant, Alfred Hitchcock, Clint Eastwood, Sophia Loren, George Lucas, Orson Welles and many of his adulthood idols had graced the red carpet. Despite his modesty, Ryan knew he belonged: his reviews set the tone and held the future for many of the films that would debut here at Cannes. The whole movie-world would be reading.

Fans of his droll and often acidic reviews were startled when they met him in person. He didn't seem like a celebrity or even one to solicit attention. His casual congeniality made him popular and it was a component of his survival as head film critic in an industry where psycho behavior was tolerated for those with box-office hits.

So, what was he doing standing in a herd for a late-night party? He had the "Cannes Disease," the contagious desperation that you had to be doing something every minute; if not, you were missing something somewhere, most likely at the event you'd heard about but decided not to go to. The constant fear was that the missed event would turn out to be the highlight of the festival. Ryan had lost his train of thought when he heard a familiar voice call his name.

"Hackbart."

Ryan turned around to spot Dennis Barlowe, his buddy from his early *Hollywood New Times* days. Barlowe was an older guy with flowing gray hair and the requisite retro-Keds tennis shoes. He was a terminal hippie whose calendar had stopped at 1969. To his credit, Ryan thought, Barlowe never wore his hair in a pony-tail, or even worse, a man-bun.

Barlowe had fallen on hard times since being laid off from an entertainment business publication. Ryan knew him from a short stint Barlowe had spent with The Hollywood New Times a couple years back. They had bonded in the newsroom with similar dark senses of humor, love of sports, and skepticism about the competence of their new publisher, Orson W. Woolsey. Barlowe now cranked out press kits for independent producers and wrote for an entertainment business blog, which was a unique hybrid of techie news and investigative stories; it often pissed off the movie and music industry, mainly because his stories were dead-on. Barlowe was respected for his skills and connections, and other journalists read his posts to get story leads. He maintained another popular blog called SinSpin, but under a pseudonym.

"So, what's going on with you?" Barlowe asked. "I just got in from Amsterdam yesterday, and the first thing I see on my room TV is a story about your scathing review of the opening night film."

"What can I tell you? I'm an exciting guy," Ryan deadpanned

"That *Ice Princess* actress was hot," Barlowe said. "I've got some of her early videos from this guy I know in Amsterdam."

"Ingrid Bjorge?"

"Yeah, they're off-the-hook sexy. I think she was about fifteen or so when she made them."

"Most actresses have something like that in their past," Ryan said.

"She did a lot of them. They all had 'blonde' in the title. *Blonde Bombshell, Blonde Girl, Ice Blonde, Blonde Desire, Wet Blonde, Blonde Booty, Arctic Blonde, Blonde-age,"* Barlowe added.

"You and your blonde fetish," Ryan said.

"I hope they have some more hot Scandinavian women here tonight," Barlowe added.

"Usually the worst movies have the best parties, so this one could be right up there," Ryan said.

"You missed a good one at the Hotel du Cap last night. Some Russian billionaire puked all over that twit from Lives of the Super Rich," Barlowe said.

"Sounds like a lot of laughs."

The line stalled. Ryan seethed: it was all so typical of the French. Year after year at Cannes, they never got it right. Ryan had taken to calling it, The French Factor, or "Le Factor Francaise," the inability of the French to handle any organizational challenge in a logical or efficient manner. His sour attitude and disgust with the French clued Ryan to the fact that he was jet-lagged and out of sorts. He usually applauded the French for their taste, diet and less-frenzied lifestyle.

He took more deep breaths and stared out over the beach, focusing on the light tower sparkling at the end of the old port.

Just when Ryan had decided to throw in the towel and go back to the hotel to catch up on sleep, the crowd finally inched forward. The great tent erection that loomed before him was said to have cost more than $2 million, exceeding even the $1 million that had been spent celebrating the Bruce Willis sci-fi monstrosity *The Fifth Element* back in 1997. That lavish affair was a dud even with Neneh Cherry performing and Jean-Paul Gaultier organizing a fashion show.

The entrance to *The Ice Princess* bash was fronted by a wild ice-sculpture in a tangle of arms, legs, butts and breasts. The men all had enormous appendages and god-like dimensions, while the women boasted rippling curves and pornographic postures. They reminded Ryan of the Vigeland erotic sculpture garden in Oslo. Surrounding the frozen orgy figures were real-life Vikings, tall and muscular blonde men in azure capes and silver Viking helmets.

Barlowe snapped a flurry of pictures on his iPhone, angling toward a gorgeous red-haired woman. He gestured to Ryan, "Get over here. I'll get your picture with this beautiful actress." The woman stepped back, but Barlowe crowded in on her. He pushed Ryan into position next to the woman and snapped the photo.

"Sorry about this," Ryan told the red-head.

"I understand you are a famous Hollywood writer," she said. "I am excited to have a selfie with you."

"Thanks."

"Do you get to meet lots of celebrities?"

"It's sort of an occupational hazard," Ryan responded.

"What?"

Barlowe pulled him away. "You're a celeb, man. You've got to cash in on this. Lighten up, dude. Work it. These babes are dying to get laid by a power-player like you."

"That's not my style."

"You are so straight-arrow, it's downright unprofessional for a film critic," Barlowe joked. "You're probably the only guy in show business who doesn't have to worry about a sexual harassment suit," he added. "I could Snapchat you here, cavorting with all these gorgeous women."

"Give me a break."

"You're such a Luddite."

"I know. I might need your help again with my laptop," Ryan said.

"I thought we straightened all that out at Sundance."

"I know, but there's always some technological weirdness here at Cannes. Our Wi-Fi is all messed up at the hotel."

They squeezed past the guards and entered the tent. The scene inside the tent was a demented Valhalla: laser lights knifed through the revelry, drums thundered, and a brass horn wailed pagan. The flooring glimmered in snowy white, and the lavishly set tables, with silver goblets and metal bowls, were centered by blue candles, their flames leaping wildly over the wax. Bordered with hot springs, the main stomping area was truly a Viking heaven, or at least, Valhalla as designed by a liquor distributor.

A ten-foot iced sculpture of a Viking warrior with a large erect penis drew a crowd. The organ was designed as a tap dispenser, with champagne flowing in a steady stream from the stiff appendage. Curious drinkers held their champagne glasses underneath the ice warrior's member, letting the golden elixir splash into their plastic glasses. "Get drunk and naked" was clearly the theme. The outer perimeters of the tent were ringed with burning fires, each manned by muscular Vikings with clubs and spears. Swirling mists of dry ice-foam sizzled up from a gurgling moat that surrounded an island of tables. All around, tribes of voluptuous blondes in lacy blue lingerie handed out shot glasses of liqueur. Barlowe grabbed one.

"Better watch it with that stuff," Ryan said.

"Why?"

"It's Aquavit. It's over 100 proof. It will knock you on your ass."

"Maybe just what I need to get some sleep," Barlowe said.

"You still got the insomnia thing?"

"Yeah, no matter where I am, or even if I'm jet-lagged, I always pop up at the crack of dawn and can't get back to sleep."

"You get in some writing then?"

"I wish," Barlowe said. "Usually, I just go for a walk on San Vicente. Before the morning joggers even."

Barlowe sipped the Scandinavian liqueur and shuddered. "This is awful. It tastes like turpentine." He shook the shot glass, letting drops of liquor fall, and pocketed it. "I've got a joke for you. If a

Harvey Wallbanger is a drink with vodka and orange juice that's topped off with Galliano, what's a Harvey Weinstein?"

"I give up," Ryan said.

"A Harvey Weinstein is vodka and orange juice topped off with Girl-iano," Barlowe said.

"Gimme a break. I'm jet-lagged."

"I've got more, but I'll save them for the end of the festival when your sense of humor is up to the quality of my material," Barlowe added. He glanced at the wine, "Wow, this is great Bordeaux." He handed Ryan a glass. "$100 a bottle at least. This guy Sevareid probably forked over at least $100 grand for the wine alone."

Ryan took a sip. "It is good, every bit as heady and robust as the Two-Buck Chuck I get at Trader Joe's," he said.

"You are such a peasant."

As usual, Barlowe had an eye for the festival freebies. He angled toward the premium bags on the dinner chairs. With their shiny azure glaze, they resembled Tiffany bags. Barlowe grabbed one and pulled back the silver strings on top, opening it. It was loaded: Saint Laurent perfume, a six-ounce bottle of Aquavit, chocolate covered strawberries, and an azure Hermes silk scarf like the one Ingrid Bjorge had worn in the *Ice Princess*.

There was also an expensive timepiece. A gold-plated Rolex watch was mounted on a dazzling glass sculpture. What did Rolex run, twelve grand? The timepiece holder had *The Ice Princess* crest embossed on it. Ryan picked it up and turned it over: the logo for Orrefors, Scandinavia's vaunted glassware company, was etched on the bottom. Evidently, the movie's producer, Gunnar Sevareid, had put more money into the party favors than the movie. About

$20,000 a bag, Ryan calculated. There were roughly 250 guests at the party. About $5 million for the goody bags? This guy caught on fast: Hollywood would be impressed.

"This is the best SWAG ever," Barlowe said. He slid to another table, glanced, and lifted another bag. A security guard appeared out of nowhere:

"One bag only, please, monsieur."

"I'm with BGK," Barlowe said. "I've got to get this to Gunnar Sevareid for a friend of his."

"I'm sorry, monsieur, only one bag. I cannot let you take it."

Barlowe shrugged and returned the bag to its table setting. "Damn, I could have sold that on eBay," he told Ryan. "If it was like the old-days in the '90s, Susanne would have filched one for me, but BGK has gone corporate. How about if I give you $5,000 for your bag?" Barlowe offered.

"No, thanks. I'm going to give it to my niece."

"You mean your niece who really is your niece? The one back in Minnesota?" Barlowe noted.

"Wisconsin," Ryan corrected.

"Whatever. But if you come to your senses and want some quick cash, you can meet me at the Arab Bank anytime."

Ryan reconsidered Barlowe's offer. A quick $5,000 would come in handy. He gazed toward a flock of blonde women beckoning from artificial ice floats in the port. Brave the waters and swim to them –

Scandinavian sirens. They drew the attention of a pack of stubby Armani-men, Sammy Glicks from Planet 90212.

Someone tapped him on his back. "I believe I know you," she said. The woman wore over-size glasses, and her cheeks sparkled with blue glitter. "Who are you, exactly, and where have I seen you?"

"I'm exactly Ryan Hackbart, and you have seen me at Jumbo's Clown Room in Hollywood." The woman gaped. "I was being facetious. I write for *The Hollywood New Times*," Ryan said.

"That's right. You're the guy who trashed the opening night movie. The one with the beautiful blonde actress," she asserted. "What was her name again?"

"Ingrid Bjorge," Ryan answered.

"Wasn't she some sort of pop star in Norway?"

"That was Bjork who was the pop star. She was Icelandic, not Norwegian," Ryan said. "She was the star of a movie here called *Dancer in the Dark*. It won the Palme d'Or in 2000."

The woman was not interested in ancient movie history. "Anyway, she's got the look, this Ingrid," whoever-she-was said.

Ryan angled toward Barlowe who was talking to a guy with the "cool filmmaker" costume: shades, stubble, baseball cap, t-shirt with the film logo and a blue *Ice Princess* scarf draped around his shoulders.

Ryan approached. Barlowe pocketed his iPhone and turned to Ryan. "So, dude, you wanna see if we can check out some women?" he asked in his best mock-California tone.

"If you want to check out women, you don't have to leave," the baseball-cap said. "You look like you could use a woman," he said to Ryan.

"I've had a crazy couple of days," Ryan said.

"You and me both," the cap said. "What do you do?"

"I'm a journalist."

"Which site?"

"*The Hollywood New Times*, but we put out a daily here too."

The baseball-cap director stood back and squinted at Ryan. He tried to focus his bloodshot eyes. "You're not Ryan somebody or other."

"Yeah, Ryan Hackbart."

The director reached back and smashed Ryan with a karate punch, driving his fist straight into his nose. Ryan stumbled backward, splashing into a hot tub. He swallowed a big chug of the chlorinated stuff, ramming his arm against the side of the tub. He was chest deep in the gurgling hot water. Mr. Baseball-Cap towered over him.

"I read your idiotic review, you ignorant son of a bitch. You douche-bag moron," the guy yelled at Ryan. He pulled a whip from one of the nearby Vikings. Snapped it toward Ryan, barely missing.

"Consider this a warning."

Two Viking security guards hurried toward them. They grabbed the baseball-cap guy, pinning his arms behind him. They dragged him away. The partygoers moved in. They crowded closer, straining to see what was going on.

Ryan hoisted himself out of the water. Barlowe pulled Ryan away. "That's Jason Pinelli," Barlowe said. "He's the guy who directed *The Ice Princess*.

"Oh shit."

"I tried to get you out of there, man," Barlowe said.

The remaining Vikings formed a wedge around Ryan and Barlowe. Ryan brushed his face. There was blood on his hands. He watched as Pinelli was dragged off through the crowd. All around, people crowded in. A barrage of cell phones pointed at Ryan, snapping away.

"Come this way," one of the Vikings said to Ryan. Just what he needed: media coverage of his being hauled out of a festival event, this time surrounded by hulks in Viking gear.

Barlowe shielded him from drunken partygoers, and Ryan ducked behind the big Viking warriors. The Vikings led the two journalists out a side exit, ushering them to the water's edge. A police boat waited. It was an inboard, its motor chugging and a bright blue light glowing on its bow.

Back behind, the band roared: horns blared and drums beat in tribal rhythm. Ryan rubbed his upper lip with a linen napkin. Lots of blood. A security guard tossed a hand-towel at Ryan.

The engine kicked in, and the boat slid backward into the water. The inboard gurgled as the boat swirled out into the bay and looped to the east. Over to his left, Ryan could see the Palais all lit up still, and back much further behind, he glimpsed the old church tower high up on the Old Town hill. It was swathed in a salmon-colored glow.

"Here, you dropped this in the Jacuzzi," Barlowe said. He handed Ryan his laminated press pass. Then pulled out a tiny digital camera and pointed it at Ryan: "Say, 'swag'."

"With blood running down my nose," Ryan said.

"Don't worry. It makes you look dangerous. I can use it for my site. You were lucky those security guys came by. Pinelli knows how to use a whip."

"What do you mean?" "He's into S & M."

"Where do you get all this stuff?"

"Just good investigative journalism," Barlowe said with a smile. Barlowe pointed to a yacht in the bay where a raging orange flame consumed the deck. "That boat's on fire."

Ryan looked toward the burning vessel. "It's a Viking burial ship."

Barlowe pointed his iPhone at the burning boat. "You're saying this is a staged fire?"

"Yes. A Viking burial is a high honor," Ryan said. "But I wonder why they're staging a burial."

"Well, you did kill their film," Barlowe joked.

Ryan hunched down as the boat kicked up speed. He gazed toward the shore. The light-drenched Carlton Hotel glistened magically, like a Disney castle. In his dazed mind, Ryan thought for an instant he could see Cary Grant and Grace Kelly on the Carlton balcony. Yes, in that brief moment as the boat bounced along on the waves, Ryan envisioned Cary Grant and Grace Kelly in Alfred

Hitchcock's *To Catch a Thief*: He in his black tux and she in her light blue gown.

Chapter 2

Day 2

"I'll give you $15,000 to get me tickets to the premieres and the hot parties," Nick Steele said. The low-budget producer put his arm around Ryan's shoulder.

"Sorry, I can't do that," Ryan answered. "Come on. I've got the cash on my yacht."

"No, I really can't," Ryan said. "There's no magic way to get into the festival. There's the French, the festival. Believe me, I can use the cash, but even if I were Brad Pitt, I couldn't do it. No one has that kind of clout at Cannes."

"Think about it," Nick said. He hurried across the Croisette toward the Majestic Hotel, where producers in the 1980s signed deals on cocktail napkins. Ryan couldn't believe it: he had been at the festival less than a day, and he had not only been punched out but encountered one of the creepier film producers, Nick Steele. Not a good omen.

He slouched in the press line outside the Palais, the imposing main venue for the Cannes Film Festival. It perched on the sweet spot of the Riviera city's beautiful beach. Ryan was still jet-lagged and also stressed out from some technical problems he had with filing his film review of the festival's opening night film. The Wi-Fi in *The*

Hollywood New Times' hotel was erratic, and he had to switch rooms to a higher floor to get the service. What else was new? This was France, where things didn't always connect. And, Ryan had to admit, he was not much of a techie. It could have been worse if Barlowe had not noticed Ryan had lost his press pass in the water. He would miss a film. It would be disastrous if *The Hollywood Reporter* or *Variety* had published their reviews and Ryan didn't publish his.

Ryan braced himself in the swirling sea of film critics. Everyone was crammed together, jostling to get into the morning's press screening of *La Grande Chevre Rouge*, a French film by one of the ardent young followers of Luc Besson. More than a few of the critics seemed spawned by a Toulouse-Lautrec etching: bearded, frumpy, angular, fat, pasty, bizarre. The natter-chatter of the crits was at full pitch even at the morning hour, and Ryan felt sympathy for the guards. In the post-journalism world, Ryan was not only competing with legitimate movie critics but bloggers and even phony reviewers paid by public-relations firms who represented the movie-makers. Ryan was thankful he had his full-time position with *The Hollywood New Times*, although with new people coming in all the time – three different owners in the last seven years – he constantly had to prove himself. He had to defend himself over and over to new executives with law degrees and MBAs who knew little about journalism or even the entertainment industry: two months ago a millennial Harvard MBA had hovered over him with a stop-watch, tabulating how long it took him to write a movie review.

With a clap of their hands, the guards motioned the critics to begin to funnel through the gated corridor. Ryan slid into the group. The guards that morning seemed particularly nasty, examining everyone's press pass with special scrutiny. Ryan pulled out his festival identification card from his wallet. He had the Carte Blanc, the white card that entitled him to free-flowing access within the Palais. With his *Carte Blanc*, Ryan virtually had the entire run of the Cannes Film Festival.

He emerged from the stockyard-like gate. He paused for a second to savor the red carpet before him. It was the fabled walkway the stars and festival dignitaries had ascended the evening before in their gowns and tuxes for the world premiere of *The Ice Princess*.

Ryan had seen *The Ice Princess* in Los Angeles, along with his fellow critics from *The Hollywood Reporter* and *Variety*. The film's Norwegian producer, Gunnar Sevareid, had arranged for a special screening so the movie-industry trade reviews would run the same day as the movie premiered at Cannes. So far, Ryan hadn't had a chance to read his own review in the stacks of *The Hollywood New Times* that were ubiquitous in all the festival hot spots – hotel lobbies, theater entrances, lounges and, most auspiciously, the Palais. It was a guilty pleasure: savoring his words on the printed page. All critics did it; none admitted to it.

He scampered up the red stairs, looking down to his left at the tourists and festival groupies who, even at this early hour, jostled outside the gates with their cameras. They didn't realize this scruffy looking bunch heading up the stairs was merely the working press, which is one of the greatest oxymorons, especially when applied to film festivals. True, he was working: Ryan would write between two and three movie reviews a day, but, bottom line, he was getting paid to watch movies. As far as jobs went, he thought of his boyhood friends in Madison who had worked in the hog-kill at Oscar Mayer or the iron foundries. He appreciated that he had a pretty cushy gig. He also wondered how many of his critical pals would be missing from this festival, downsized in the new post-print age. Film critics were disappearing but bloggers and tweeters glutted cyberspace with their uninformed balderdash.

The theater was, as usual, packed, and that's why Ryan always preferred to sit high up in the balcony. The balcony was designed more like a basketball arena than a theater, so steep it almost felt like it tilted forward. He climbed as high as possible, securing an aisle seat with a clear view.

He always loved it when the loudspeaker announced in French that the movie was about to begin. On the big Lumiere screen, golden steps shimmered up through an azure blue sea. The uplifting image was musically enhanced by the romantic piano glissando of Carnival of the Animals. The trickling keys transported everyone into a blissful realm. Ryan loved it: it was the one moment, or twenty-nine seconds, when everything about Cannes was perfect, exciting, and serene.

The thirtieth second resounded with a harsh bang. Down below, French gendarmes sprinted from the side aisles. They tromped onto the stage. A commander barked out orders. The crowd hushed.

People swirled around in their seats. A team of police charged up the aisles. Ryan craned his neck to see what was going on downstairs. He was jolted by a thunderous clomping to his right. A regiment of National Police barged into the balcony. They lined the front railing and sprinted into position, two feet apart, along the walls. A unit assembled at each stairway. Ryan wondered what was going on: terrorists, a bomb scare? His mind raced: the blue-shirted police marched in precise cadence up the stairs. In their wake, everyone cowered. The cops were only a dozen or so rows below him. Everyone craned up, looking to see where they'd go. Up higher, closer.

The leader stopped abruptly at Ryan's aisle, slamming his foot down hard on the stair. He looked straight down at Ryan.

"Monsieur Hackbart," he said.

"Yes. I mean 'oui'," Ryan said.

"Come with me."

"What?"

"Please," he said, gesturing with his hands. "Please get up, monsieur. You must come with us."

"What's going on?" Ryan asked.

"Monsieur Hackbart. You must come. It is the law."

Ryan's stomach flopped. His body sagged. He tried to stand. He slipped back down. The gendarmes pulled him up. He bumped against the side of the burgundy chair. He felt weak, and he started to breathe out of his mouth. Everything was a blur. What was going on? Was this a dream? Some sort of crazy, jet-lagged nightmare? If it was a dream, it was too vivid. He could see too many faces.

The sunlight smashed him in the face as he was escorted out of the balcony tunnel. The police hurried him along. People darted in and out in front of him, snapping away on their cell phones. The cops maneuvered Ryan across the entrance-way, past the clear windows. Out beyond, he could see the shiny blue sea, a great day. They pulled him toward the escalator. Everywhere he looked, he saw gendarmes. They tugged him down to the next level. His knees buckled.

The police dragged him upright and formed a cordon out the door. Hundreds of police and military, local and national, lined the stairway. They stood in a tight, straight row, all the way down the red carpet. Beyond the barricades and walkways, a row of police cars. Their blue lights flashed against the morning sunlight.

The tourists pushed forward against the steel gates. Ryan could hear the newspaper-guy who was always out front of the Palais. His Gallic rasp pierced the pandemonium: "Murder. Murder. Star actress of *The Ice Princess* murdered. Voici, *Le Figaro.*"

"Murder?" Murder at the festival?" What did he have to do with a murder? *The Ice Princess'* star actress was murdered?

The police escorted Ryan straight to a police car and pushed him down into the backseat, not bothering to cushion his head. Two gendarmes sandwiched Ryan in the middle. His knees nearly jammed his chin. The driver swung the car forward. The four gendarmes in the car all stared straight ahead. The sirens wailed that awful blaring "hee-yaw, hee-yaw, hee-yaw" sound that Ryan hated: Jason Bourne speeding through Paris, all the cops in the world in pursuit.

They sped through the intersection, past the little park on the right. They turned right at the next intersection, barreling past La Pizza. The cavalcade swung up a steep side street by the train station. They stopped at a bleak, modern cement building with glass fronts and three flags, the headquarters of the French National Police.

The gendarmes yanked him from the police car. Surrounded him. They were all nearly six inches shorter than Ryan. He felt like the Hulk.

The French National Police headquarters peers down at the Cannes central train station. It is a cement bulk that hovers over a five-intersection traffic wheel. The gendarmes hurried Ryan through the reception, which resembled a cheap hotel lobby, Plexiglas and gray. They guided him down a narrow brown hallway. They propelled him into a room far down on the left. It was slightly larger than a bread box and painted gas-chamber green.

A man in his mid-fifties, wearing a dull black suit perched behind a table. He studied a copy of the day's *Hollywood New Times.* The page was opened to Ryan's review of *The Ice Princess*. He looked at Ryan. Then, he looked down at *The Hollywood New Times.*

Back up at Ryan. "We have some questions for you, Monsieur Hackbart," he said in a dull monotone.

"Please tell me what is going on?" Ryan's voice cracked and his mouth was dry. He pushed the words out. "What is all this about? Why was I dragged down here in a police motorcade?"

The man looked back up at him. "Monsieur Hackbart, my name is Inspector Geoffrey Montand. I wish to talk about your film critique."

"You brought me down here for a movie review?"

"In your criticism of *The Ice Princess* film you wrote, 'The dialogue is so bad one hopes the film's signature blue scarf would be stuffed down Ingrid Bjorge's throat so we wouldn't have to hear her utter another word."

"What do you mean 'stuffed down her throat'? I never wrote that."

"It is right here – 'one hopes the film's signature blue scarf would be stuffed down Ingrid Bjorge's throat.'"

"Can I see?"

The policeman shoved the review across the table. Ryan grabbed it. His hands quivered. He scanned the opening paragraph where he had talked about the beauty of Ingrid Bjorge and her screen presence. None of that was there.

"These are not my words," Ryan said. "Somebody has messed with my review."

"I do not understand."

"Someone hacked up my review."

"Again, I do not understand."

"Sometimes to fit things in, to get a review or story into the space a newspaper has for the day, the editors cut your writing. Usually they will take a line or two off the bottom of a paragraph, or condense things. This is appalling. It's a butcher job."

"A butcher job?" The man looked straight at Ryan, not blinking.

"Yes, it blatantly misrepresented my thoughts. I would never take such a vulgar, aggressive tone. It's so internet."

"Again, I do not understand."

"Someone on our staff cut up the review, so it would fit into the paper we have here at the festival," Ryan explained.

"'Cut up,' interesting choice of words," the policeman said.

"What's going on? Are you the review police?"

The man did not respond. Once again, he looked down at the review and then up at Ryan. "You say you don't know why you were brought here?"

"Yes, what is going on? I heard people yelling out 'murder' as I was dragged here."

"Monsieur, the actress Ingrid Bjorge was murdered in the early evening yesterday. We put the time around eighteen hundred hours, or six in the evening," the detective said.

"That's horrible, but I don't see how it involves me."

"Where were you last night?"

"I walked around, nowhere specifically. I was getting re-adjusted to the fact that I was in Cannes. It was my first day here. It was a very long trip from California."

"Did you go to the premiere of *The Ice Princess*?" the detective asked.

"No, I saw the film at an advance press screening in Los Angeles last week." The detective picked up the review.

"You wrote she should have the scarf stuffed down her throat."

In his nervous fog, it finally hit Ryan. "Are you trying to tell me that Ingrid Bjorge was killed by having the scarf stuffed down her throat?"

"That is the way, yes. It is the way she was killed," the detective said. "We found the scarf in her mouth." The detective folded his hands, confidently placing them on the table. "Just like you said to do in your film critique."

"I told you, someone changed my review. Besides, you don't think anyone would be so dumb as to write in a review about stuffing something down an actress's throat and then actually kill her that way?"

The inspector stared at Ryan. He didn't blink. Ryan could see he had missed a spot shaving on the left side of his chin. The pores on the inspector's face bunched around his lip. The eyebrows were thick and curly. The man resembled a fat Inspector Clouseau from *The Pink Panther*.

"It's all so *Basic Instinct*," Ryan finally said.

"Basic instinct?"

"The movie with Sharon Stone and Michael Douglas," Ryan said. "Sharon Stone was this sexy but psychopathic novelist who wrote a book about a murder, and then one was committed in exactly the same way. She convinced Michael Douglas, the alcoholic police detective that she couldn't have done it because no one would be stupid enough to write in advance about a crime they were going to commit."

"You are telling me you know an old movie with Sharon Stone where someone was killed like this?"

"That's misinterpreting what I just told you," Ryan said. "What I'm saying is this reminds me of that movie."

Ryan realized he was working his way into a hole: wasn't Sharon Stone guilty at the end of the movie? He remembered a final shot of a knife under the bed when she and Michael Douglas got it on for the last time. He realized he had better shut up, and that part about the drunken detective had not gone over well.

Maybe he was still jet-lagged, and he would wake up in his tiny French bed with the hard, pretzel-shaped pillow half under his neck and find the alarm was about to go off. He looked around. Everything was too clear and too detailed for a dream. No, he was not having a nightmare. He was in a nightmare. He was in a foreign country. He was in France, where they were not renowned for doing anything in a logical or sensible way, a country where Jean Valjean had been locked away in jail for stealing a loaf of bread. Or the man who was clamped inside an iron mask. Did they still use the guillotine?

The detective did not say anything for a long minute. Finally, he spoke. "Is there anyone you were with between the time of eighteen and twenty hundred hours, between six and eight in the evening?" he asked.

"No," Ryan answered. "I just ambled around and went to the Monoprix to buy bed-time snacks for the festival, but I forgot to buy sunscreen." He tried to control his breathing. "Then, I went to Le Petit Splendid for a couple of beers. But, it was pretty crowded with a bunch of Brits. I didn't see anyone I knew. Then I went to the Carlton."

"The Carlton? For what?"

"I had to use the restroom there," Ryan said. "The beer had set in."

"You went to the Carlton Hotel to use their toilet?"

"Yes, the Carlton is the only spot along the Croisette where there is a good public bathroom on the first floor. I sometimes use it as a pit stop."

The detective stared straight at Ryan, not responding. "I can prove it," Ryan said. "It's got a marble sink and real towels. They even pipe in classical music. I remember they were playing Chopin's Polonaise in A-flat Major when I was there. You can check it out."

"So you admit it, you were at the Carlton Hotel."

"Admit? Well, yes, I was at the Carlton."

"You were at the Carlton because you like the toilet there. Because it is marble in the wash basins, and they play Chopin."

"Yes, public bathrooms are, basically, non-existent at the festival," Ryan repeated. "You need festival passes to get into the hotels and the restaurants don't allow it." He knew that sounded idiotic, but it was the truth.

The inspector made a scribble and hoisted himself up from his chair. He left the room. Ryan's over-charged brain started to settle and he realized that Ingrid Bjorge must have been killed at the Carlton. He was in the building, and he'd given out the lame excuse he liked the first-floor public bathroom.

Ryan clicked on his cellphone. He saw a picture of himself on his site page: "Hollywood Critic Top Suspect in Cannes Murder." The whole world knew more about what was going on with him than Ryan knew himself. He was the star in an international media storm. Or was he the fall guy for a murder?

Time stopped. No one returned. Ryan's mind ran crazy. He always over-analyzed things and sometimes thought out everyday problems in terms of movie plots. His writer's brain warp-sped to the worst-case scenario: Was he a pawn and voodoo doll for anti-American sentiment? Was this a latter-day Dreyfuss Affair? Would the French march him to the guillotine? Slice his head off –"Mais, Il est un Americain. C'est bien dommage."

He sucked in deep breaths. He pushed his chair back. The metal scraped on the floor. He got up, stretched. Took three steps, and then he was at the wall. He peered around. Two-way mirrors? He didn't see anything that looked like one. But then, what did he know about new police technology? They must be watching him. He would sit down and remain cool, or, at least not move around. He couldn't look guilty, but wouldn't someone who was audacious and crazed enough to kill an actress before she went on the red carpet, wouldn't he be shrewd and cunning enough to know how to behave? Yes, so if he acted cool, maybe they would think that he was guilty? Ryan tried to stop conjecturing, over-analyzing something he didn't have a clue about, trying to connect lines to lines that weren't even there.

The door opened and the detective entered. Closed the door. He handed Ryan a sheaf of papers.

"What are these?" Ryan asked.

"For your convenience, they are in English. When you sign them, you can go."

"What do you mean, sign them? These are four pages and I don't have a lawyer."

"It is a standard release form. It states you agree not to leave the country, until we are satisfied with your innocence. And we must have your passport."

"I can't stay here if you go on and on with an investigation. That could take months."

"You are over-reacting, monsieur. Once we rule you out as the murderer, you will be able to go."

"Rule me out. What does that mean? You'll be investigating me, following me around?"

"We will be following procedure, like we always do," the detective said.

"And if I don't sign this thing?"

"Then we will be forced to detain you here," the detective answered.

"Well, I'll get a habeas corpus," Ryan countered.

"This is not America, monsieur. If you do not sign, you could be here for the rest of the festival. You would not be able to do your film critiques for your important Hollywood newspaper."

"I need to call my editor, Tim Daniels. He can bring you my passport." Ryan punched in his cell and made the call. "He'll be here in about an hour," he told the detective.

The detective handed him the release form. "Do you get to meet a lot of celebrities in your work?" he asked.

"What?"

"Have you ever met Kylie Jenner?"

"You seem kind of wigged out," Tim Daniels said as Ryan emerged from the rear exit of the Cannes Police station. Tim was the news editor at the paper and Ryan's best friend on the editorial desk. After he had delivered Ryan's passport to the Cannes Police, Tim had waited for Ryan behind the police station's rear exit. He was a tall Virginian whose easy-going manner belied a tenacious nature.

"Thanks for coming to get me," Ryan said. "Who hacked up my review?"

"Our new Russian correspondent, Dragan Dylko. He's filling in on the copy desk part-time when he's not on a story."

"What is this Russian guy doing here anyway?"

"What can I tell you? It came from up-top. Woolsey met him at some symposium up in Palo Alto. There are some big film-funding deals coming out of Russia. He can get these stories for us, so we're pretty much stuck with him."

"A number's geek, who's probably in tight with the Russian mob, edits my opening night film review," Ryan muttered.

"That's a little paranoid, don't you think?" Tim said.

"Paranoid? I've just been dragged in by half the French police force for murdering the star of the Cannes Film Festival's opening night premiere. It's not paranoid, it's merely reacting to this whole pile of crap," Ryan said. "Look, I think I need a lawyer. This is all too crazy."

"Don't worry, the paper has plenty of lawyers," Tim said.

"I don't mean libel lawyers. I mean criminal lawyers. I'm not going to get railroaded because I'm defended by a guy whose specialty is intellectual property rights."

"Calm down. I hear you," Tim answered. "Just don't worry, don't get yourself all riled up. They'll probably get the real killer within a day or so."

"Yeah, but this isn't an episode of *48 Hours*," Ryan said. "Look, the question remains: Why would anyone mess with my review? Change it in such a hostile way. This isn't some college prank. Why would someone do this? What's the motive? There's got to be something more behind this than making me look like an idiot."

Tim grimaced and pulled out a *Hollywood New Times* tennis visor from his back pocket. "Better put this on. The sun's already wicked." Ryan fit the visor on his head and headed down the old cobblestone hill. Tim pointed in the opposite direction. "Safer," he said. “They’re swarming all over the front of the station. You’re their celebrity suspect.” He patted Ryan on the back. “Someday we’ll all have a drink back at Musso’s and laugh about it. You’ll have scads of women writing you now they’ve seen your picture on TV and on all these websites.”

“I can find enough wacko women on my own, thank you,” Ryan said.

“Henri is picking us up. Remember, the guy who was our French office gofer the last couple festivals.”

“Yeah, how could I forget? He was always pestering me for party invitations. Back in 2017, he RSVP’d in my name to the Weinstein Company party on the Palais rooftop,” Ryan said. “When I got there, the guards wouldn’t let me in. They said, I was already there. It turned out he had used my name.”

“Well, did you get in?”

“Yeah, Harvey happened to be right there and got me in.”

“As long as he didn’t grope you,” Tim added. “Come on, guy, you’re the big story. Every cable channel and newspaper in the world is showing your picture and will have you in the story.”

“Well, just as long as Stan Peck doesn’t write it up for us.”

“I think he’s too busy focusing on his new fave, this billionaire guy Sevareid from *The Ice Princess*. Peck went on and on last night about what a Renaissance man he is. Sevareid has some personal Picassos up in his suite at the Carlton. He won’t travel without them.”

“I can relate to that,” Ryan said. “I never leave home without my signed poster of *Dirty Harry.”*

"Glad to see you've still got your sense of humor," Tim said.

They trudged up the hill through the Old Section of Cannes, an area dating back to the 1400s. At the peak, the street hair-pinned to the right and back down in a Grand Prix-like turn. Tim was a sinewy guy in good condition, and although Ryan was in great shape from his daily three-mile runs, he gasped for breath. His chest tightened. He stopped, and Tim waited. "Take your time," Tim said. "Your system has had a shock." Tim pointed to a black skull that was displayed on the door of an old stone building. It was a wrought-iron face-mask of the Man in the Iron Mask. Ryan approached the door and read the inscription. "This is where they held the guy in the iron mask," Tim said. "The guy Alexandre Dumas wrote about it in his novel, *The Man in the Iron Mask*. I didn't know it was here."

"Just when I thought this festival wasn't bizarre enough for me," Ryan said.

"Don't worry, I've heard the French don't put people in iron masks anymore, except if you kill an actress at the Cannes Film Festival," Tim joked.

A green Renault pulled up and Henri honked the horn. Henri was French, charismatic and served as, essentially, *The Hollywood New Times* fixer at Cannes. Tim opened the back door for Ryan. Henri reached back across the seat, punched Ryan on the shoulder. "Un celebrity, n'est-ce pas?" he said. Henri jolted the tiny car into action. Ryan tried not to watch as Henri took his hands off the wheel to light up a cigarette. Tim glanced back at Ryan, shrugging his shoulders as

Henri slammed on the horn and yelled at an old man who was trying to cross the street.

"Next time you get arrested, I'll bring both of us helmets too," Tim said to Ryan.

They careened Formula One-style through the crowded streets, filled with vegetable and flower stands. Ryan felt as if he was speeding through a grocery store. Henri yanked on the wheel, barely missed a group of old women.

"Better luck next time," Tim said.

"You can't toot your horn, or yell at these old people because they do not hear so well," Henri said.

Before Henri was able to run down any elderly or infirm pedestrians, he commandeered the little green Renault down a side street, looping in behind *The Hollywood New Times*' hotel. The building was hemmed in by a patch of derelict buildings. Ryan hadn't been to this side of the hotel since his first year at Cannes when he'd gotten lost trying to find his way back from a drinking night at the Petit Splendid bar. The back area was glutted with out-of-control vines and heaped with patches of thick, green rubbery plants. Wild flowers butted through the tangled growth, even though the suffocating foliage pressed them down. On the far wall, a thicket of roses protruded; they were spindly and discolored.

Ryan's joints cracked as he wiggled got out of the tiny car. He bent over and reached down for a toe-stretch. He swung back and forth, rotating his hips. He needed a run. Henri plucked a cigarette pack out of his shirt pocket. He lit up. He extended the pack to Ryan and then pulled it back. "I did not remember you do not smoke, monsieur," he said.

"I could use one of those," Tim said.

"Since when do you smoke?" Ryan asked.

"I always smoke during this festival. Stan Peck does too," Tim said.

"No kidding?"

Henri nodded to Ryan. "I know we have had our misunderstandings in that past, but if I can do anything to smooth things over for you while you are here, just say so. When you live here all the time, you get to know the people who are the real-life people."

"Thanks," Ryan answered. "I hope you know a lot of cops."

"More than you think," Henri said.

"Yeah, Henri. You are the man," Tim said. "I still can't believe you got our Irish correspondent out of that $20,000 bill for damages at the Eden-Roc."

As Henri and Tim reminisced about parties-of-destruction past, Ryan stretched his muscles. He could feel his heartbeat. He stared intently at the flowers, trying to emotionally transport himself to a more natural realm. With its thick mosses and overgrown vegetation, the back entrance had the unkempt appearance of a South American hideaway. It was sinister, like out of a Gabriel Garcia Marquez novel where a dying dictator might spend his doddering days with the spiders and insects. Ryan gazed up to the trees through the cigarette smoke, half-expecting to see hideous birds or, more likely, vultures lurking about.

Chapter 3

"I can't take any more parties!"

"I know what you mean. By the time they got us back from that Russian billionaire's yacht, it was nearly 4:30. This is the second year in a row where somebody stole my shoes. I don't know why they make you take off your shoes when you go on a yacht."

Ryan couldn't help but overhear the conversation from the next table at the Carlton Intercontinental Hotel's patio restaurant. The jaded exchange between the women re-affirmed to Ryan that he was still among the chattering classes. It was late morning, and the discreet stirring of the coffee spoons and the fluttering of the napkins flavored the pricey serenity. Nearby, a buffet table boasted silver coffee pots and a large, ornate urn that looked like Louis XIV might have used it. Ryan savored the French vanilla aroma as it wafted across the sun-streaked patio of the festival's flagship hotel.

Even to the most jaded of jet-setters, Cannes' seductive powers were intoxicating. With the succulent blue of its waters, the regal red of its carpet, and the inviting creams of its sandy shore, Cannes was a grand-ole temptress. A white-clothed table was filled with mounds of croissants, strawberries, blueberries, kiwi, and cheeses. Amid the culinary splendor, Ryan felt lousy. He had taken two Tylenol, but he still felt sore after his hot-tub encounter. Besides his aches and pains, he also felt he needed an emotional pick-me-up. Ryan waited for

Delisha Blair, a friend from LA who was a Victoria's Secret model. They had met two years earlier at a Warner Bros. premiere party on top of a parking garage in Westwood Village. Ryan knew Delisha functioned on model's time, anywhere from fifteen to thirty minutes late. She was worth it, though. He recalled the sleek, gold dress she had found in a thrift shop on Melrose for the Oscars the year he had taken her as his date. The dress was a stunner that had easily outpaced all the Christian Diors, Armanis, Pradas, and gowns of the other houses who had vied to make their mark on the red carpet.

In recent years, the Victoria's Secret charity fashion bash at Cannes had garnered such extraordinary press coverage that it upset all the festival-heads, those beard-and-beret types who thought the festival was about "film" and "*les auteurs*." The contemporary *auteurs*, at least at this festival, were the fashion designers. The stars were the lingerie models, Ryan mused. The two worlds of film and fashion had intersected at Cannes: Director Sofia Coppola had a successful background as a fashion designer before she won the Cannes' Best Director Award in 2017, Ryan recalled.

"Fancy meeting you here," the singsong voice rang out.

Delisha had come up from behind. She squeezed Ryan on the shoulders as she circled around the table. "Sorry, I'm late, but I slept through my travel alarm. I'm not used to the buzz it makes." Delisha was a stunning beauty – African-American, Jamaican, Dutch, and Cherokee. She had been born and raised in West Philadelphia and attended Temple University on a track scholarship. Ryan's private name for her was 'Philly Masala.'

He hadn't seen her for nearly a year, but Delisha was even prettier than he remembered. She wore a white terry-cloth jump suit with a silk azure scarf draped from her neck. Prior to her Victoria's Secret modeling, Delisha had done some sultry ads for another lingerie line, but had left them when they suggested she be part of their skydiving team where the models would jump from planes in their undies over famous golf resorts.

Delisha reached across the table and took his hand. "You have no idea how great it was to get your text. I was so worried about you. I can't believe anyone would be stupid enough to think you murdered someone, especially the police."

"I'm shocked myself," Ryan said.

"Sweetie, what is going to happen? Do you think they will find the real killer?"

"I don't know what to think," Ryan answered. "I simply don't know enough about the dead actress, or the people around her. It makes no sense."

"See, there you are," Delisha said. "It doesn't make any sense you would kill her."

"It's so bizarre. The reason they brought me in was about something in my review that I didn't even write," Ryan said.

"What do you mean, didn't write?"

"Some new editor changed my copy," he said.

"But they can't do that. You are a respected critic."

"The paper has been in this crazy cost-cutting mode, and he's a freelancer who's got connections with big Russian investment money, so he can get us stories."

"That is whack." She handed him a shiny gold ticket. "It's for our Pres de Printemps fashion show at the Miramar Hotel. It's something Victoria's Secret has never done this early in the festival."

Ryan took the ticket. "Thanks, I can't wait to see it."

"I know a hand-written note would be more appropriate for a gentleman of your sophistication, but what's a modern-girl to do?"

"Are you saying I'm old?" Ryan grinned.

"You're the perfect vintage," Delisha said. She leaned forward to Ryan and frowned. "Sweetie, you look so wiped out."

"I'm still on L.A. time," Ryan answered. "I'm worried that someone is setting me up as a murderer."

"Let me know if there's anything I can do."

"I think I've got to find the one-armed man myself," Ryan said.

"One-armed man? What are you talking about?"

"*The Fugitive*," Ryan said. "Harrison Ford has to find the one-armed man who killed his wife before the authorities catch him and put him back on Death Row."

"Is this one of those old movies you're always talking about?" she asked.

"Not old, 1994. It starred Harrison Ford. Tommy Lee Jones won Best Supporting Actor for his portrayal of U.S. Marshall Girard."

"Well, since I was born in 1998, you can excuse me for missing it. But I do know who Harrison Ford is," she said. "He's the old guy who crashed his plane in Santa Monica."

"You're right about that," Ryan said. "Well, it's a similar situation, the pursued-pursuer plot-line," Ryan answered.

"So you're saying you're Harrison Ford here, and if you don't find out who killed the actress, you're going to Death Row?"

"Well, the French police didn't seem to have too much on the ball when they questioned me," Ryan said.

Delisha's lips curved into a flirtatious smile. She reached out, took his hands, and began to massage them. Ryan relaxed, then he straightened up. He saw people beyond the restaurant gate pointing their cellphones at him. He couldn't even have a simple breakfast with an old friend without people intruding into his life.

Delisha clutched his hands more firmly and slowly withdrew her touch. She pointed upward to the rounded blue spires that topped off the front corners of the fabled Carlton Hotel. "Your directions were perfect. I'm glad you told me to look for the big white hotel with the blue Dairy Queen cones on the top ends."

"Those aren't really ice-cream cones. They are a woman's nipples."

Delisha craned her neck, squinted at the Carlton's roof-top. "They are not. They're much too pointy."

"No, it's true. A rich Russian prince built this hotel in the early 1900s. He had the architect incorporate his favorite mistress's breasts into the design."

Delisha grinned. “You are always messing with me.”

“I would never deceive a woman of your sophistication and standing in the community,” he deadpanned.

She reached across the table and pinched his cheek. “It’s so good to see you,” she said “Don’t worry. I’m sure they’ll find out who did it soon.”

Ryan noted she wasn’t wearing a ring on her left hand, not even a friendship ring. He hoped she wasn’t still partying on the fringes of the Lakers/Clippers basketball circuit and the whole predatory jock-celebrity game in LA.

“I never thought I’d ever be in the south of France,” she said. “I always read about it in my art books, and saw photos of this beautiful area, but I never thought I’d be lucky enough to be here one day.”

“That’s right, you were an art major at Temple.”

“I love the Impressionists,” she said. “Matisse mainly, but also Seurat.”

The waiter appeared. “Mademoiselle would you care to order?”

Delisha grinned. “You are always messing with me.”

“Strawberries et les autres fruits et water gas,” she said.

“Moi aussi,” Ryan said. The waiter jotted down the order and departed.

“There, we’ve used our entire repertoire of French,” Delisha said.

“Not quite. I also know how to say, ‘L’addition, s’il vous plait,’” Ryan joked. “And, ‘Donnez-moi une Coca-Cola.’”

"I'm sorry for the sunglasses," Delisha said. "I don't mean to be rude, but the sun here is so bright."

"I know. Idiot me, I forgot to get sunscreen."

"Don't go another day without it," she said. "The ultraviolet here is horrible." She rubbed his cheek. "And you've got such a luscious complexion."

Jean-Robie Ginibre, the hotel concierge approached. Jean-Robie was continental-suave with wavy black hair, sprinkled with gray. Ryan had met him several festivals back when he had done a feature story on the Carlton Hotel's place in festival history.

"Monsieur Hackbart, my favorite opinion-maker for the cultural elite and, as of this week, celebrity murder suspect," Jean-Robie cracked. He hugged Ryan in a continental way.

"Jean-Robie, it's great to see you. I'd like you to meet Delisha Blair, my favorite supermodel."

"I'm not a supermodel, but I'm pleased to meet you, Jean-Robie," Delisha said.

Jean-Robie took Delisha's hand and kissed it, a la Maurice Chevalier.

"Jean-Robie is the head concierge here at the Carlton," Ryan said. "He won't admit to it, but it's the most powerful position at the film festival."

"Monsieur Hackbart is good always with the jokes," Jean-Robie said. He turned to Ryan with a twinkle in his eye. "If there is anything I can do for you during the festival – provide a hiding place, lend you toiletries, supply you with an alibi, let me know?"

"Thanks, you never know when I might need an alibi."

"Especially when one breakfasts with such a beautiful woman," Jean-Robie said. "I'm sorry, I must attend to business." Out of the corner of his eye, Ryan spotted Nick Steele and his brother Boris Steele by the buffet table, two of Hollywood's sleaziest producers. The downside of film festivals was that Ryan encountered people whom he always managed to avoid in LA.

He nodded to Jean-Robie. "I feel like I'm back on old Hollywood Boulevard, east of Vine," Ryan said.

Jean-Robie followed his gaze to the producers. "Yes, they are, perhaps, my greatest challenge in all the festival," Jean-Robie said. "They have rented one of our best suites for an office. Unfortunately, they think our restaurant lounge area is an extension of their offices."

"Jean-Robie, is it true those blue things on the top ends of the hotel are nipples?" Delisha asked.

"Yes, you know your Cannes history, mademoiselle. Prince Vladimir modeled them after the breasts of his beloved courtesan. Not many people know that these days. They think they are some sort of holiday ornament."

"Thanks, Jean-Robie," Ryan said. "You are always a source of enlightenment."

Jean-Robie bowed and turned to mingle with the guests at the next table. "Just because you weren't fooling me about those boobs on top of the hotel doesn't mean you can get away with other things at this festival," Delisha said.

"At least things of a verbal nature."

"Well, if I ever decide to use my vast resources to build a luxury hotel, I will surely consider topping it with your luscious breasts."

"Then you'd have to charge a lot more than this place does for rooms," she said.

"Some suites here go for nearly $30,000 a night during the festival," he said. "With my two goodies on the front top, you'd have to double that," she said.

"Didn't this hotel have some sort of big jewelry heist a few years ago?"

"Yes, a jewel thief stole $136 million worth of jewels here at the Carlton in 2013," Ryan said. "This festival can be 'open season' for thieves. So, be careful."

"Well, I don't have to worry. I left all my diamonds and pearls back in L.A.," she joked.

Delisha arched her shoulders back, allowing the morning sun and breezes to caress her hair. She glanced up as someone tapped Ryan from the back. Ryan turned to see Stan Peck, his least favorite journalist and, since last fall the chief film reporter at Ryan's own company, *The Hollywood New Times*. Peck sported a Hawaiian shirt, paisley sun visor and round, blue metallic sunglasses.

"Where's your cigarette holder, Hunter?" Ryan asked.

"Slightly funny," Peck answered. "I hoped to catch a few words with you about your scathing review of *The Ice Princess*. It's already the talk of the festival. Well, at least it was till the murder of the lead actress," he continued. "That wasn't you, by the way, trying to distract attention from your damning review?"

"My review was rather gentle considering it was the worst opening night film I've ever seen at Cannes."

"Any theories on why the French police think you were involved with Ingrid Bjorge's murder?" Peck asked. "Why they thought it had to do with your review?"

"None whatsoever," Ryan said.

"Was it, perhaps, a suicide? Something the police and *The Ice Princess* people are hiding? Maybe Ingrid Bjorge was so upset with your review she took the only way out."

"I've never known an actress to pass up a red-carpet opportunity," Ryan said.

Peck peered at Delisha. "I recognize you from somewhere."

"Men sometimes say that," she said.

"Well, obviously Ryan's fortunes are rising," Peck said. "Not only is he in the international spotlight, he's having breakfast with the one of the most beautiful women in Cannes. Who would have thought our unassuming movie critic here would have turned into James Bond?"

"I see Ryan more as Clark Kent," Delisha said. "You might see the gifted wordsmith, but I know the Superman side of him." She stared through his sunglasses.

"Sorry to interrupt your breakfast," Peck finally said. He patted Ryan on the shoulder. "By the way, I loved your *Ice Princess* lead: 'Big guns, big gadgets, big boobs, big hair, and big dud.' He tapped Ryan on the shoulder once again before he sauntered off.

"What was that?" Delisha asked.

"He's our paper's head film reporter."

"He's so smug. Why didn't you say something?"

"Not saying anything to a guy like Stan Peck is the worst thing you can do to him. He's left with nothing to distort," Ryan answered.

"I thought you said his name was Hunter."

"I was being sarcastic."

"Some sort of guy thing?"

"A gonzo-guy thing," Ryan said.

"I don't get it, but I love it when you're using your intelligence to be bad," Delisha said. "It's a definite turn-on." She leaned forward. "It must be exciting to have everyone at the festival talking about your review."

"Yes, I have to confess it is kind of a rush seeing some guy in a beret dragging on a cigarette, sipping coffee and reading my review."

"I didn't know how much power you had," she said. "You could destroy someone's career with your reviews."

"I never thought of it like that, not at all," Ryan said. "I look at it as discovering new talent or pointing out excellence."

Her eyes sparkled, and she leaned forward. "You are a major player here."

"Only when I'm dining with you," Ryan said.

The waiter appeared with Delisha's fruit plate. It was resplendent with all shapes and colors of fruit. "It looks like the chef has studied Cézanne," Ryan said.

"Cézanne would put the kiwi closer to the middle, and he'd have a pear near the edge," Delisha said. "But you're right, it's an inspired arrangement. I didn't know you knew art."

"I don't know anything about art, but I know strawberries," Ryan said. He reached over and swiped one of her strawberries. "I've got a party invite for tomorrow night at a villa up in the hills. The company that owns Italian TV is throwing it."

"I'd love to go," Delisha answered. "But what would your wife say?"

"Wow, it has been a while since we've seen each other," Ryan answered. "The divorce went through about two months ago."

"Well, if it's any consolation, I never liked what's-her-name anyway," Delisha said.

"Things were kind of crazy for me at that time," Ryan said.

"Well, I hope things are better for you now," she said.

"I hate to admit it, but when I look back, she fell for me because I took her to exciting premieres and things, introduced her to stars. It wasn't me at all. It was the event," Ryan said. "Bottom line, I've sworn off actresses."

"What about lingerie models?" she asked.

"Lingerie models are way out of my league," he said. "Where did you get that scarf?"

She glanced at the azure silk scarf draped over her shoulders. She pulled it from her neck. "We all took them. They delivered all the wrong lingerie. I liked the blue color."

"They delivered lingerie you weren't going to wear?" Ryan asked.

"Yes, there was some sort of mix-up with the shipping company that was delivering our line from the airport," she said. "They brought these huge boxes of this blue lingerie. But it wasn't Victoria's Secret."

"Was it all light blue?"

"How did you know?"

"That was the color they wore in *The Ice Princess*."

"I didn't know blue was in."

Ryan picked up the bill and calculated in his mind: 82 euros for two fruit plates and coffee. That was roughly the same amount in dollars. He pulled out a 100 euro note, and collected the receipt. Bernie had specifically told Ryan to increase his per diem expenditures. The previous year Ryan's travel expenses had been roughly one-quarter of the other staff members, and it had caused the company accountant to question the much higher expenses of his colleagues. His co-workers were not pleased.

Delisha grimaced at a tiny silver shopping bag she had brought with her. "I never thought about it, but I bought some things yesterday I was thinking about returning today, and I don't want to take them to our Victoria's Secret brunch."

"I can take it. I'll give it back to you after the party tomorrow night."

She handed him the bag and sashayed off, her azure silk scarf shimmering in the morning sun. Ryan watched her go. On cue, she turned and gave him an air-kiss. Ryan watched her scurry down the outer stairs, as every male diner gaped in her wake.

Nick Steele approached. The sleazy producer seemed to be everywhere. "I see you are a great man with the ladies," Steele said.

"Circumstantial evidence," Ryan said.

"Your lady is beautiful. I hope it was an after-breakfast," he said. Nick patted him on the shoulder. "You and your lady should team up. You could direct her and make some big money. The German market loves women of her look."

"Got a screening, Nick," Ryan said. He got up from the table. "Good luck with your foreign sales."

"We have already had good luck. Your publisher Mr. Woolsey says you will be doing a story on us."

"What?"

"Yes, I had an earlier breakfast with Mr. Woolsey, at the Hotel du Cap. He promised me you would write a special mid-Cannes feature. We have a big deal to announce."

"I'll have to check my screening schedule. It's tight."

"We will make it work for you, find a convenient time. I must leave. I am late for another breakfast. This one's on a yacht, and I have to take one of those little boats to get to it." Nick hurried off, nearly trampling a designer-dog that a woman had leashed to her breakfast chair. She waved her hands in the air and unloaded angry French at him. Nick Steele gestured to a waiter, pointed at the dog and yelled, "Remove that dog!"

"But it eeeez not my dawg," Ryan muttered to himself a la one of his favorite *Pink Panther* lines. He smiled: just the pick-me-up he needed.

Ryan darted between a Bentley and a motorcycle as he angled onto the Croisette. On the walkway he was engulfed by a swarm of Evian girls, cheerleader types in blue-and-red shorts and tight white t-shirts handing out bottles of the favored water. An Evian cutie jammed a water bottle into him. "Hey, you're the critic who killed the actress!" the girl exclaimed. She grabbed onto his shoulder, swung into him, and shot a selfie. She held it up to the other girls. "Wait till everyone sees this. I'm in Cannes with the murderer!" The other girls jostled enthusiastically, regarding Ryan as a true celebrity, an internationally known murder suspect, someone their friends back home would know about. They rushed around him. He smiled for their selfies.

As they wiggled around him, Ryan spotted a photographer clicking away at them. His good-humor turned to worry: how was he ever going to get to the bottom of whatever-the-hell was happening to him if even the t-shirt girls recognized him? Worse, the paparazzi were obviously following him.

He angled over to a bench behind a patch of orange-and-yellow peonies. He sat down, tried to collect himself. He needed his morning run, a ritual he missed.

He took deep breaths: four-count in, four-count hold, four-count out. It was just the beginning of the festival, but he was exhausted.

With people not factoring in the time difference with the United States, Ryan had been up the entire night, fielding calls and tons of e-mails and texts from friends, distant relatives, his sister, and people he hadn't heard from in years. Ryan also had numerous cell messages from women he did not know. How had his private cell-phone number gotten out? How had he come to the point where everyone in the world could reach him? He had gotten numerous calls from a guy who claimed to be Howard Stern. The New Yawk-talking caller wanted to know whether Ryan thought Ingrid had great buns for spanking.

He turned off his cell and gazed out across the aqua blue sea. To his right, the hotel staffs were positioning umbrellas that centered the outdoor restaurant tables. The blue-and-white umbrella tops jutted up like blossoming flowers on the sandy beach. Soon, they would be surrounded by diners in expensive casual-wear ordering shrimp salads, sipping white wines, and feigning fitness by decrying the luscious tortes, eclairs, sorbets, cakes, and icing-coated delicacies the tuxedoed waiters dazzled before them. He reflected that the Carlton Pier, as it was called, would be a good place to take Delisha to lunch, once this fest settled down for him. He pictured her glee when a friendly waiter would dribble exotic sauces on whatever new thing she would order. Delisha would not be one to just order the safe salad, but, rather, would sample something she couldn't pronounce and experience something new.

In its unique way, the Cannes Film Festival was like a giant Rorschach test. Each festival attendee had his or her own personal bounds regarding the festival, and Ryan's friends and family back in the states had their own individual interests: his sister (the setting), Shan (parties), James (hedge funds), Lauren (shopping), Syria (guys), Britt (shoes), Stumpf (wines), Rich (topless beaches), Meghan (fashion), Ro (cosmetics), and, alas, his friend Scott (films).

And now, a new one for everyone (murder).

Chapter 4

The circus was in town: CNN, PBS, Fox, MSNBC, CBS, NBC, ABC, and BBC – every multi-letter monster of the media universe had landed on Cannes' shores with their cables, wires, satellites, and well-coiffed correspondents. Big News and cyber-tech had stormed the azure-waters of Cannes's beaches. The tabloids and TV entertainment stations had gone crazy. For them, nothing this wonderful had happened since Lady Di had been killed.

The so-called mainstream press was jetting "special" correspondents to develop the story, or, in the case of the info-entertainment news magazines, do "in-depth" programs on the murder, and on the murdered actress Ingrid Bjorge. Her killing had made worldwide headlines and, for TV news executives, it couldn't have come at a better time. It was a viewer windfall.

Ryan's cellphone pinged incessantly. He finally turned it off, and spotted Barlowe headed his way. "I assume you'll be at the festival press conference about the killing," Barlowe said by way of greeting.

"No way. I'll be mobbed with crazy journalists and paparazzi if I go to that press conference," Ryan said. "I'll have even more phony stories written about me."

"Don't sweat it. I'll be your eyes and ears," Barlowe said. "You still sound a little paranoid."

"I need to be. I don't have much confidence in the police here, and I'm not going to end up being the fall guy in all this," Ryan said.

"Everybody's on this. The cops or a good investigative journalist will come up with something."

"The journalists are what I'm worried about," Ryan said. "I've already run into that idiot woman from MSNBC who's been pestering me with out-to-lunch questions about conspiracies."

"So, go Trump on them. Start tweeting," Barlowe encouraged. "Start putting out your own theories on the murder." Barlowe slapped Ryan on the back: "Expand your brand, dude! Make hay while the sun shines. You're failing to see the great opportunity this whole murder thing gives you."

Ryan shrugged, recalling the nutty coverage that had already sprung up around the murder. The *Los Angeles Times* wrote that an animated series on Ingrid's life was in the pipeline at Spike TV. *The Washington Post* reported that *The Ice Princess*' producer, Gunnar Sevareid, had "suspicious" ties with Texan entrepreneurs and had made overtures to buy the Dallas Cowboys football team from Jerry Jones. CNN proclaimed Donald Trump had once tried to buy the Intercontinental Carlton Hotel where the murder took place, implying his minions would have had insider knowledge of the hotel's innards and... ratings roll...perhaps had something to do with the murder.

Le Figaro had concentrated on two groups in France suspected of bombings in Paris. *Le Monde* editorialized the festival had taken on too much of a Hollywood flavor. The media, and the entertainment press, saw Ingrid's murder as a "blonde" sex story. And, in the case of the Hollywood trade-paper websites, the murder was covered as a "movie-deal" story with a box-office slant. Ryan had become the sorry straight man in this news farce, a celebrity suspect, as it were.

"You look awful," Bernie said.

"Getting dragged in by the police and ambushed at a party is not the way I like to start out a festival," Ryan said.

Bernie patted him on the shoulder and then sat down at the white modular desk in the hotel room that served as the office of *Hollywood New Times*. Bernie was the newspaper's executive editor. He had been an end-of-bench guy on Syracuse University's basketball team in the early '90s. His gangling height was a drawback in France. He was in a constant contortion during the festival, sore from squeezing his long legs into the tiny French furniture.

"This whole thing wouldn't have happened if someone hadn't butchered my review," Ryan said.

"We're all behind you here," Bernie said. "If you need to take some time off, or collect yourself, go ahead."

"Thanks. I think I'm better off going on with my schedule, picking up my review routine."

"So, what about the cops?" Bernie asked. "Do you think it went okay?"

"I'm not sure. I couldn't read the main guy who was questioning me," Ryan said. "He was so literal. It took me a while to convince him somebody butchered my copy." Ryan noticed his voice quaver. He had been so shaken and unglued since being dragged in as a murder suspect, he hadn't had time to reflect about Ingrid Bjorge's death. Ryan realized he didn't know much about her, other than the scant details the media kit had provided.

He had re-read Ingrid Bjorge's bio, and wondered how much of it was true. Like most biographies of newcomers, it didn't say much that was concrete except she had won some provincial beauty contests and studied acting in Oslo at something called Der Institut som Gjovik. According to *The Ice Princess* press kit biography, Ingrid Bjorge had won a beauty contest in Tromso, a tiny city above the Arctic Circle on the northern coast of Norway. She had been discovered at a 7-Eleven during the 1994 Winter Olympics at Lillehammer when she was a toddler. Her discovery had been by a director for ESPN, Jason Pinelli, who had morphed into the "hot new" director, the "auteur" who had sucker-punched Ryan the night before.

Ryan wandered toward Bernie's desk. "I've already left a message with Dylko about messing up your copy," Bernie said.

"I can't believe we've got someone who doesn't know anything about movies editing my review of the opening night film," Ryan complained. "He distorted the writing. He made me sound imbecilic and vile: 'The star actress should have the signature blue scarf stuffed down her throat'– that's like a bad college newspaper."

"Orson feels he's vital here, and I don't have anyone else to back-up Tim on the copy desk," Bernie said. "I'll take care of it. I know you've been under a lot of strain. Only Tim touches your copy from now on."

"Well, then there's the obvious question: why hasn't this guy Dylko been dragged in for questioning?" Ryan exclaimed. "He's the one who wrote she should have the blue scarf stuffed down her throat."

"I don't know, maybe he has," Bernie said. "I've been in and out and haven't seen him around. He's working on this big Russian funding story for us. Don't worry, I'm sure the French police are going to solve it."

"The French police, are you kidding me? I'd feel more confident if Inspector Clouseau were on it," Ryan said. "These guys are the Keystone Kops."

Ryan looked away, tried to contain himself. He knew Bernie was the man in the middle. The newspaper itself was in a transitional mess, not as reliable or bold as when the seventh wife of the original owner ran the paper by her instincts. The current publisher, Orson W. Woolsey, was a Stanford law-school grad who excelled at hosting marketing seminars and talking "brand-expansion."

The Hollywood New Times was covering Cannes with virtually a skeleton crew compared to its main competitors, *The Hollywood Reporter*, *Deadline.com*, and *Variety*. Ryan had learned from a friend in accounting that the new publisher, Woolsey, would get a million-dollar incentive bonus with the new parent company if he kept costs below a certain level. That meant the higher paid, experienced reporters were driven out: they were laid off and replaced by recent college grads. The studios, streamers, and the stars could bully and intimidate rookie reporters. What passed for entertainment news nowadays was usually just publicists' spin.

Ryan drifted into the office's reception area. His mailbox was crammed. Basically, a wad of movie invites, press releases, and outdated announcements. He recalled a time, just a few years ago, when the classier party invitations came in lush envelopes. Amid the announcements and various party invites, Ryan found that Henri had left him a note the day before, imploring him to get Ingrid Bjorge's autograph. Guess it is too late to honor that request, Ryan thought. He picked up a copy of that day's *Hollywood New Times* from Tim's desk and flung it toward the wastebasket.

"Are you sure you're all right?" Bernie asked. "This murder thing is a big story, you know."

"I can give you an exclusive interview any time you want," Ryan answered.

"We don't want you quoted, on anything."

"I was joking," Ryan said.

"Someone knocking off this actress could spur a deal. It puts a whole new spin on the opening night and certainly thrusts the film into another realm," Bernie added. "The movie is much bigger now after the murder."

"So, her death was a good career move?" Ryan deadpanned.

"Yes, absolutely," Bernie said. He never got Ryan's dry sense of humor. Ryan turned away; he was in no shape to carry on this kind of conversation any longer, and feared he might say something offensive to his editor, who was on his side.

"The rumor is Netflix might be interested in the movie now with the murder," Tim said.

"What?" Ryan asked. "Sorry, I didn't hear what you said."

"You should get some rest," Bernie answered. He turned to Tim. "We should have someone see about Amazon too. Go see Jeff Bezos out on the yacht," he said. "Also, Universal might be interested. Have someone call the Black Tower."

"It's the middle of the night in LA," Tim pointed out.

"Damn, Cannes sucks," Bernie said. "I hate everything about this place, weird time zone, bad Wi-Fi. Get someone on Paramount too."

"Who?" Tim asked. "We've got Peck on this murder thing, and with the cutback he's our only experienced film reporter."

Since he wasn't bleeding all over the floor or ranting and raving, concern for Ryan had ended. The "click, click, click" of it all set in as the desk people hunched over their keyboards. Ryan nudged Tim as he headed for the door.

"Have you seen this guy Dylko around?" Ryan asked.

"No, he always files electronically," Tim said.

"I still would like to hear his version of messing up my review."

"The review was already in the system when I pulled it up."

"That's kind of surprising," Ryan said. "The Wi-Fi Airplane Mode was kind of crazy on the plane. I didn't think my transmission worked."

"Whatever," Tim said. "We've all been concerned about you. You've gone through an ordeal. Let the other guys pick up the slack. You need a breather, take a couple days. Go to the beach, get laid. You always work too much. Do what everyone else does in Cannes."

"Thanks, maybe I will just concentrate on the Competition Films. But I've got to do the Matt Damon movie later in the week."

"Okay, but till then, try to chill."

A tall, red-haired man in large, black-rimmed glasses approached Ryan. "You're Ryan Hackbart?"

"Right."

"I've got something for you." He handed Ryan a large envelope. "Come see this."

"Sorry, I've already got my review schedule."

"No, your publisher Mr. Woolsey said I should talk to you."

"You've got to walk with me then," Ryan said. "I'm heading to a screening." Ryan grimaced: Almost anyone could walk in to *The Hollywood New Times* office, and did. Publicists, delivery guys, hotel staff, and other journalists were in and out all day long. This despite the fact that thievery was rampant at the festival. Ryan had heard that the MTV people had been burglarized at their festival headquarters.

Ryan headed to the main lobby and hurried out of the hotel. The red-haired man followed and guided Ryan to a wagon that was designed as a stage. Scarlet letters proclaimed: “The Globe Theater.” Seven cats perched on it. They wore elaborate and colorful costumes, regal battle outfits. The man handed Ryan a business card. In an Old-English font, it read: “Giles G. Hall, Shakespearean Feline Amusements.”

“My cats do Shakespeare,” he said. “Look, at the costumes I’ve done. They’re perfect for the Elizabethan period, although I did dumb them down for today’s audience.”

“This is remarkable, especially the cats’ running shoes,” Ryan said. “I review movies. You must have misunderstood Mr. Woolsey. Your story is not for me.”

“Yes, but your Mr. Woolsey said you were highly educated and had studied at the prestigious University of Southern California.”

“Sorry, I’m late for an important screening,” Ryan said. “I’ve got your card and later, if I get a window during the festival, I’ll contact you.”

Ryan hurried down the walkway outside the hotel. When he was safely out of the Shakespearean loon’s sight, he checked his festival book for a mid-afternoon movie to review. Cannes was a grueling game for a film critic. Ryan did what he considered a “five” everyday: some days he would see three movies and write two reviews; the next day, two movies and three reviews. The trick was to keep up with the pace. Cannes was like a marathon, you had to keep going. But already, Ryan was behind. This was the second day and he still hadn’t filed a review. Usually, he would have filed at least three or four by this time in the festival. And, unlike many critics who were not gifted writers, Ryan felt an obligation to entertain, as well as analyze and inform. He couldn't bear to write a boring review. Too many film critics were wooden writers or, worse, boring academics whose reviews were never read by anyone except tenured college professors, or those with comparable disposable time.

He searched the daily festival screening guide and found an independent U.S. film that was showing at the Palais at 3:30. The cast included Rihanna, James Parsons, Michael Madsen, and Shaquille O'Neal.

The press auditorium at the Palais asserts its importance with 322 bright red seats. Less than thirty-six hours after the murder of Ingrid Bjorge, the room was packed with more than 400 entertainment journalists. Amid the world's foremost movie scribes, there were only a few regular investigative journalists. Although the top crime and news reporters were flying in from all destinations, the coverage for the murder was presently in the hands of those who wrote movie reviews, projected box-office figures, interviewed celebrities, or, most closely related, covered entertainment-industry parties.

Many of the more-connected journalists had already jumped into the assignment by calling Beverly Hills, trying to reach their favored stars and having them offer speculation on the murder. Only the time zone difference impeded their efforts to get the opinions of the hottest celebrities about what had occurred on that awful night minutes before the opening premiere of the Cannes Film Festival.

Gwyneth Paltrow's "people" were reportedly preparing an in-depth think- piece on her theories that the Norwegian actress's murder had been perpetrated by multinational oil companies in collusion with corporate skin-care companies that endangered holistic health. The actress's publicity team had slated their client for a female-hygiene party at the Carlton Pier, but they wished to bump up her presence to "the murder window."

The "window" had become increasingly crowded with even more than the usual publicity parasites, those who showed up to use the festival as a backdrop for self-promotion. The Rev. Al Sharpton was slated to deliver a speech at the Gray d'Albion, presumably tying the murder to worsening race-relations, while Kris Jenner would be offering unique insight at a soiree at the Hotel du Cap-Eden-Roc, based on her former friendship with Nicole Simpson, another blonde celebrity murder victim; coincidentally, Jenner would also announce a new Kardashian spa-franchise.

The auditorium bustled with technicians staking their digital turf. TV camera crews and agitated news people maneuvered for position. Multilingual tempers soared as Lt. Roger Savin entered the room from behind the stage.

Roger Savin was the liaison du presse of the Cannes Police Department. He endured relentless pressure and input on how to serve up this spectacular case to the world press. Lt. Savin couldn't pinpoint who all his other bosses were in this murder investigation: his superiors within the department, the Cannes city fathers, the festival itself, or even the Hollywood movie people. It was the sort of crisis that could only be a black mark on the festival, the city, the police department, and the French tourism business, now all a-dither about its notorious limelight. The young actress's murder was impacting a lot of people, and it was making them nuts.

Lt. Roger Savin had held the post of liaison du presse for the Cannes Film Festival for the past two years. His day-job throughout the rest of the year was to handle public relations for the Picasso Museum in nearby Antibes. During his stint as director of communications at the Picasso, the main gallery had been robbed of valuable Impressionist art, not to mention some early Picassos. Foiling art crime had led Lt. Savin into contact with the Cannes police. Fortunately for both the museum and for him, the artwork had been recovered. The press never got wind of things, and the police department was impressed with his crisis-management skills. He had also warded off news of a plot to steal Marc Chagall paintings and even sketches from artist/filmmaker Jean Cocteau that were displayed among the Riviera's vaunted art museums.

"I cannot start the press conference until you quiet down," Lt. Savin said as he peered out at the hyperactive crowd of journalists, all pushing forward. "If you stand back, you all can see much better. If you're too close down here, you'll not get the correct angles for the coverage your publications need."

After a rock-star-length delay, the panel participants entered. They had been transported by an elevator that brought them up to the stage from the Palais's inner bowels. It was a marvelous contraption that had been specifically designed to facilitate quick getaways for movie-star panelists. A quick hush swept over the room as the participants entered: Jason Pinelli, the director of *The Ice Princess,* with the *de rigueur* facial stubble and a muscle shirt revealing several tattoos; Gunnar Sevareid, the tall, silver-haired producer of *The Ice Princess*; Honoree Humbert, one of the associate directors of the festival; the coroner from Nice, and two gendarmes.

Lt. Savin perched at the center of the table and tapped on his microphone. After a solemn and perfunctory introduction of the panelists, Lt. Savin addressed the throng. "You all have your official press statement," he said. "We will now take questions."

"We understand you have suspects," someone shouted out.

"At the present time, we have interviewed a number of people. No one has been charged, and no one is being held," Lt. Savin responded.

Lt. Savin proceeded. He picked a familiar face in the middle of the front row, one whose photo the Beverly Hills publicity woman had given him. It was the film reporter from the "Los Angeles Times": "good to make them feel involved," the publicist had told him. Savin pointed to the writer. "What about the Hollywood film critic, Ryan Hackbart?" the scribe yelled out.

"We questioned him, but, as of yet, we have found no concrete evidence to tie him to the crime," Savin said.

The room erupted into a shouting match. Lt. Savin watched it all, and did not move. He finally pointed to another reporter whose face he recognized from his briefing photos. A big-time New Yorker, he recalled. "Reports have circulated that the murder was sexually motivated," the *New York Post* reporter asked.

"We suspect it was done by someone who knew her well or cared a great deal about her," Lt. Savin answered. "The particulars we cannot divulge."

"What about the Russians?" a CNN talking-head called out.

"There is no evidence it was a political crime," Savin emphasized. Furious, multilingual shouting erupted, but Lt. Savin quelled the noise with easy aplomb. He orchestrated the next barrage of questions with crisp dispatch, all about mundane matters: When was the body discovered (around 6:30 p.m.), by whom (the film's producer Gunnar Sevareid when he came to pick her up), what were the funeral arrangements (she would be sent back to Oslo for burial), when did they expect future developments (could be any minute, could be days, weeks).

Lt. Savin next called on an older man down front with a pointy beard who, he recalled, was from Cahiers du Cinema. The French journalist launched into an oration that referenced Roman Polanski, the French New Wave, and Brigitte Bardot, but never formulated a specific question. Lt. Savin followed up by selecting an MTV reporter for the next question.

"How much did the party for *The Ice Princess* cost and, in light of the murder, is Rihanna still going to appear for her film promo?"

"We have not heard back from her people," Lt. Savin answered.

Lt. Savin squelched a perverse grin as discussion turned to Rihanna and various hip-hop Illuminati. "We will take one more question and then we must adjourn," he announced. "There is a press conference here for the Peruvian film in five minutes."

"Are you a neo-Nazi?" the reporter from *Le Monde* barked at Gunnar Sevareid.

The imposing Scandinavian withered the questioner with an icy stare. Before Sevareid could respond, the festival's associate director jumped in, wrenching his microphone from the table. "You must remember this festival has always been anti-fascist," he emphasized. "The Cannes Film Festival was begun in 1938 as an opposition to the Venice Film Festival, a propaganda tool of Benito Mussolini."

The entire press corps seemed to shrink back, as if the associate festival director's remonstrance was aimed at each and every one of them. Cannes 1: Press 0, Savin calculated. He could already envision many of their preposterous stories – "Nazis. Drugs. Trump. Rihanna. Kinky Sex."

It had taken less than forty-eight hours for *The Ice Princess* to resurrect itself from Ryan's scathing review. The movie was suddenly, "hot," the talk of the festival. The buzz resounded all along the Croisette from the Miramar to the Palais, and bloggers bombarded "insight" from the Carlton to Kathmandu.

On this remarkable day of filmic ascension, Ryan, had become a household name. Unfortunately, his recognition was not as a film critic, but, rather, as a murder suspect. That he'd been cleared by the French police of any suspicion did not factor in: the onslaught of news did not have time to clarify. In the foggy world of instant-information, Ryan's name would be forever clouded. Half-baked stories had appeared worldwide: The *New York Times*, in a showy foray into Ryan's past, had referred to him as a "failed hockey player." Failed? He had played hockey as a freshman in college to release stress and had given it up after a year. Worse, the *Washington Post* had misspelled his name as "Hackfart." Ryan could already hear the bad jokes his buddies would make of that. "Hack," "Fart" – he tried not to think of t-shirts. And, of course, other news agencies had plagiarized the *Times* and *Post* and were circulating the same nonsense.

Ryan slumped in a burgundy art-deco chair in the lobby of *The Hollywood New Times* hotel. None of the furniture was in sync with the spine or the human anatomy. If Ryan had been a true conspiracy theorist, rather than one in development, he would have noted that the furniture maker had to be in collusion with a spa or chiropractic clinic.

He tried to get comfortable, but he was fidgeting in part because he was waiting for *The Hollywood New Times*' media-relations person, Lauren Perrino. The flak was a hyperactive ditz, unendurable at any hour, much less 8 a.m. when Ryan had agreed to meet her. She had left a hysterical message on his cell the previous night, using the word "emergency" at least a dozen times. Like many successful people in her profession, she was OCD, ADHD, and WTF.

Ryan sipped on a large coffee with cream, "Cafe Americain," as the French called it. As he waited, he glanced up to see a young woman bolt out of the elevator. She was rail thin with long, straight, bottle-blonde hair. Her skin was carrot-colored. Ryan wondered what combination of nutrients, lotions, or sun lamps accounted for the strange hue. Even at the early hour, she had the crisp stride characteristic of someone in the public-relations business, extreme urgency mixed with maximum confusion. She strode toward him. "Ryan, I'm Giselle from BGK. I've been reading all about you."

"Does it say that I have a three-book deal with Knopf and am handsome?" Ryan's dry sense of humor was particularly ineffective at the early hour.

"This murder has been such a headache for us all," the publicist said. "We can hardly service any of our clients." She sat down and punched at her iPad, brushed Ryan on the knee. "I'm sorry about Jason. He's nice and a cool guy."

"Contrary to what people who have worked with him say."

"This is his first big movie, and when he read your review, he lost it."

"Well, I hope he's pacing himself," Ryan said. "He'll have a lot of critics to punch out, plus the people who pay money to see the movie."

"I left some stacks of hand-written party invites by the door to your offices, but no one was there yet," she said.

"I was just there. And it was open."

"I must have missed them." She pushed her overflowing festival bag toward his feet. "Will you be at the MTV party? Everyone says it will be the bomb. Lil Wayne might perform."

"No, thanks. I get beat up at your parties."

"Great," she said as she hurried out the door.

Ryan glanced at the front page of The Hollywood New Times. There was a front-page editorial from his publisher, Orson W. Woolsey, whose "Trade Wind" column featured his picture. Woolsey's writing was solemn and stiff, reflective of his entertainment law background in contract-writing.

Lauren Perrino appeared from behind him. "You're innocent, of course," Lauren said as she pushed a table out of the way, nearly knocking an ashtray to the floor as she sat down.

"Certainly innocent of killing Ingrid Bjorge," Ryan answered.

"Orson thinks it's important you keep a low profile on this and not do any interviews."

"That's what I thought he'd think. Besides, I've got too many films to review. As usual, I'm going up against about a dozen critics from *Variety*, and *The Hollywood Reporter* has its A-team."

"This has been a real black mark on the paper," she said as she shuffled through a thick stack of interview requests, faxes. "It's hurting our brand."

"It's not done a lot for my reputation either," he said.

Lauren pulled a letter from the stack. The stationery glistened. It was shiny white with stark black Asian lettering on the top. "Look at these. They're all in Japanese, or Chinese, or Filipino-ese, or something. Who knows what kind of creepy publications they are."

"The world is full of creepy publications, not just those devoted to the entertainment business," Ryan said. Irony or self-reflection did not abuse Lauren. She had been deluged with requests for interviews with Ryan. Many wanted to grill him on the air and get him, a la some old Perry Mason episode, to fess up. Scoop! *E: Entertainment!* solves the Cannes murder as the resident bimbette tricks the truth out of film critic/murderer Ryan Hackbart.

"Geraldo Rivera's people have been calling constantly about you," Lauren said.

"Ask him where he gets his mustache done," Ryan said. Lauren frowned. Ryan knew he'd have to tone it down. Lauren was a notorious well-poisoner, and he didn't need any bad word from her getting back to Woolsey.

"I hope you're getting enough sleep," Lauren said.

"I don't think I slept at all last night. I've still got this headache from when I got punched," he said.

Lauren jammed the interview requests for Ryan back into her folder. "It's ridiculous that I don't even have an assistant. I'm getting pretty tired of having to deal with all these press people, answering all their invasive questions," she said. "You don't happen to have a cigarette on you, do you?"

"I don't smoke."

"Me neither. I quit two years ago, but the last twenty-four hours have me craving," Lauren sighed.

"This festival has got everybody smoking again."

Lauren swooped up, brush-kissed him, and headed toward the elevator. As she turned, Stan Peck nearly ran her down. It was a fortuitous meeting. Lauren was able to bum a cigarette.

"There's a lot of people out there who still think you're guilty. You killed that blonde actress," Peck said to Ryan by way of a good-morning.

"That's idiotic," Ryan answered.

"They think she invited you to her hotel because she thought you were a big Hollywood critic and could do her some good down the line," Peck said. "She then had sex with you, and you got carried away and killed her."

"That's nuts. It's beyond nuts."

"I've heard it from a number of people. Alvy Berkowitz over at Miradel says it's entirely plausible."

"Alvy Berkowitz is a nerd and a complete idiot when it comes to developing scenarios," Ryan said.

"But Alvy knows the marketplace, and that is the jury," Peck said. He bit into a croissant and pushed it aside. "This murder of yours is screwing up my coverage. I've had to go to a stupid press conference about it when I should have been having breakfast with Nelson Jefferson and the TriCoast people."

By doing nothing, Ryan was screwing up everyone's festival.

Chapter 5

"Tyra, Tyra, Tyra!" The words did not come tripping off the tongue like "Lo-li-ta." Rather the two syllables blasted out – "Ty- rah, Ty-rah. Ty-rah" – much like a football cheer. The French mob was calling for Tyra Banks, the famous supermodel turned TV producer who had come to epitomize the fashion line's notion of high glamour and to epitomize the ideal of feminine beauty. Expectations were high for this year's show, positioned to set internet records over past successes when such superstar models as Stephanie Seymour, Shakira, Gisele Bundchen, and Daniela Pestova lit up the runway.

The street and sidewalk area outside of the Hotel Martinez roared as paparazzi jostled for position and fashion photographers, celebrity staffers, lingerie connoisseurs, and movie-fans craned their necks for a look at the comings-and-goings of the Victoria's Secret fashion models. Ryan savored the spectacle. He felt energized: he had churned out a very fast review that morning. It was a pithy dismissal of an English film in the venerable movie tradition of massive furniture and the age of the powdered wig. He had even managed to get in a jog in the rose garden before showering and downing two chocolate-filled croissants.

Ryan entered the Hotel Martinez and hurried across its lime-carpeted, art-deco lobby. He dodged workmen who had just finished draping a huge Victoria's Secret banner on the wall. The Victoria's

Secret charity bash would be held shortly in the hotel's main ballroom. The lingerie show had been the unabashed hit of the festival in recent years, beginning as an AIDS fund-raiser. Much to the snotty displeasure of festival purists, the lingerie line's annual catwalk extravaganza had become a permanent fixture.

The haunting saxophone strains of Last *Tango in Paris* gushed through the hotel lobby as Ryan hurried to the Victoria's Secret Charity Fashion Show. Gato Barbieri's raunchy and lilting sax always made him melancholy – he loved the score – but it was too early in the day for such sad strains. He maneuvered through the clogged lobby, pausing at a glass case that signaled the corridor to the Salle De Gaulle where the fash-bash was being staged. Ryan recalled that the case usually featured jewelry but today the signature blue scarf of *The Ice Princess* movie was featured. The azure scarf was draped around a jagged rock.

A woman tapped him on the shoulder. "I know who killed that actress," she said.

"You do?" Ryan responded.

The woman draped her arm around him and shot a selfie. "Yes, it's obvious, it was the director. They were having an affair."

"How do you know that?" Ryan asked.

"Because I know story structure. I was in development for Josh Brolin," she said.

Ryan nodded and presented his ticket to a man in a tuxedo at the door. Two women in sexy maroon teddies escorted him to his seat. To his amazement, it was in the front row, to the right of the runway.

He was seated in a section of cocktail tables roped-off in red velvet. Ryan joked to the guy at the next table, "Me without my digital."

"I'd lend you mine, but I left it in the suite. My kids always ridicule me because I don't have the latest gadget they're putting out this week," the gent said with a thick nasal tone. Ryan flinched. It was Mick Jagger. The Rolling Stone sat primly next to him with a sly grin across his face. He sported a parrot-green blazer and sipped from a water bottle.

"How's your movie production company going?" Ryan asked with a crag in his voice.

"A few projects in the pipeline," Mick said. "How is your murder spree going?"

"I'm easing off a bit till the end of the festival, Ryan said. "Why? Need anyone whacked?"

"I'll send you my list," Mick answered and turned back toward the stage. What was he doing sitting next to Mick Jagger? And the really crazy part – Mick had recognized him, obviously from the press coverage. No use looking a gift horse in the mouth, Ryan reasoned, no matter how bizarrely inspired. Bottom line, he had a fantastic ringside seat. He would be able to see the models as they entered the runway. Maybe his new notoriety had moved him up a notch in the social whirl. The promise of watching leggy lingerie models in a sanctioned social activity while seated next to his all-time favorite, rock star made Ryan nearly pinch himself. Only minutes earlier, in his dark mood, he had imagined himself in a dungeon-like French prison. And now he was runway-side at the sexiest fashion event of the year.

The invariable screeching of the microphones brought him back to his senses. The crowd quieted and the lights dimmed. A Mediterranean man in a white tuxedo appeared from behind the curtain and took center stage. "On this festive occasion, we must pay a moment of silence to the young actress, Ingrid Bjork, whose life was lost before it began." Nothing like using a beautiful woman's death to spur product interest, Ryan mused. Next time, get the name correct.

The room burst into applause at the end of the three seconds of silence, torture to many who had to quiet their electronics for the entire duration. The audience cheered as a fresh-faced model with shifting blonde hair sashayed down the ramp. Her apple-colored skin glowed over an emerald green teddy: the panty cut up between her thighs. She took three long strides down the runway before she was bombarded with floodlights and the rattlesnake-sounds of the digital cameras. The models pranced out with Busby-Berkeley precision every four or five seconds. A Nigerian with no hair paraded in a bridal-like, lacy two-piece. Several more beauties, in an array of shapes, sizes and colors promenaded before him – all united in their defiant attitudes. Ryan grinned: diversity and multiculturalism in its finest display.

Ryan paid uneven attention, gaping for Delisha. He sat up straight as he spied her at the top of the runway. Delisha enlivened a lacy burgundy V-string and a black garter belt snapped down to matching stockings. Smoky and sizzling. She sashayed with a snap, with the perfect high arch to her butt. As she approached the end of the runway, she feinted left and flipped a down-spin, a playful twirl that won her the event's most enthusiastic applause. The applause rippled and the music crescendo-ed. Although the sounds were dopey Euro-rock, the notes brought just the right carefree zest to the show. The show climaxed moments later when Delisha swung her hips back and forth – roughly to Juan les Pins on the east and Saint Tropez on the west -- as she teased in an azure teddy. Its skimpy lines jutted up her hips, conveying the illusion of no clothing at all.

Ryan turned to get Mick's reaction, but he had already left, smartly having slipped through the crowd when all attention was on the stage.

For the finale, the models strutted to the center of the stage. They formed a kick line. The sound system crackled into a rap version of Jacques Offenbach's "Can-Can" as the beauties thrust their legs in unison, right/left, right/left, to whistles, applause, and shout-outs.

As the applause still rippled through the room, Ryan followed Mick's gambit and slipped out. He hurried down the hallway and out of the lobby. The hotel's exterior was jammed with onlookers. The afternoon sun sliced down over the old buildings and straight into his face. Ryan maneuvered his way through the throng.

He hurried up the sidewalk to the Rue d'Antibes, pumped by the models-and-Mick experience. The store windows along the shopping area were as alluring as ever. Filled with succulent chocolates and candied fruit decorations, they were an enticing vision, especially with the pretty French clerks with their auburn hair and colorful nails in the background. Each boutique was filled with fruits and "les parfums," emoluments and lotions – all dripping with seductive promises.

Ryan glanced over at the train track behind the trees. Every-day people waited for their commute home, unaware and uninterested in what lingerie models or rock 'n' roll icons were doing a hundred or so yards away.

A jazz bar across the street, the Anaconda Room, gleamed with an old-style window display: a saxophone and a trumpet perched on a red velvet cloth. Like a 1920s expatriate-type joint.

"Thinking of drilling somebody's film to relieve the stress?"

Ryan turned. It was Barlowe. "You're right about needing to relieve the stress," Ryan answered. "Good to see you. Usually, I never run into you this much at Cannes."

"That's a good sign. It means you're not hiding out in movie theaters like you usually do," Barlowe joked.

"Isn't it kind of early in the day for you?" Ryan joked. "Barely afternoon."

"I'm on a new health-kick regimen," Barlowe said. "I still have some of that quality product I got in Amsterdam."

"No, thanks. I've got to keep my wits."

Barlowe pointed to the window of the jazz club. "So, are you thinking of checking out the Anaconda Room?"

"No time, but I love the window display. It's so Cole Porter. Plus, I love the tenor sax," Ryan said.

"Those are all musical props. It's not really a jazz-club. Senegalese girls come up from Africa to work the festival," Barlowe explained. "This is their room."

"Seriously?"

"And you're into black girls, right?"

"What?"

"I hear you've been seen with a dusky beauty," Barlowe said.

"Where did you hear that?"

"I didn't hear it. It's all over the internet." Barlowe clicked on his cell. He scrolled and pulled up a story. It was topped by a picture of Ryan and Delisha at breakfast at the Carlton. "You're a rock star, man."

Ryan stared at the internet photos of his breakfast with Delisha. It was true: people clearly recognized him. Strangers all around, peeping at him. This thing wouldn't stop.

Barlowe gestured back toward the Anaconda Room. "You should check out those African babes. They've got those great French/African accents. Plus, they have those outrageous butts."

"Just what I don't need," Ryan groused.

"This murder thing has got you uptight," Barlowe said. "Your man Henri is throwing one of his parties later in the festival. You should go this year."

"Not in another seedy warehouse. I heard people got mugged last year."

"There you go again, looking at the downside. Besides, this one's a converted warehouse. Very upscale, and Henri tells me that he knows the people who are providing security."

"Parties that start at 4 a.m. aren't exactly conducive to doing my job," Ryan said.

"You really missed one last year. There were these great Russian hookers who were into blow-jobs," Barlowe said. "I hear they're operating again down by the Dick Dock."

"Dick Dock?"

"Yeah, that's what they're calling the Old Port, this year. Just down from La Pizza. These Russian babes are crazy sexy."

"I've sworn off Russian hookers as a protest over Putin's policies."

Barlowe grinned: "I might steal that line for the festival," He angled off into the crowd, toting a cell phone in each hand.

Ryan shielded his eyes from the sun that jutted down from high over the Mediterranean. Delisha had been right about the sunscreen. With his fair complexion, he needed ultra-violet protection. He maneuvered his way across the crowded street, glanced back at the Anaconda Room: Russian mobsters, hookers, underwear models, and hucksters: *Cannes, how do I love thee? Let me count the ways.*

A gray-haired Gypsy approached him. It was a guy that Ryan recognized from previous years. He escorted a little girl, who handed out roses. During the festival, this little girl worked from dawn till past midnight. The festival had been trying to clean up on the Gypsies, but they always reappeared. Ryan skirted out of the way, torn between giving the Gypsy money for exploiting the little girl. Then, he saw the child's eyes, turned back and hurried over to them. He pulled out his wallet and handed a 10 Euro note to the little girl. She looked up at him, and then the man smiled at Ryan and grabbed the bill from her hand.

Ryan looked closely at the girl. Her eyes were slack, dead. She had probably been up till late at night, being dragged through Cannes. From expensive restaurant to expensive hotel. Her father – if he was her father – hustling money from inebriated, expense-account-rich festival goers. Ryan suspected he was being duped, but he knew he couldn't help but give something and hope it would help the little girl. Next time he would take them to a fruit stand and buy her something nourishing.

Back behind him he heard a roar of squealing applause. Some star, or wannabe star, or has-been had evidently emerged from the hotel. Or, even bigger, the festival's really big stars … the Victoria's Secret models.

Norwegian billionaire turned movie producer Gunnar Sevareid peered down at the Croisette, Cannes' gorgeous beach walkway, from his luxury suite at the Carlton Hotel. He watched as a gush of photographers had swarmed down the walkway, chasing a flock of

Victoria's Secret models that had strategically exited the hotel to attract maximum attention.

The silver-haired Norwegian leaned over to view the entrance where the poster for his film, *The Ice Princess*, perched in festival splendor. Sevareid had reserved seven suites at the Carlton, the unofficial flagship hotel of that glamorous Cannes Film Festival. The chairman and president of VikFilms, and also the majority owner of a multi-tier corporation encompassing North Sea fishing, minerals, natural gas, and oil exploration, Gunnar Sevareid had an estimated worth of $97.7 billion in U.S. dollars. Forbes tabulated him as one of the world's four richest men, in the company of Jeff Bezos, Bill Gates, and Warren Buffett. There were other billionaires, but Forbes did not have access to Russian gangster accounts, or sundry third-world despots. At seventy-four, Sevareid was bored with the routine of running a fishing/mineral/oil conglomerate.

Gunnar Sevareid was six feet five and ruggedly handsome in a Nordic way: thick silver hair, a firm chin, and sparkling blue eyes. His cheekbones were high, graced with supple, age-defiant skin. When Gunnar Sevareid made an entrance in Alpha-male domains, it was as if a powerful avenger had charged in to wipe out the vermin. The $35,000 a day tab for the Imperial Suite, which he had booked for the entire festival, did not make a dent in Sevareid's ledger line – it was mere petty cash. The four-bedroom, balcony suite perched on the southeast corner of the luxury hotel. His private bathroom was adorned in blue Brazilian marble and included a massive jet-tub.

From his Carlton balcony, Gunnar Sevareid savored the Mediterranean breezes, so different from the raging winds he had experienced most of his life on the North Sea. Their soft, sensual overtures he speculated were no more than a brush-kiss – don't expect more. Sevareid refocused; he would not allow his down-moods to ruin his festival. He had been preparing for more than a year for the movie-world and Cannes. He had marveled at how shady industrialists, garbage-collection moguls, used-car dealers, dry-cleaning merchants, and criminal-arms traders had made easy entrée into the Hollywood community. He was stunned at how they were embraced once they started investing in movies or new technologies. It was surreal how foreign gangsters won admiration from entertainment-world professionals. Most recently, a Russian billionaire gangster had entered the fray, buying up a Canadian movie company and hanging out with major Hollywood types.

Gunnar Sevareid had prepared for becoming a "major player" in Hollywood, or whatever people called "Hollywood" these days. He had secured the representation of BGK, the powerful public relations entity headed up by publicist-for-the-stars Susanne Clearidge. Bulldozing his way into the movie business improved his mood. The depression had subsided, the illness that had plagued him his entire life. New medication had "evened" him out. He was glad he had not taken it earlier in his life; the manic craziness had propelled him to greatness. For the festival, he knew he needed that old-edge: he had prepared for Cannes by weaning off his main med, Desoxyn, but the accompanying insomnia tormented him.

Sevareid had battled the insomnia since his arrival at Cannes by reading. He had delved into F. Scott Fitzgerald and was surprised to learn that the novelist had sojourned not far from Cannes in Juan les Pins while enjoying the celebrity of his first novel, *This Side of Paradise*, and beginning *The Great Gatsby*.

He sipped his coffee, enjoying the quiet. He speculated on who the C.I.A. would have at the film festival, considering its awful terrorist risk. As he stared out at the many yachts in the harbor and the super yachts further out in the bay, Sevareid recalled the best time he had ever had on a yacht – more than twenty years before – when he had taken the most beautiful blonde woman out on his boat near his hometown on the northern Norwegian coast.

Gunnar Sevareid munched on his Klivar chocolate, savoring what he had already set in motion for the foolish bastards who ruined his opening night film gala and killed his lead actress.

Like many crazy bastards throughout history, Gunnar Sevareid was hell-bent on saving the world.

Much colder than the beaches of Cannes where Gunnar Sevareid plotted his revenge, the coastal town of Bodo, Norway, was seared by a frigid wind. A hellish outpost that hovers just inside the Arctic Circle, Bodo is the town closest to Norway's northern border with Russia, eight miles away. Asbjorn Magnusson adjusted his scarf and zipped up his heavy-duty, insulated jacket. He was a member of a private infantry brigade, a clandestine component of Gunnar

Sevareid's oil-and-mineral empire. He turned off his Volvo snowmobile. His thick white snowsuit made him virtually invisible. The terrain was too remote and unpredictable for high-tech tracking. Virtually Google-proof.

Magnusson scoped his high-tech rifle, a VO Vapen Swedish hunting rifle, a preferred weapon for big-game. Today, his big-game targets were transporters of the Russian military. On the frozen Arctic terrain, the Russian troops traveled on reindeer sleighs; the animals were more reliable on the frozen tundra than high-tech military vehicles.

Magnusson squeezed: his first target crumpled, a perfect head-shot between the eyes. Then the second target, the third. The fourth, the fifth, and the sixth. The reindeer staggered, lurched in the deep snow. All kill-shots, if his weapon had not been loaded with animal tranquilizer instead of bullets. Six heavily tranquilized reindeer. They would recover and survive. His employer had insisted that the reindeer not be fatally harmed, but he had no such concern for the Russian troops who would never make it back to their base on foot.

Chapter 6

"This is so glamorous, freezing our asses off waiting for those little pricks," one of the thong models said as Ryan hopped off a tender, a transport boat that carried guests to the super yacht Orgasmo. The yacht 500 meters off the end of the old harbor at Cannes. As per Cannes regulations, any vessel that exceeded 60 meters had to stay one-quarter mile off shore.

The thong model sprayed sunscreen across her shoulders, and adjusted her orange, string bikini. "You don't speak English, I hope," she said to Ryan. "I didn't mean for you to hear what I just said."

"I do speak English, but I didn't hear a word about freezing your asses," he said.

"Oh, my God, it's you," the orange-thong girl exclaimed. "Don't you remember, the other night at the party? We took a selfie." It clicked for Ryan: she was the pretty, red-haired actress with whom Barlowe had paired him for a photo.

Christened "Orgasmo," the private yacht belonged to a Russian fertilizer billionaire, Nikita Besova, which the brothers Steele, Nick and Boris, had procured for Hands-On Films' worldwide splash at the Cannes Film Festival. Besova had granted them limited use of the yacht for the first part of the festival as part of a film production agreement.

The mega-yacht Orgasmo stretched 150 meters and cost more than $300 million. With its conspicuous luxury, the vessel had glided into the waters off Cannes like an old-time movie harlot. Once a former Soviet military ship, it had been revived by a business consortium in Minsk as a pleasure dome on the seas. Befitting its military heritage, the yacht was equipped with anti-aircraft artillery, as well as three mini-submarines with special rocket launchers. Orgasmo was fortified with state-of-the-art electronic fences that extended more than 4,000 yards. In addition, the super-yacht was equipped with a special wing that housed 50 men and women from a maritime security company out of Vladivostok. Some masqueraded as yacht guests for undercover intelligence-gathering during the vessel's festival parties.

Orgasmo now sizzled with the A-list sheen of an ostentatious luxury yacht. Its owner, Russian oligarch Nikita Besova, had made billions in fertilizer, oil, and minerals. It was rumored that he had gone to military school with Vladimir Putin.

The thong model hugged Ryan again, and he speculated about how many photos and videos were being snapped of them. Still, she was a beauty and Ryan was admittedly turned on. He would have to stop regarding everything, especially being approached by attractive women, as part of a plot to frame him.

From the front deck, Nick yelled out to him. "Do not be stealing my pussy!"

"I must leave," the model said. She skirted away as Nick approached. Ryan cringed at Nick's crudeness. Today, Nick was bare-chested, and drenched in tanning oil.

"I knew you would be a natural in handling the actresses," he exclaimed.

"I met her the other night at *The Ice Princess* party," Ryan noted.

"Watch out for her," Nick said. "She thinks she is a serious actress."

Of the two brothers (they were rumored to be half-brothers), Nick was the more outgoing, while Boris was dour, a behind-the-scenes businessman. Ryan was still shocked he had been assigned to do a profile on the two producers as part of *The Hollywood New Times*' special Cannes section. But, then again, he speculated his opportunistic new publisher, Orson W. Woolsey, was using Ryan's notoriety to "expand the brand." He also surmised that Hands-On must have purchased a boatload of ads in *The Hollywood New Times* to justify this advertorial.

Nick gestured to the yacht. "It is outrageous, right?" he said. "I will never go back to staying in a hotel again."

"You've got a great location, so close to the Palais," Ryan said.

"I named it Orgasmo for the Russian owner," Nick said. "It had a very boring name in Russian before the festival, but I got the idea from the name of that other yacht, the Eros."

"Isn't that Barry Diller's yacht?"

"Yes, if a big-shot like Diller can give his yacht a sexy name, why can't the rest of us?"

"You have a point," Ryan noted.

Hands-On had prospered, producing sadistic adventure movies that usually involved a forbidding terrain, constant gunfire, gruesome murders and no plot. Sometimes, they sold the same movie to the same people twice by just changing the title. The investors hardly ever looked at them anyway, just sent them out to the theaters in third-world markets or to streaming sites.

"We will have a great festival. We have videos of Ingrid Bjorge's early acting," Nick blurted.

"You've got worldwide attention with her," Ryan said.

"Yes, I spotted that blonde two years ago when I was in Amsterdam. She did some great videos, and I secured the rights. I saw her talent."

"Who would think someday she would be the star actress of the opening night film at Cannes?" Ryan said.

Nick lit a Dunhill cigarette. "Usually, I don't smoke. It's a vile habit, but this festival is so overwhelming, I allot myself six a day."

"One of our reporters does the same thing," Ryan said.

He stood back as Nick shouted orders at a team of two flunkies, one with a light meter and one with a handful of towels. Nick wrapped his arm around Ryan's shoulder. "Shower scenes are always good, especially if they're on the beach at Cannes."

"She's pretty," Ryan said, nodding toward the orange-thong model.

"They all are," Nick said. He took one last drag of the cigarette and sauntered over to a waste container. He glared at the sea, pointing toward a clump of debris floating in the surf. "People are such pigs," he said. "I remember when we first came here in 1986. That was the year they had all the US battleships and Reagan was shelling Libya," he said. "It was better then. There was not a bit of filth in the water. Now look at it."

Two other actresses sauntered from the yacht. One was black with crinkled red hair and paraded in a bright yellow thong. The other was a Mediterranean-skinned girl with a gold bottom and no top, just a hand towel draped over her shoulders. Both wore dark-blue cop's hats and carried red batons. Metallic gold hand-cuffs jangled from their bikini bottoms.

"Get under the shower and get your nipples hard," Nick called out. "Where is my blonde? She wins some pussy porn-star award, and she thinks she can blow me off." He waved his hands at two deckhands who toted a huge winter backdrop. "I have wasted a whole set for that blonde!" As Nick ranted, Boris emerged from the yacht. He approached Ryan and stood next to him without saying a word. Boris was not known for his charm.

"Goldie Jolie did not show," Nick yelled over to him.

"So, get another one with bigger tits" Boris said. "What's the difference? Blondes all look alike."

"I signed this one, and she's the one I need. I have a vision for this shoot. She has the special look," Nick said.

"Believe me, from what I've heard about this Goldie, she will never show up," Boris said. He turned to Ryan. "Sometimes I think

Nick takes this directing thing too seriously. This place is crawling with blondes, especially with convergence."

"Convergence?"

"Yes, a theory of mine," Boris said. "The adult-video world and the Hollywood movie world are converging. Many top performers in porn have crossed over into mainstream movies," Boris said. He reached into his coat pocket and handed Ryan a news clipping from Variety. "Jiz Biz Whiz," the headline read. In real English, that translated to adult DVDs and on-demand cable porn haul in mega-tons of money.

"Adult entertainment grosses more in a year than the NFL, the NBA, and Major League Baseball combined," Boris said. "The ancillary sales – personalized dildos, lingerie lines, and love toys - are even more phenomenal."

As Ryan processed this unique theory of the state of modern cinema being driven by sex toys, he spotted Henri from *The Hollywood New Times* office coming from the yacht. Henri headed toward Boris, but then turned away. Boris hurried after him. Ryan watched, wondering if Henri had spotted him and for some reason wanted to avoid being seen. He wondered if Henri might have instigated the idea of linking Nick and Boris to *The Hollywood New Times*. He seemed to know everyone at the festival, and all the ins-and-outs of how things really got done.

Ryan turned to see Nick had approached him from the side. The producer put his arm around Ryan's shoulders. "You look a little sickly."

"No, I was just thinking I need some sunscreen," Ryan said. "Someone reminded me of that the other day. I forgot to pack it. With my complexion, I get burned fast."

"Go down into my private bathroom. I have just the stuff for you there," Nick said. "It's in my medicine chest. But take off your shoes before you get on the yacht."

"Thank you. I will." Ryan needed a break from Nick. He hustled onto the yacht. He padded onto the dark wooded-deck and ducked his head as he went down into the cabin. He maneuvered down its four steps and entered a dining room. The room was empty except for a shiny black table with eight chairs. It was stacked with dirty highball glasses.

"Nick sent me down to get some sunscreen in his bathroom," Ryan said. The kid pointed toward the back of the yacht. Ryan headed down the hallway and entered what looked like the living-room area. Unlike the photos of yachts he had seen in magazines, this one didn't have a dark-wooded interior with a stately shelf adorned by nautical pieces. The walls were plastered with bright purple wallpaper that featured gold etchings of naked men and women in sexual positions: Kama Sutra kitsch.

Ryan followed a small hallway to the right, and behind it found a video room, complete with all the gadgetry and toys, most prominently an Avid editing machine. Ryan poked his way into the bowels of the vessel, toward a room at the end. It was a large bathroom, with a hot tub and a stall shower. He opened the medicine chest, one of those round ones like they used to have in the Old Spice commercials Ryan enjoyed as a kid.

It was filled with every color of Trojan condom in the universe – orange, purple, blue, gold. Bottles of cologne, tweezers, and one of those electric nose-hair clippers were crammed inside. Amid the mess, there was a small box full of packets. Ryan took one out. It was light green and proclaimed "Androgel 1%." in dark green letters. Below that, it said in parentheses "testosterone gel." Other than the testosterone gel, there were two prescription bottles, Hydrocodone and Vicodin. He unscrewed the cap and jiggled out a Vicodin capsule. He stuffed it in his pocket. Why not? A necessary precaution for what could happen down the line: he was already half-delirious with lack of sleep and constant worry. And, worse, his head still ached from Pinelli's punch. The painkiller might be a blessing.

Ryan glanced around the medicine cabinet. He noticed a Ziploc bag. Inside were two white cotton panties. Both were ripped in several places. Next to the Ziploc a container was filled with plastic packets. Some were red, some were yellow, like ketchup/mustard packets. Ryan slit open the top of a red one, squeezed. Watery goo oozed out, filmier than usual sunscreen. Ryan rubbed it on his hands, then smoothed it across his forehead and nose. He slipped several of the sunscreen packets into his pocket.

"What are you doing?"

Ryan whirled around. "I'm getting some sunscreen," he answered.

"Oh, it is you, Mr. Hackbart. I did not recognize you," Boris said. "Hand me a couple packets. I feel heat coming on."

"Which ones? Red or yellow?"

"Red," Boris said. "Nick prefers the yellow ones, slightly higher protection."

"Who markets this sunscreen? It beats carrying around a tube with you," Ryan said.

"It is something Nick arranged. The plastic-wrap guys who do our DVDs are into other packaging too. They are making big money." Boris turned around and headed up top. Ryan followed him up the stairway, feeling somewhat bummed at his prescription-pill theft.

Ryan patted more sunscreen on his forehead as he walked across the deck. It was much stickier than the Aveeno he was used to. He squinted in the direction of the bikini-girl shoot. Nick swung his arms around, like a coked-up music conductor. The girls giggled and squealed happily, as if they were having a great romp in the hot sun. They rubbed their breasts with the soap, lathering up and cupping their breasts with their hands. "Well, what did you think? It will go down as one of the greatest topless shower scenes in the history of movies, don't you think?" he asked Ryan.

Ryan paused, trying to formulate an answer.

"You didn't like it? Something was wrong?" Nick asked. "Their boobs aren't good enough, not big enough? Not what you're used to?"

"If you're doing a sexy shower scene, you should only have the girls rub their breasts for a second at the beginning," Ryan said. "Then, you have them sponge their stomachs, rub their arms, rub their upper legs, but not their breasts."

"Their stomachs? Are you crazy? This is a tit shot."

"That's right," Ryan said. "And if you've got them rubbing and cleaning their breasts, what is the viewer going to see? Hands and rags and soap. By having them rub their breasts, you're blocking the view."

"You are a genius," Nick said. He let out a shrill whistle and gestured to the cameramen. "We need another take." He slapped Ryan across the back, beaming. "Where do you come up with such good ideas? You have obviously rubbed a lot of tits."

"I've just seen a lot of old Roger Corman movies," Ryan answered. "The second scene in those movies is typically the locker-room scene, where all the girls from the swim team, the volleyball team, or the cheerleading squad undress and shower."

"Yes, the money scene," Nick said. He waved the girls back to the shower pole. Ryan looked out and saw the "actresses" returning from the boat. He could have kicked himself. Now they would have to freeze again so this little sleaze-bag could get his shot. The girl in the orange thong caught his gaze. Ryan approached her.

"I'm so sorry," he said. "I didn't mean to say anything and subject you to that again."

"Don't sweat it," she said. "You can make it up to me, though. Take me to a premiere or a party."

"I'm pretty swamped with all the reviews I have to write."

"Well, I give good after-party," she winked. "I need your advice on breaking into real acting."

"Well, I'm not connected with acting," Ryan answered.

"I was thinking of making a sex video to get noticed, like Kim Kardashian did."

"There are better ways."

"Well, I've heard sleeping with a producer is only going to get you a sexual disease," she said. "Plus, I hear after this Weinstein guy got busted, all the producers are pussies."

"I wouldn't believe that," Ryan said. "There are still a lot of predators out there. Plus, sleeping with them would only make you a MAW."

"What's that?"

"Model- Actress-Whatever," Ryan said. "Hollywood players prey on beautiful and ambitious girls. They go through them and lead them on, but they never cast MAWs in their movies. They discard them."

"You make it sound so cruel," she said.

"It can be."

"So, doing this nude project might not be the right path?"

"I couldn't say. I tend to be kind of old-fashioned. My advice would be to get in as many plays as possible in LA. The agents still scout there."

"Maybe someday you can write a review of me in a big movie. I've got to read a new script for a shoot we're doing later today," she said.

"What's the story line?" Ryan asked.

"I get gang-raped by cops and robbers."

"What? You have multiple partners?"

"I don't know how many. I'll have to read the script first," she said.

She hugged Ryan and scampered back toward the yacht. Ryan hoped he had given her the right advice. He turned and stared off at the blue sea. He speculated on what career advice he should give himself. In his darker moments, Ryan reflected on the demise of his own profession, the on-staff film critic. Many of his colleagues at big-city papers had been given pink slips, replaced by the syndicated movie critics. Reuters and some new syndicate in Europe picked up his reviews from *The Hollywood New Times* for their major markets. No telling how many critics Ryan himself had caused to be down-sized. In the not-too-distant future people would pull up "film critic" on Wikipedia and learn about the strange profession that had run through late twentieth century and fizzled out in the first part of the twenty-first. It was time for him to position himself for a new stage. Ryan hated transitions. He'd ruminate about it after the festival. He just had to hunker down and survive this one.

Nick startled him out of his funk. He playfully clasped his arm around Ryan's neck. "I'm serious. Would you like to direct for me? Fifteen-hundred cash a day and all the pussy you can eat."

"Not for me," Ryan answered.

"Yes, you are a true film-critic type, more interested in art. Have you gotten enough for your story?"

Ryan looked back and saw the girls all squatted and huddled under their towels, trying to get warm. "Yes, I've seen enough."

Ryan hurried along the walkway of the Old Port. He darted around a white convertible Rolls Royce. Tourists had lined up to get their photo taken in front of the vehicle by a tuxedoed photographer for a preposterous 35 Euros. He turned right and headed toward the Croisette. The festival's first weekend also coincided with France's Labor Day. The Croisette was inundated with French tourists who had come to gape at the festival people, spot a star, or be able to tell their friends they were there the year an actress was killed. In the real world, it was Sunday.

He picked up his step, neatly skipping around the guy who always painted himself completely in silver and stood motionless as tourists or first-time festival types stopped to gape, and toss coins onto his plate. Up ahead, Ryan spotted Cossack soldiers promenading down the Croisette perched atop impressive stallions. They were part of Nikita Besova's festival splash: Orgasmo had transported nine Arabian stallions, as well as former Soviet military soldiers who would ride them up and down the Croisette during the festival. The soldiers were selected for their dark, swarthy looks or, as described by *The Hollywood Reporter*: "They all looked like Joe Stalin on speed." Most had participated in the violent mayhem during Russia's annexation of the Crimea from Ukraine. The two riders at the front of the promenade had earned special tattoos for their brutal participation at the so-called Pussy Riot during the 2014 Winter Olympics in Sochi. They had tear-gassed and bullied a band that had performed a song mocking Putin.

The "Cossacks" now "patrolled" the shore of the most glamorous film festival in the world. The horsemen could barely control themselves with the abundance of beautiful women. The beauties, however, paid no attention to the Cossacks because they had no money to spend on them or could do nothing for their movie careers. The riders felt they were the only men in Cannes who were not getting laid, and they were not happy about it.

The whole walkway was packed, and it was in this glob of humanity where the festival made a quick fade into everyday tourists – older men and women, paunchy voyeurs, teens – meandered along the beach-front walk. "Hey, Hackbart!" Stan Peck burst out from the pack. "You haven't returned any of my messages," Peck said. "I'd like to get your side of the story." Peck pulled out a digital recorder. "So, set the record straight for me on this murder. Your side."

"My side of the story is irrelevant, as I've told you before," Ryan answered. "The police asked me in for questioning, and were satisfied with my answers. I know nothing about the murder."

"You know it's ironic that you, a member of the press, aren't talking to me, another member of the press."

"I'm an ironical guy. You can quote me on that."

"Seriously, you were hauled in. You said in your review that she should be strangled."

"I criticized the dialogue. A new editor mangled it with the scarf thing. The police understood," Ryan answered.

"You've been keeping some beautiful company, I've noticed," Peck said. "Being a murder suspect, has it increased your allure with women?"

"I'm running late for a screening." Ryan hurried away. He angled left across the Croisette. Despite the momentary high of jerking Peck around, Ryan was pissed at himself for giving Peck between-the-lines hints about the police interrogation. He hadn't said anything Peck could misquote, but he knew Peck had read him correctly. Peck would know Ryan was still bothered by the police interrogation.

Ryan took deep breaths as he approached the Carlton Hotel. Four seconds in, pause, four seconds out. He sucked in the cool sea air, preparing for the Galois smoke in the screening line. Smoke and screen, his brain clicked with the word association. That's what this festival was about: smoke and screen. Namely, hype and illusion.

As usual during the festival, the Carlton's entrance-way was decked out with a large movie poster. In years past, guests had exited through Pierce Brosnan's legs in *Tomorrow Never Dies*, or under Tom Cruise's wheels as he soared atop a motorcycle in *Mission*

Impossible. This year the grand hotel's entrance was encased in a spectacular poster, rimmed with jagged slices of ice. It was adorned in various shades of blue. It was, of course, for *The Ice Princess*.

Up above, three small planes looped their way through the light blue sky. Further out was a blimp. It was red and yellow with the Hands-On logo encrusted across its breadth. Once again, he mused about how much of the festival didn't have to do with movies at all. The fashion aspect of film festivals and awards shows had heated up in the '80s when the fashion people began to notice they could use the long walk to the Oscars as a fashion show for their lines. Armani had set up shop in 1988 and with a shrewd fashion manager had snagged some of the bigger stars to wear his fashions. Ryan had heard there had been fights over who wore what, and snooty houses were exclusive to certain actresses. "No, we can't dress Halle. We only do Jennifer Aniston."

Jewelers had gotten into the act too, and such houses as Harry Winston began loaning out massive amounts of gems to Oscar-goers. Then they were chastened by bad experiences when certain stars became too greedy and insisted they keep the jewels. Now there were contracts to protect the merchants from the more larcenous of the beautiful people.

Every now and then, things clicked beautifully: Uma Thurman in her lilac Prada: The fashion line was launched on the strength of Oscar showing, vaulting from a handbag house to a full-fashion behemoth. Ryan wondered what Ingrid would have been wearing that night. Probably something in azure blue. Enough fashion and thoughts of Ingrid. He was amazed at how personally he had taken her death.

Chapter 7

Day 5

The first van had already left, and the rest of *The Hollywood New Times* staff was stuffed into the second van. It was poised to head to Grasse for a night of R & R. The entire newspaper crew had been invited, courtesy of Berlusconi Communications, to a party at a chateau the conglomerate had leased in the perfume country, just outside of Cannes.

Ryan stood uneasily by the door, enduring the glare of the driver. He had convinced him to wait for Delisha, his model friend. Ryan sported his ubiquitous blue sport coat and a crisp white shirt, but he had enlivened it with a purple-bow tie. It had been a favorite of Delisha on the occasions he had taken her to events back in LA. Just as the driver yelled something at him in unfriendly French, Delisha arrived, blasting down the Croisette on her micro-scooter.

She was decked out in a one-piece silver mini-skirt with a sleeveless top and a low, jagged neckline. She wore a delicate pair of silver slippers. Her hair fluttered in the early evening breeze, showing off pearl ear-rings, and the light-blue scarf adorned her neck. The driver gave Ryan an appreciative glance, acknowledging that Delisha was worth the wait.

Delisha swung into the first pair of open seats, wiggling over toward the window. “Sorry, I’m late,” she said as she slid a kiss onto Ryan’s cheek. *The Hollywood New Times* publicist, Lauren Perrino, sat on the opposite side of the aisle. Lauren glanced dismissively at Ryan and then out the window.

“You were terrific at the fashion show,” Ryan said.

“Thanks, it was off-the-hook.”

Lauren leaned over. “Ryan, you haven’t introduced anyone to your date yet. She’s so beautiful, so I can see why you want to keep her to yourself,” she said.

“Lauren, this is Delisha.” Ryan said.

“Hi, Lauren. Your blouse is slamming,” Delisha said.

“Thank you, it's Armani,” Lauren said. “What do you think about Ryan being a celebrity?”

“He’s always been a celebrity to me,” Delisha said.

Lauren did not respond. She opened her wallet, pulled out a hand mirror. A photo of a dog was embedded on the back.

“Is that your dog?” Delisha asked.

“Yes, he’s new. I named him Bruce.”

“Is Bruce gay?” Delisha asked.

“What made you say that?”

“Well, when I was first starting out and doing stage plays, Bruce was usually the name of a gay character in the play,” Delisha said.

“Well, Bruce is definitely not gay, but I’d be perfectly happy if he was,” Lauren snapped.

“I’ll bet you miss him,” Delisha added.

"Yes, I do. Of course, he's well taken care of. I got him a reservation at the Canine Country Club on Melrose," Lauren said.

"That's sweet."

"Cameron Diaz just loves him," Lauren said.

"Cameron Diaz knows your dog?"

"Yes. I walk Bruce sometimes in the Hollywood Hills when I go to visit my friend Cochise," Lauren said. "Cameron lives up the drive. We run into her on Sunday afternoons. She always plays with Bruce."

Lauren handed the photo to Ryan. "Nice dog," he said. "To me, it looks like Bruce might be bisexual or even gender nonconforming."

"That sounds like something only you would think," Lauren said.

"Or, he could be a heterosexual male, but just likes to bark a lot," Delisha joked.

"He's not bisexual, and even if he was, it would be fine with me," Lauren said. With that pronouncement, Lauren snatched the photo and turned away.

Ryan wrapped his arm around Delisha's shoulder. She yanked a wad of business cards out of her mini-purse. She handed them to Ryan.

"You've collected all these cards since I saw you last?"

"People keep handing them to me," she said. "I didn't know anyone used business cards anymore," she said. Ryan did not curb her enthusiasm by noting most of the cards were from older, tech-challenged guys who had one thing on their minds.

The minibus began to sway as it wound out along the country road. It circled past the flower market and up the hill, and then headed onto one of the narrow freeways that rimmed the city. As Delisha lolled on his shoulder, Ryan gazed out at the old stone farmhouses and animals. Goats grazed on the hillside. Bougainvillea caressed the old stone barns. Wildflowers sprouted in patches of purple, orange, and yellow. All along the route, roses bloomed. "Slow down and smell the roses," he told himself.

Down to its essential mission, the ride itself was ironic: they were traveling to a gala event through some of the most bucolic and cherished hillsides in the world, in the prettiest month and during the golden time of the day – and what was it all for? So a newly acquired media conglomerate could host opinion makers, or deal-makers to elbow in their agendas for whatever they were doing.

Delisha fell asleep. The next hour passed in a swoon of green countryside and Delisha's rhythmic breathing. Eventually, the little bus turned off the main road onto a long paved drive and chugged up a steep hillside. It was surrounded by a stone wall. Eight security guards in high-fascist uniforms manned the entrance-way.

"What's the delay? Who are these people?" Lauren Perrino barked to no one in particular. "What do they think we are, terrorists?"

The driver pressed the lever, and the door whooshed open. Lauren elbowed her way past everyone, and emerged first. Several security guards formed a corridor from the bus to the chateau.

Ryan and Delisha proceeded through a cobbled courtyard and onto lavish, multi-tier grounds. Delisha sparkled as the early evening sun's rays cascaded off her silver dress, bouncing off in a fitting electric glow.

Roses caressed the upper terrace, arching all along the stone walls. On the terrace, a twelve-piece orchestra bounced through the last refrain of Swing, Swing, Swing. The Benny Goodman sounds belted out their raunchy, primitive call, jolting everyone into a festive state. Waiters pirouetted, swirling with their silver trays of champagne, assorted wines, and a cornucopia of colorful, sculptured hors d'oeuvre.

A phalanx of wine stewards poured Bordeaux at a white-linen table. Delisha pulled off a glass while Ryan watched the steward pour the same expensive Chateau de Rothschild Bordeaux brand that Gunnar Sevareid had procured for The Ice Princess party. The wine distributors must make a fortune at this festival, Ryan calculated. Delisha sipped on her drink and snuggled up against him. "How's your wine?" he asked.

"Good, I guess. I never really drink wine," she said. "Someone told me this stuff costs about $300 a bottle."

She glanced at the bottles, noting the label. She watched as a steward gathered the empties and placed them in vintage, dark-brown wooden wine cases, all tastefully imprinted with the most colorful and impressive stamps and pedigrees. "If I could get one of these empty bottles I could refill it with some Boone Apple and serve it at my next dinner party," she joked.

"Now you're talking my kind of party," Ryan said.

The strains of Lauren Perrino's shrill bellow punctured the evening's patter: "You call these hors d'oeuvres?"

Ryan slid his hand to Delisha's waist, and guided her to the far end of the deck. Stone vases with purple and orange roses lined the perimeter. A hundred-foot length of granite stairs descended toward a reflecting pool. A young woman dangled her feet in the water. She splashed and laughed to herself. Further down below, the lush green grounds were edged with rose bushes. To the right tennis courts rested, partially secluded in the lines of fir trees. A hedged wall about four feet high separated the courts from the chateau. And, far down the hillside, the farmhouse lights flickered, as if they were part of the party design.

"I love it that the band is doing Benny Goodman," Ryan said.

"That's what those songs are?"

"Yes, from the big-band era. It was a more civilized time when people regularly got dressed up and went out for dinner and danced under the stars."

"Seriously?"

"Yes, places like the Aragon Ballroom in Chicago where my grandparents used to go. In Santa Monica, the pier had an Aragon Ballroom on the end. It was famous for its sophisticated Saturday night dances."

"They got all dressed up to go to the Santa Monica Pier?"

"Well, it was a different time," Ryan answered.

"I do love these old songs, though. They've got so many instruments," Delisha added. "I'm going to have to tell my grandma about this party. She is always complaining that people my age don't have as much fun as they used to when she was young."

"She might be right," Ryan said.

"The night is still young," she said. "Besides, I don't always tell her everything." Ryan relaxed, and put his arm around her waist. They savored the sight. More than two hundred A-list party-goers circulated, not counting the legions of waiters and armies of security people. George and Amal Clooney chatted with David Geffen and Brittany Baker, while Barry Diller and Diane von Furstenberg maneuvered toward Leonardo Di Caprio and his svelte date.

"Do you know many people here?" Delisha asked.

Ryan nodded. "I recognize a few bigwigs."

In their tuxes and jewels, they all looked important, but Ryan reasoned most of the attendees were management wonks in charge of conglomerate-owned media companies. Ryan spotted his old buddy Barlowe with Nick Steele, not surprising since Barlowe was always on the prowl for "actresses" and Steele had a stable on his yacht. Ryan took Delisha by the arm and guided her out of Steele's range. He steered her past tennis courts, and through a maze of small evergreens. Delisha squeezed his hand again, and he stroked the inside of her thumb.

Overhead, the true stars had arrived for the party. Ryan felt as if he were encased in some kind of magical, snow-globe world. He felt as if stardust was sprinkling down on them. Strolling with Delisha through the rose gardens in Provence as an invited guest at an impossible-ticket party at the Cannes Film Festival – everything was suddenly right.

"Do you have a girlfriend now?" she asked.

"I haven't dated since the divorce."

"'Dated,' now there's a concept from the past," she said. "What about that publicist you were seeing?"

"Well, we're friends."

"You always seem to drift into the friend-zone," Delisha said.

"Yes, I'm so sick of hearing, 'You're such a nice guy with a great sense of humor, but'."

"Don't worry, sweetie," Delisha said. "I think you've just got to expand your horizons. The only women you are meeting are actresses and publicists, and, basically, they're all self-involved."

"But I am expanding my range," he said.

"You are?"

"Yes, I'm expanding my circle to include lingerie models," Ryan said.

She laughed and punched him on the shoulder: "Touché! Your luck seems about as good as mine," she said. "I'm a real loser-magnet. I think I've had it with Purvis."

"What's he doing these days?" Ryan asked.

"After he got cut from the Clippers, he went to play in Italy. I haven't seen him for three months."

"You and he have quite a history."

"Well, that's the word for him, history." She looked up at Ryan. "I need this festival to take my mind off him. I need a break."

"That's what festivals are for, or should be for," Ryan added.

She touched his hair. "You're still Mr. Frizzy." Delisha wrapped her arms around his shoulders, pulled him toward her, and kissed him. Ryan slid his arms around her waist, drifting into her. She stretched backward, looked to the side, and then pulled him down into the shrubs. Ryan landed backward on his elbows and looked up at her. She flipped her hair back, arched her neck, and nuzzled straight into him. He caressed the cleft of her neck. She swirled her lips against his. In the distance, he barely heard the "thud, thud, thud" of the fireworks and the applause of the revelers — "ooohs" and "aaahs."

Overhead the sky erupted with a swirl of reds, pinks, greens, blues, and oranges and, best, the silver down-shimmer. Ryan held Delisha snugly as they watched the magical sky-drops. "I hope you're not going to compare this to an old movie," she said.

"No, I would never compare it to the blast of fireworks over the Carlton Hotel as Cary Grant and Grace Kelly, he in his black tux and she in her blue dress, stood at the door to her bedroom in the 1955 classic To Catch a Thief."

Delisha squealed and pinched him on the shoulder. "I'm going to have to discipline you, young man. I told you, 'no talking about old movies when I'm trying to make you.'"

She rubbed up against him, playfully punching and slapping. Ryan pulled her toward him. As he kissed her, he detected the sneering puss of Lauren Perrino. The little twit was hunched over, gaping in between the two bushes. Her head tilted like one of those hideous close-ups in the horror movies: Bette Davis/Susan Sarandon eyes. "This is a respectable, black-tie party," she called out. "Robert De Niro is supposed to come with all the Tribeca people. Show some decency!" She swirled and hurried off.

"That woman needs to get laid," Delisha said. She smiled at Ryan. "And she's not the only one, Monsieur Old Movies."

"That's an inspired notion. But just not here," Ryan said.

"I didn't mean we'd do it here. Besides, this setting isn't romantic enough." She laughed. "See, I'm even picking up on your weird sense of humor. You're rubbing off on me. And I'll be rubbing off on you later."

For once, Ryan did not ruin the moment with word-play. Up above, the fireworks sputtered to their finale. On cue, the band slid into "Star Dust." The solo trombone nuzzled into the cusp of the Hoagy Carmichael classic. As the horn took hold of the melody and lifted "Star Dust" over the garden walls and up into the rose-scented sky, Ryan held Delisha. And he whispered into her ear the sprinkle of the last refrain: "The melody haunts my reverie, and I am once again with you."

"Stop talking," she said.

"How did you enjoy the fireworks?"

"They were fantastic," Delisha said. "But I'm still waiting for the grand finale, or should, I say, 'climax'?"

She squeezed Ryan's hand and flashed a smile toward The Hollywood New Times' editor, Bernie Shore. Bernie was multitasking: trying to devour the teeming plate of delectations, as well as to make conversation. It was a particular challenge since he talked with his hands, and his chin pointed toward Delisha's chest.

"Bernie, this is Delisha," Ryan finally said.

The newsman reached out and pawed at her hand with his napkin. "How have you found the festival?"

"I haven't been able to get to it yet," Delisha answered.

Bernie stopped gnawing and gaped at Delisha. "Who are you here with?"

"I'm here with the lingerie."

Bernie started to choke and threw a quick glance at Ryan. The old newshound in him wanted to know what someone could be doing here if it wasn't for the deal-making at the festival, and the horny old goat in him wanted to know what this silver-spangled beauty was doing with his mild-mannered, senior film critic. It didn't compute, so he turned to business. "No word yet on whether Lionsgate is going to pick up The Ice Princess. What do you think?" he asked Ryan.

"I haven't really thought about it," Ryan said.

Bernie turned to Delisha. "You'll have to have Ryan introduce you to Robert De Niro. He's supposed to show up later on."

"No way am I going to let De Niro get near her," Ryan said.

"By the way, Dragan Dylko is here somewhere," Bernie said. "He's pissed off that you accused him of sabotaging your Ice Princess review."

"I didn't accuse him," Ryan said. "I want to talk to him. See what happened."

"Well, keep your guard up. He's a hothead, and he's been looking for you,"

Bernie said.

"Don't worry, I've already been sucker-punched at one party. I'm not angling for another."

"He's wearing a gold tux. He told me he has scored an interview with Nikita Besova."

"Who?"

"Nikita Besova is a mega-billionaire Russian and he is soon to be a major player in entertainment product. Woolsey had a breakfast with him at the Eden Roc this morning and found out he's setting up a state-of-the-art studio in Moscow. He is going to call it The Eisenstein Institute, in honor of some old-time Russian filmmaker."

"Sergei Eisenstein. Battleship Potemkin," Ryan added.

"Anyway, Dylko is going to have it for us exclusive."

Delisha arched her back and looked out over Bernie's shoulder. A crowd milled around the little reflecting pool. Delisha pulled away.

She brushed past Bernie, and dashed toward the group. Ryan hurried after her.

In the midst of the crowd, a woman floated face down in the water. Her black gown crinkled over her body. "I wonder if it's some sort of performance art," a male voice said.

"It's a bit off-color, even for the French absurdists," a woman in a lime-colored tunic added.

Delisha jumped into the pool. She grabbed the woman in the pool and pulled her up by the neck. The water splashed up. "Are you, okay? Talk to me!" Delisha called out. She swirled the woman around. The woman's eyes were blank. Her jowls gushed out. Delisha shook her and threw her over the side of the pool. The woman's head bounced on the tile, and Delisha jumped out and crouched over her. She dug into her mouth with her thumbs. Delisha pinched the woman's nose tight and cupped her mouth over the woman's lips, blowing deeply. Delisha threw her head back again and sucked in huge lungs of air. She forced the oxygen into the woman's mouth. Delisha pulled her head up, flipped her hair back, and pushed down hard over the woman. Up, down. Up, down. She forced her palms into the woman's chest, pressing firmly. On the fifth thrust, the woman blasted out water. She wheezed like a tire had hit a nail. She coughed, sucking in air, trying to grab air through her eruptions. She shuddered, splashing and spewing out more water – straight at Delisha.

"You're okay! You're okay," Delisha sang out.

The crowd muttered, quieted, and someone began to clap. Everyone joined in. A man grabbed a shawl from his date and put it around Delisha's shoulders. People began to whoop and cheer, all in their respective languages. Ryan bent down and hugged Delisha, steadying her and helping her to her feet. Ryan led her away from the edge of the pool.

"Delisha, you just saved someone's life!" She looked back, watching protectively as people ministered to the woman. She began to cry. "It's all right. Delisha, you just saved that woman's life," Ryan exclaimed.

"Were they going to let her die?"

"I don't know. It was too bizarre. They didn't want to look foolish and jump in the water if it was some sort of performance-art or prank."

"What is it with these movie people?"

"They're not necessarily bad. They're all in their own little worlds, chattering about their deal memos, Russian financing, and up-coming projects," Ryan said. "It's not that they're callous, or even horrible people, they're just self-absorbed and insecure." He wrapped his arm around her shoulders, leading her away from the pool. They sat on one of the stone ledges. She cried softly. Ryan held her firmly and rocked her in his arms. People looked on from their distance, and the security team formed a wall around them.

Ryan could see the party-goers were chirping enthusiastically, lifting champagne glasses. The party had new energy. Nick Steele approached, elbowing his way past the guards. Ryan cringed. He'd want to film Delisha in her wet, clingy dress and star her in one of his sleazy productions.

"I heard everything about your girlfriend's brave rescue," Nick said. He leaned down over Delisha and turned to Ryan. "Is your girlfriend all right, Mr. Hackbart?"

"Yes, Nick."

"Your girlfriend is a hero. She is a true-life hero, not a movie hero," he said. "I have been called for an important meeting. It is from a big investor for my new film. He's got oil money and fertilizer megabucks. We are taking a meeting in his limo on the way to another party."

He reached into his pocket and pulled out a key. He handed it to Ryan. "This is the key to my Aston Martin. You should not have to ride back in a bus filled with common people. Your girlfriend is royalty, and you my friend, are obviously a prince for being with her."

"I've never driven an Aston Martin before," Ryan said.

"Then, here is your opportunity. This one is the same model as the one Pierce Brosnan drove when he was James Bond, that one with Halle Berry in the orange bikini." He sneaked a glance at Delisha. He turned back to Ryan. "It is down by the valets. Put it through its paces with your lovely girlfriend," Nick said. "The moon is becoming full, and it will be a beautiful drive for you two."

"Okay, and I'll get it right back to you."

"Just drop it by the yacht. I want to talk to you anyway about directing one of my movies. I liked your suggestions for that scene the other day."

"Good evening, beautiful lady," Nick said to Delisha as he hurried off.

"Does he want you to direct something?" Delisha asked.

"No, nothing I would be interested in," Ryan answered. "He was just being kind, trying to make me look good in front of you."

Chapter 8

There were enough security guards to stock an island dictatorship. Instead of colorful uniforms with feathered hats, gaudy medals, and polished swords, the party's front-guard boasted black Armani tuxedos, silver cummerbunds, and azure bow-ties. The well-dressed unit stood at attention at the mansion's gate. Despite their disciplined pose, their eyes riveted on Delisha.

Within seconds, one of the attendants had pulled up with the car, and at least half the squadron had rushed to help Delisha into the passenger side of the gleaming Aston Martin V12. Another attendant brought Delisha her microscooter that she had left in the van. He bowed like a knight-of-old and presented it to her. She reciprocated with a curtsy and slid into the classic vehicle. "Allons y," Delisha called out, bestowing a celebratory wave on the riveted attendants.

Ryan hunched up against the steering wheel, not used to its position in what he knew as the passenger-side of the front seat. He idled as the iron gates snapped open, spreading their steel in a deferential backward swoop, like an old-fashioned English servant. Once they had gotten the clear sailing salute from the guards, Ryan punched the pedal. They flew through the estate's stone-lined entrance.

Ryan fingered the wooden steering wheel. Three prongs with the perfect diameter of a race car. Delisha clasped his hand. "Home, James!"

"Bond, James Bond," Ryan called out in his best 007 accent.

Delisha giggled and planted a quick kiss on his neck. For the moment, Ryan felt like the glamorous super-agent. Like the celebrated and handsome James Bond, he was behind the wheel of an Aston Martin with a ravishing beauty next to him. The trouble was: he didn't know how to work a stick shift. Maybe, if it was all downhill, they could continue in a single gear.

They glided down the curving hill from the chateau, and Ryan could feel Delisha's aura, not only the silver sparkle from her dress in the pitch-black night but also her utter ease and genuine goodness, the qualities that had nourished the full potential out of the occasion. Most people, and Ryan feared this included him, make nothing "special" out of "special occasions." They merely take cautious refuge in the trappings – the setting, the dress, the food – and just mingle about, making insipid comments on the obvious grandeur of the occasion.

"You're grinding. You've got to let it out," Delisha said.

"I haven't driven a manual since high school."

Delisha slid over and grabbed the gear handle. "You just steer."

With Delisha on the gears, Ryan wound his way aggressively through the zigzags and turns of the old road – down and up and back around. Their looping descent back to the real world was appropriate. A direct drop down the hill from the magnificence of the chateau to the everyday world would have been too abrupt a transition, like an astronaut burning up on re-entry.

Up above, the moon darted and winked between the branches and the spring leaves of the sycamores and eucalyptus. The nocturnal fragrances mingled with the lush leather interior. With the soft night air whisking over the windshield and forming a cushion over them, Ryan navigated the road's curves. The wine had loosened him, and he felt the May breeze. The car glided downward, descending through the rolling turns, winding down in long patches of graceful arcs. Ryan relaxed his grip on the wheel, gaining confidence, knowing Delisha had the real stuff.

Delisha down-shifted, but the car shot forward. He spun the steering wheel, barely missing a head-on into a stone wall. He eased his foot from the accelerator. They skidded and blasted into the road's upward loop.

"Oh, my god. You've got to slow down," Delisha called out.

"I am!"

They careened straight toward the stone wall. Ryan pulled the car a hard left, dovetailing it away from the wall. Sparks flew as it scraped against the stone. The car fishtailed, swerving, picking up speed. "Damn!" Ryan yelled. He had nicked James Bond's perfect automobile. He eased up on the gas, but the entire section of the stretch was lined with the chest-high stone walls, and backed by thick eucalyptus trees. Ryan whipped the car through the turns. With its perfect calibration, the Aston Martin seemed to thrive on the crazed drive. Yet, the downward incline was too steep. It felt like they were on an ice chute. Ryan whipped the wheel, left and right, left and right. Delisha double-shifted into as low a gear as the engine would allow. The hairpin turns snapped him, faster and faster. Ryan tightened his grip. He felt like they were riding on the back of a coiled snake, as the car whipped against the big stone wall. Tree branches snapped out, the moon smacked through – like the opening scene of Great Expectations.

No going left or right. Ryan needed an opening. He swerved left. Spotted what looked like a clearing. Behind it, only the moon, the stars, and black emptiness.

The Aston Martin lifted up, like Thelma and Louise soaring off into the Grand Canyon. In that millisecond, Ryan's life did not flash before his eyes; only an awful pang that he wanted more time with Delisha.

Silence screamed for a beat; then it was: "Thud! Thud! Thud!" The sound reverberated like giant kettledrums. The impact jolted Ryan. A pain shot up from his knees. Then, a bounce, thud, bounce – the vehicle had landed. Ryan jolted forward against the steering wheel. Delisha's arm shot out, smacking him in the nose. They skidded and swirled, sliding and whipping sideways in moist grass.

"We're going to be alive. We're going to be alive!" Delisha shouted. The sports car down swirled into a leisurely dizzying whirl. Its headlights sprayed in every direction, its arc like a figure-skater in the glorious slow-motion twirl of a gold-medal finale. They had survived, spinning in a soft country field, under the stars and a mature moon. As they revolved to a stop, Ryan spotted only gray.

Everything looked like big soft blankets. No, it wasn't blankets. It was a flock of sheep and goats. The car slid to a stop, and the animals scampered away.

Delisha planted a big kiss on Ryan's forehead. "That was fun. Can we do it again?"

Her dress, with the jagged lines around her left breast, was delectably ripped. Ryan pulled her toward him. Once again, the moon was in just the right position. Ryan caressed Delisha. He blew into her ear and rubbed the back of her neck.

"I've got to be on top," she said.

"We can't risk driving that car back," Ryan said as he hopped into his pants.

"You mean leave it here?"

"We can't risk it any further without brakes," Ryan said.

"Where are my panties? You threw them somewhere."

"One of the goats probably ate them."

"You are so bad," Delisha said. "You are a beast!"

"Since you're not wearing panties, we could make love again."

"'Make love'? You are so old-fashioned. I love it, but no. I need to get back. I've got a crazy day tomorrow. What are we going to do?"

"I think our best bet is to have you make like Claudette Colbert."

"Who?"

"Claudette Colbert," he said. "The world's greatest movie hitchhiker."

"She was some sort of world traveler?"

"No, she was an actress. She was beautiful and resourceful, a lot like you," he said. "There was this terrific movie, It Happened One Night, the first movie to win all the five top Academy Awards. She and Clark Gable are out on the road in the middle of nowhere. He starts to hitchhike and everybody drives by them without stopping. You know what happened next?"

"Of course, I know what happened. You don't have to watch old movies to know that." She glanced dismissively at him. She ambled out to the side of the road, and stuck out her leg, pulled up her skirt.

"We'll travel first-class for the rest of our lives with those beauties. Around the world, at least," Ryan said.

They waited roughly twenty minutes, huddling together on the side of the road. It was the wee-small, Sinatra hours. They sat down. Ryan clasped his arms around Delisha and wrapped his legs around her. She positioned her bottom onto his lap, wiggling into the perfect place.

Ryan didn't know about Elysian Fields, or Strawberry Fields, or any other fields of ecstasy, but this sheep and goat field was easily the most blissful spot he had ever been in. Spread out with an amorous Delisha squeezed up against him, watching the moon slide into the sun, and the night sounds blend into the morning's hum, Ryan had never been happier.

When the festival clock struck midnight, he feared, he would be back to real life, or as close to real life as a film-critic gets. The ramifications of the evening sped through his mind: He had to explain to Nick what had happened to the car. He had damaged an ultra-expensive vehicle, James Bond's car, no less. Why couldn't he just stay here with Delisha, and the goats and the sheep in the field? In the perfume country with the roses?

A sharp white light flickered down from the heavens and hills. It beamed on and off, as it moved back and forth on the winding road. A vehicle was heading their way. Ryan squeezed Delisha's shoulders.

"Girl, I need you to do your thing."

Delisha wiggled up to her feet. Her tiny dress had been perfect earlier, but now it was smudged and torn. She stumbled as she moved toward the road. She yawned and leaned out over the pavement, sticking out her thumb, thrusting up her butt.

The black Mercedes SL500 purred to a halt.

The driver was muscular, tattooed, and mute. His chest stretched a black tux, tatts protruded over his collar and beard stubble strafed his bowtie. He barely glanced at Ryan and Delisha when they fitted themselves into the backseat. As the luxury car cruised, Delisha snuggled against Ryan and fell asleep. In the distance, the awakenings and mewing of the farm animals drifted into the experience: the splendid setting, the delirious lovemaking, the crazed exhilaration of near-death in an outrageously expensive sports car had touched and excited every nerve in Ryan's brain and body. And now, the wonderfully romantic thrust of riding in the back of an S-class Mercedes, slinking down the mountain to the crystal-blue seaside. The smooth dip of the ride transported Ryan into a blissful limbo. He had experienced a great primitive, sexual stimulant: goats had surrounded them, symbolically enough, he thought. Ryan drifted into a slumber, a mini-dream with goats bleating. He opened his eyes, and in his overly-drenched sensory state he conjectured that he would forever associate a goat's bleat with Delisha. Would he always have some sort of Pavlovian response – any time he would encounter a goat – would he become passionately aroused? Would he put on his horns again, and rut feverishly with the nearest maiden? "But, Your Honor, I heard a goat call out to me."

Ryan and Delisha inhaled the intoxicating scent, and their breathing fell into the same rhythm. Ryan began to focus. Down to the left, he could see the haunches of Cannes. He detected a whiff of the sea, sneaking in over the beach. Delisha took a deep breath, and her eyes popped open.

"Where are we?" she asked.

"We're just outside of Cannes."

"What time is it?"

"It's almost 4:30."

"Oh, no! I've got to be at the hotel and all packed and everything. I can't screw this up." She sniffed her arms and her breasts. "I smell like a pig farm."

He stuck his nose between her breasts. "You smell delicious."

Up front, the driver glanced at his rear-view mirror. Ryan caught a flash of his dark eyes.

"Oh, my god, I've got to ride in a limo to Saint Tropez with Zoë Saldana. And I've got sheep manure all over me."

"Zoë is probably having her own adventures and is worried about sitting next to you," Ryan said.

"But hers couldn't have been as good as my adventures," Delisha said. "It smells in here. I'm stinking up the whole car."

"Don't worry. We'll get there early enough and you can do a real quickie shower," Ryan said.

"This is important for me. Image is everything with these lingerie people," she said. "They're very anal, excuse the bun-pun. If they find out I'm late because I've been out in a field with a bunch of goats sexing you, they're not going to be happy."

The driver pulled off-road and into a thick grove. The Mercedes purred to a halt. The driver got out of the vehicle. It was still dark, but Ryan could make out the dagger-shaped tattoos that covered his neck. The driver moved into the bushes. From the splashing noises, Ryan didn't have to ask what he was doing.

"Monsieur, monsieur," the driver's voice rang out. Ryan leaned over to see the man gesturing to him. Ryan got out of the car and headed over to the driver. The man zipped up his pants and in the same motion pulled out a knife. He flashed it at Ryan. The big guy moved closer, muttering in some dialect Ryan didn't recognize.

"I'm a film critic! I'm a film critic," Ryan yelled.

The man lunged at him. Ryan sidestepped, and in a split-second, he latched onto the man's arm, twisted and dislodged the knife. Ryan thrust him to the ground, kicked the knife away just as Delisha jumped out of the car. She charged up behind Ryan. The man slid back, shifting his body along the thick grass. He tried to get up, but Delisha tore into him, pummeled him with her fists and kicked him in the balls.

"You stank-ass bitch!" Delisha screamed. She punched him in the head. Blood gushed from the man's nose. She jumped on him, went straight for the eyes. Ryan jumped in, pulled her arm away, and yanked her off the man. Delisha broke free from Ryan. She spotted the knife in the grass; its blade sparkled in the moon's shaft. She grabbed it, whirled toward the man. He ducked but she caught him with an upper slash. Blood spurted from his shoulder. His knees sank, but he charged straight at Delisha. As he grabbed for her neck, Ryan caught him with a roundhouse kick to the head. He crumpled, unconscious.

Delisha hovered over him. "Bitch was going to kill you," she exclaimed. He grabbed Delisha's hand, but she pulled away. Leaned over the man. Ripped at the top of his shirt. A jagged tattoo circled his collarbone. Delisha leaned over closer, peering down at the tattoo. "Hey, he's got these spires on his chest, like the top of the Carlton," she said. "Three of them."

"Come on. Don't be touching things. We've got to get out of here. It will be light soon. I should call someone," Ryan said. "The police."

"No way! Someone wants you killed, sweetie, and the police here are not your friend." She squeezed his hand. She picked up the blade. "This is titanium. I could have used one like this back in the day."

The Mercedes 500 SL was an automatic so Ryan took the wheel. Delisha stretched out in the front seat. "You were in a zone there, girl. Where did you learn to use a knife like that?"

"West Philly," she said. "'Someone comes at you with a knife. You take out a hatchet and cut off his arm'," she said. "You know who said that?"

"One of your homeys?"

"No, Bill Clinton." She pressed her hand against his knee. "Don't worry, sweetie. No one will connect us to this guy. The police here already have too much else to do," she said.

"Yeah, like framing me."

"It's not necessarily you," she said. "He wanted to rape me. "Nobody rapes me. Bitch was not going to get away with it. No way!"

Ryan glanced over at her. She was likely right. Maybe, it wasn't all about him. Delisha was off-the-charts sexy, and her skirt was torn. Still, it was too much of a coincidence: First, the brakes failed on the car he was driving, and, then, a follow-up killer was sent to ensure the job went right. Just when he thought he was in the clear, Ryan was an accomplice to beating a man nearly to death. Or was he dead?

Who was this guy? Was he trying to kill him, or was his victim supposed to have been Nick, who was supposed to have been in that James Bond car?

His mind raced. Had they left any evidence? Oh no, his stomach sank: DNA could link him. It could put him at the scene of another crime, and this time the evidence would not just be circumstantial; it could be physical. Would the French police have a crack CSI team? With the luck he had been having, they certainly would. Plus, he would have to get Delisha to get rid of that knife.

As he drove toward the outer edges of Cannes, he noticed the car's navigation system. It had been pre-set. If he followed its predetermined path, it might lead to something. It might clue to him what all this was about. It was a risk, but he followed the glowing directional.

Ryan pulled to a stop in an industrial section of the Old Town. It was poorly lit and not the kind of place that would be brimming with security cameras. He parked, turned off the engine, and scoured the surroundings. The area was blighted, abandoned warehouse buildings smeared with graffiti. Not the vision of Cannes that the world saw on their TV screens. Why had the driver's navigation system taken them here? To this derelict place? He peered up to find the address that had been input as the vehicle's destination. It looked like an abandoned market. A red-and-yellow poster was plastered on the doorway. In dagger-like letters, it read: "Ru' De Mor'G." The hip-hop type spelling was superimposed over a club scene, with dancers toting automatic, Marvel Comics-like weapons. As he tried to get his bearings, Delisha crawled out from the car. She stretched, and bent over for toe-touches. She paused to rub off grass stains from her right butt cheek. “I wish you hadn’t thrown away my panties,” she said.

“A beauty with that booty shouldn’t wear panties.”

“I’m serious,” she said. She grabbed his hand. “Don’t you go overthinking everything and worrying about that guy. It was his fault. He was going to rape me. He would have killed us, and no one can connect us to him anyway,” she said. She pulled back, sniffed. “What is that smell?” she said. “I thought it was me, but this is something else.”

They peered at the trunk. Ryan snapped the lock switch. The trunk clicked open. The inside trunk lights flashed on: a body, gold tux, and a cord tied around the victim’s neck.

“Oh, my god. A gold tux. This could be that guy who messed with your review,” Delisha exclaimed.

Ryan leaned over. A festival I.D. badge was pinned to the corpse’s breast pocket. It read “Dragan Dylko.” Ryan looked closer. “He’s been strangled and shot. There’s blood from the back of his head. Somebody executed him!” The blood had seeped onto the trunk’s carpet. It looked black in the dim light. “We can’t be tied to this. We can’t have fingerprints. Close the trunk. And, wipe down anything with your scarf that we might have touched.”

She grabbed the trunk and pushed it down into place. Her blue scarf shone in the dawn's darkness as she wiped down the vehicle. She pulled out her cell, and clicked on her directional App. "We're actually not all that far from the Croisette," she said. She opened the car door with the scarf and yanked out her microscooter.

They angled toward a narrow sidewalk and walked as close to the buildings as possible. She took his hand. "If you don't mind, can I take a shower at your place? I just remembered you've still got that bag of lingerie and party dress I left with you at breakfast that day. I could wear that."

"Sure, go ahead. Etienne should be at the desk. Or, maybe that Moroccan woman. Just ask for my key card. Tell them I'm on my way. I've got to walk around a bit, need to clear my head," Ryan said.

She kissed him. "Sweetie, remember it's always darkest before the dawn." Cliché or not, Ryan believed her.

Since Ryan didn't have Nick's cell number and couldn't text him, he decided to stop off at Nick's yacht. Tell him what had happened. Or, considering the hour, at least leave Nick a note. He couldn't believe he had damaged a James Bond car. And had transported a corpse, Dragan Dylko, the person he had accused of altering his review. He tried to compose himself. Deep breaths: four seconds in, one-second pause, four seconds out.

He hurried down one of the side streets, sat down on the edge of an historic fountain. His hands quivered. Ryan was sleep-deprived and sweat had dried on his body. He couldn't put it off any longer: he had to solve what was happening to him, stop all this before he was killed or arrested for murder, or some other thug attacked him.

Despite the danger, and the craziness, Ryan felt invigorated: endorphins soared in him. He realized his life had just taken on the magical moments of his all-time favorite movies: he had been gifted with the explosions of fireworks over the Riviera sky like Cary Grant and Grace Kelly experienced in To Catch A Thief when they gazed into each other's eyes at her Carlton Hotel room door, he in his tux and she in her blue gown. Was he in some sort of altered state or had he just realized real life could be as good as the movies, even the dangerous parts? Better than the movies, especially if you're just watching them and escaping real emotions in the process. That was a new thought. Well, he could chew on it and over analyze it later.

Incredibly, Ryan found himself in a magical, emotional place, and he owed it to himself to make the most of it. His world had taken on a new dimension, not safe and planned, but out of control. He tried to frame what was happening to him in terms of movies; in a manner, movies were his religion, his bible, his way of explaining things. Making sense of his universe. Instead of ancient mythical stories, Ryan thought in terms of movie narratives. He let his mind wander, recalling some familiar scenes of movie heroism: like Cary Grant in North by Northwest, Ryan had careened along a dangerously scenic road out of control in an expensive automobile. Also like the advertising executive Grant, Ryan had accidentally plummeted into some sort of international criminal scenario. Ryan couldn't figure out why people were trying to do him in. He was a film critic, not a spy, not a terrorist, not a criminal, not a MacGuffin. "I'm an advertising man, not a red-herring. I've got two ex-wives and several bartenders that are counting on me," he uttered. The Cary Grant-line from North by Northwest made him laugh. Ryan had unintentionally landed in a world of danger, like his favorite movie hero Cary Grant. And, like Harrison Ford in Indiana Jones, Ryan was careening back and forth between a quiet intellectual life and a world of dangerous adventure.

Again, he flashed to movies – the one with Dustin Hoffman and Steve McQueen on that French prison island. He couldn't even think of the title. And Ryan never forgot film facts. That told him he was stressed and off his game. Perhaps he was going insane with all the pressure. No time, for that: Ryan wasn't going to star as somebody's fall guy and rot in a French prison. He hurried down the old cobblestone street toward the harbor. He just didn't need any more superhero stuff. Or more people trying to kill him. Or more murders he could be tied to.

He glanced up at the ancient cathedral on the hilltop in Old Town. The clock's arms bent out at ten minutes to five, splayed in different directions – like his upcoming day, he feared.

Chapter 9

Day 6

The city's sidewalks near the Palais were wet and slick at the early hour. The cleaning crews had hosed them off before dawn, leaving Cannes's walkways with a sparkling sheen. Ryan hurried past La Pizza. Its scarlet awning was rolled up, and its chairs stacked neatly. He passed several seafood restaurants across from the Old Port. Something caught his eye on the sidewalk: he jumped back. He had nearly stepped on a severed fish head. He stopped: four breaths in, four breaths out.

Ryan lingered a moment on the walk, facing the luxury yachts in the Old Port. A pack of compact cars swerved sharply around the forty-five-degree angle turn in front of the Sofitel Hotel. The city's service workers were hurrying to their posts – to change the beds, serve the coffee, sweep the floors, and perform their duties during the busy festival day. No one would write a review on what they had done. Nobody would be impressed enough with their daily contribution to option their next project. There would be no pictures in the papers or on websites of their accomplishments. Nor, would there be any self-congratulatory awards shows for them to celebrate their achievements. To the film festival participants' way of thinking, these people were just the "extras" in life.

Ryan gazed out across the inlet. The Palais loomed in the early-morning gray. Awash in its dull white, with harsh creases of windows and balconies, the big edifice looked like an aged sea monster, thickened and crusted by salt. In its subdued morning state, the central headquarters for the Cannes Film Festival didn't exude the domineering countenance it would take on later in the day when it would once again assert itself as the place to be, the palace of dreams and glory.

On this Riviera sunrise, after an evening with Delisha that had ended with Ryan punching out a stranger, and later finding the corpse of the Russian journalist with whom he had a well-known dispute, Ryan's world was now unfathomable to him. He grimaced as the sea slapped the sides of the luxury yachts. No one was around. He vaulted over the little gate onto a vessel that Nick Steele and Boris used when they weren't ensconced on the Russian's super-yacht. He crossed onto the deck, his black party shoes squeaking. Oddly enough, there didn't seem to be any morning-after party debris on the deck. Ryan looked over to the other mega-yachts. No early risers, but three yachts down a crew member sprayed down the vessel's deck.

Ryan rapped on the main door, steadily and more forcefully. No answer. Ryan circled across the back of the deck. Maybe there was a window or another entrance. Ryan rapped on a porthole pane. Nothing. Something was out of whack. Even with Nick not around, the yacht should have been in after-party disarray: bimbo tracings, cigarette butts, joints, liquor bottles. But it was ship-shape, with even a swabbed deck. He shielded his face. He touched on his cell and speed-dialed Barlowe's number. With his insomnia, Barlowe was always an early-riser. "Dennis, Dennis pick-up...Damn, Dennis! I need to talk to you. Call me when you get this!"

Ryan trudged back toward the Old Town. Sat down on a bench next to the proud stone building that used to the Cannes mayoral office, but was now some sort of tourism landmark. He called Barlowe again, hoping that he was on one of his early morning walks. Still no luck. Ryan started to drift off. "Hey, I got your message, but your voice-mail is messed up." Ryan jolted, looked up. Barlowe stood over him, peering down at the bench. He wore a jogging suit and designer Nikes. "Come on. My place is just up the hill," Barlowe said. "I've got just the cure for whatever is ailing you."

"I'm pretty wiped out."

"Great purple bowtie, by the way." Barlowe said.

They trudged up hill, through the old neighborhood. Linens and clothes hung from crammed balconies. It was not the Cannes you saw in the postcards of glamorous stone buildings with geraniums in pots and pastel-colored clothes dangling on clotheslines.

Barlowe ducked into an entryway, and hurried up a steep stone stairwell. The building was ill-tended. Graffiti on the stone walls. The stairway angled back and forth. Barlowe's room was at the top. He opened the door. It creaked as they entered. Barlowe pulled open a shade. "Voila," he pointed out to a view of the Old Port. It was like a picture postcard: yachts, dark-blue evening sky, and a ripening moon.

"You've got the best view in Cannes," Ryan said. "You can see the Palais from here."

"Not only have I got this great view, but I've got the best stuff," Barlowe answered. "You've come to the right place." He opened a drawer and removed a leather shaving kit. Pulled out a packet of grass and a bottle of pills. "Now, why do you look so freaked out?"

Ryan gagged. He woke up. His head throbbed. He was stripped down to his shorts. His pants were heaped in a corner. He pulled himself off a tiny couch. Barlowe was gone. The early morning sun sheered the old wood floor into an abrupt divide, half dark and half-light. Bright orange walls were draped with beads in a wild array, strung from ceiling cords. A tiny bureau was crammed with tchotchkes, mainly biblical figures. A poster for *The Ten Commandments* was taped to a wall. Not the classic, Charlton Heston poster, it was designed like a video-game advertisement. A Darth Vader-ish Moses wielded an electric tablet in his left arm, while holding aloft a Star Wars-like light saber. The tiny boudoir was jammed with mismatched furniture and souvenir oddities. Three Vegas-style lamps, all with different colored bulbs, distinguished the living area/kitchenette. Ryan recalled the décor of his mom's crazy aunt's home in Oconomowoc, Wisconsin – the old lady with the two monkeys named Claude and Maude.

Ryan's phone was neatly placed on top of his pants. Stashed in a corner were a Groucho Marx-mask and an Elmer Fudd cap. Plus, several tubes of makeup and a box of diverse mustaches. Odd, but Barlowe had told him that he sometimes had to investigate stories incognito. He wrote about dangerous people. DVDs were scattered in the corner. One stood out: a younger Ingrid Bjorge perched atop a rock, gazing out to a harsh sea. Had they watched porn? Had Barlowe given him some of his Amsterdam stash? Ryan couldn't remember.

He splashed water over his face. Where was Barlowe? He glanced at his phone: 8:05. He pulled on his tuxedo shirt and hopped into his pants. He unlatched the door and hurried out.

Ryan perambulated down the old winding walk through the Old Town. He got his wind, and accelerated into a light jog. The Croisette was mostly deserted and he scurried along the walks that soon would be trampled by festival-goers; the outdoor cafes that would later be filled with coffee-sippers and cellphone-punchers. Ryan stopped to catch his breath. That he was winded told him that he was off his game. He usually knocked out his daily three miles with ease. Now he gasped after less than a quarter-mile. He caught his breath in front of the Palais. Workmen vacuumed the red carpet, making it ready for the celebrities and movers-and-shakers. With the sunlight still not reaching it, the red carpet now looked to Ryan like a scab of blood.

“You look like you’ve been through a war,” Stan Peck sneered as Ryan zipped past him in the hotel lobby. Peck was spread out at the table nearest the elevator, breakfasting on croissants and pawing at the morning-delivery of movie-world publications. “You and your underwear model must have had some night.”

Ryan knew better than to answer. A hotel attendant wheeled out a cart filled with cheeses, slices of ham, croissants, strawberries, pitchers of grapefruit, and orange juice. Ryan grabbed a handful of berries and cheese from the cart. He poured a grapefruit juice. His hands shook as he gulped the juice.

“You ought to chill out,” Peck said. “Have you been doing drugs or drinking too much?”

“If I had, I wouldn’t be standing upright,” Ryan said.

Peck rubbed his hands together. “No one, not even *The Hollywood Reporter*, came close to getting my story. Everyone will be talking about it all over the Croisette today. I’ll be doing some CNN or E!” he gushed. “Maybe even CNBC with the business angle.”

“Way to go,” Ryan said. He wondered if it was another one of his “scoops” Peck had purloined by simply reading his friend Dennis Barlowe’s website.

“I’ve got it exclusively. There's more bidding on *The Ice Princess* than any other film in the history of the festival.” Peck said. “*Ice Princess* could be the biggest European film ever. And I dug out the entire story. They think it could appeal to real people no matter what elitist film critics think."

Ryan knew better than to take Peck's bait of the film-critic jab, or, worse, question Peck's sources. The elevator jutted and rumbled to the fourth floor. Ryan approached his room and slid the entry card into the door slot. It clicked and he entered. Delisha perched on the bed, wearing scarlet, lacy panties and a matching bra. And she was bald.

"What's up?" she asked. She was examining the dead man's knife. "Kizlyar, never heard of that brand."

"I wish you'd get rid of that. It could link us to that guy," Ryan said.

"Sweetie, you need protection, and this is all we've got." She stuffed the knife into her bag. "Your water takes a while to warm up."

"What happened to your hair?" he finally asked.

"You don't know black-girls' hair. It's dry and brittle," Delisha explained. "We wear wigs rather than have to fuss with it every day."

"You do?"

"Yes, haven't you figured that out yet? When a woman has one style one day, and another entirely different do and color the next, it doesn't set off your alarm bells?"

"I guess I never thought about it," Ryan said.

She pulled a purple Afro out of her bag and put it on. "Well?"

"You look great, but I wouldn't have recognized you if I saw you like that."

"Precisely," she answered. "But you would have recognized my butt and boobs," she said.

"How could I not?" Ryan noted. "Best in the world!"

She adjusted her new look in front of the mirror. "You could use a shower," Delisha said.

"I'm still debating whether to go to the police," he said.

"You can't go to the police."

"Well, if I don't, they will come for me."

"Be a good boy for a change. You take your shower. Let me think."

"I'm screwed no matter what we come up with," Ryan said.

"Take your shower. Clear your head."

Ryan headed into the bathroom. A handwritten note perched on the top of the sink. It was written on the hotel's stationery, and it had his handwriting. He didn't remember writing anything. He picked it up.

"Dear Everyone: I have decided to do this because I just can't undergo the psychological torture anymore, nor will I be able to endure the shame of a trial and certainly not French prison. Please have my body shipped back to the United States and buried. Also, please donate $5,000 to Southern California University's film school for a scholarship in my name." The note bore Ryan's signature and was dated May 15, yesterday.

Ryan read it again. Whoever wrote this suicide note certainly got his slanted handwriting down pat, and replicated his signature. But, they had screwed up – *USC, or University of Southern California.*

Not Southern California University, dummy! Ryan reasoned a foreigner had written the note.

He stepped into the shower, jamming his shoulders as close to the warm spray as he could stand. His neck cracked, and he twisted his torso, loosening his hips and spine. Not surprising, considering the crazy night he had gone through. He toweled down and grabbed a pair of jeans off the hamper. He squeezed into his black *Terminator 2* t-shirt – a lucky shirt that James Cameron had given him – and re-entered the bedroom. Delisha was now topped with a shoulder-length purple wig. Ryan handed Delisha the note.

"What's this?" she asked.

"Someone is trying to frame me. Whoever killed Ingrid Bjorge is still trying to pin it on me. And they're certainly the same ones who killed Dragan Dylko. Now, they're making it look like I wrote this suicide note."

"This is whack," she said. "I saw it in the bathroom, but didn't read it. I thought it was some of your movie notes."

"I think I should alert the authorities."

"You can't take it to the police yet. You should tweet to get your side of the story out there. You do have a Twitter account, don't you?"

"Yes, but I hardly use it," he admitted.

"Well, you need to get your side of things out there. Go Trump on these bitches," she said. "I know someone who used to tweet for Ashton Kutcher. How about if I set you up with her?"

"Seriously?"

"You're not using social media to your full advantage," she said. She got up from the bed and sauntered across the room. Ryan tried not to stare. "I've got to get dressed for my Victoria's thing. Is it okay if I pick out something from your wardrobe to wear to Saint Tropez? A cool t-shirt? Any *Hollywood New Times* ones?"

"There's some in the top drawer."

A loud rap jolted the door. "Later. Come back, later," Ryan said. The knock erupted again. "Later, après noon, after mid-demi."

"Monsieur Hackbart. Open up! We are the police."

Before either Ryan or Delisha could move, the door burst open, and two cops pushed their way into the room. Both were muscular and tall. They brandished red-and-yellow nightsticks with gold handcuffs strapped to their belts.

"Monsieur Hackbart, you are under the arrest for murder."

"Murder? I didn't kill anyone."

"Monsieur, a Russian journalist who has been working for your newspaper company has been murdered. You must come with us immediately."

"But I haven't killed anyone! In fact, someone is trying to kill me. Look at this!" Ryan thrust the suicide note at them. The lead officer read it, stashed it in his pocket. "Hey, that's mine," Ryan shouted.

"Monsieur Hackbart, your suicide note is now evidence."

"But it's not my note. I didn't write it. This note has USC screwed up. Some foreigner calls it Southern California University."

"I do not understand your point," the cop said.

"Exactly. Foreigners wouldn't."

"This note seems to prove you intended to commit suicide before we could come to detain you," the cop said. "We received a mobile photo of you, standing over Mr. Dylko near the Old Town."

"Yes, he was already dead. He was stuffed in the trunk of this Mercedes," Ryan said. "I didn't kill him."

"That is a very creative story, monsieur," the muscled-up cop said.

"No, it's not creative at all," Ryan replied. "The same thing happened to Cary Grant at the United Nations in *North by Northwest* when they snapped a picture of him with a knife over a dead body."

"What has that to do with anything?" the taller cop said. "You're under arrest." He grabbed Ryan,

"He's been with me," Delisha yelled. "We've been sexing all night."

"I am sorry, but we have proof this man is a murderer," the tall cop said.

"Listen, bitch, I need you to give us your badge numbers," Delisha barked at the bigger cop. She grabbed her silver scooter from the floor and swatted him straight in the face. It cracked against his skull. She knocked the cuffs out of the other cop's hand. Ryan elbowed the second cop, straight to the chin, lifting up. He pivoted and nailed him with a karate punch to the face. Before the second cop could get up, Delisha kicked him in the face. She grabbed Ryan. "Come on!" she yelled.

They dashed from the room, sprinted down the hallway. They bolted down the stairs in the dark. They burst into the lobby, plowing through a group of hotel maids. They sprinted out of the entrance-way and swung a sharp right on the little gravel driveway, running toward the Rue d'Antibes.

"The police will hunt us down," Ryan yelled.

"They weren't cops!" Delisha barked.

"What?"

Ryan and Delisha scrambled along the tiny side street, past the real estate agencies and the yacht brokerages. They scampered past the early morning pedestrians. Delisha was a former collegiate track star, and Ryan tried to keep up. People paused to stare: a disheveled man chasing a purple-haired black woman in burgundy lingerie was an occurrence that exceeded even the usual film-festival shenanigans.

Delisha stopped and plopped her scooter down. "Get on," she yelled as Ryan caught up. She placed her left foot in the front of the scooter. "Put your right foot down. We can balance that way." He grabbed her from behind, his right foot on the scooter board and his left foot to the side. They took off, like a rowing team. As they picked up speed, surging down the street, they swung into heavy traffic. Rush-hour cars and motorcycles whizzed past. Ryan and Delisha weaved in and out of the traffic. They accelerated straight toward one of the green cannonball-sized barriers that separated the sidewalk from the one-lane drive, narrowly missing it. But, their greatest obstacle was not the thick green cannonballs or the speeding traffic but the little old ladies walking their poodles for their morning duty. Delisha swerved the board a hard left and it sailed out from under them, nearly missing a dog and sending it into a yelping fit. It cascaded onto the sidewalk, sending pedestrians dashing out of its way.

Delisha bounced back against Ryan. "I'll run one way, you the other." She took off without waiting for an answer. Ryan watched her sprint down the sidewalk. All eyes were glued to the purple-haired black woman in the lacy burgundy lingerie. After Delisha disappeared along the sidewalk, Ryan slid his way back into the crowd. He nestled against a Tabac shop window. Glancing back, he spotted the two cops. They zeroed in on him. He dashed off, darting among pedestrians. He sprinted down the walkway, approached the fountain at the corner by the Gray d'Albion hotel. Ryan leaned into the turn, and sprinted past the fountain, nearly careening into the little newsstand on the corner. He high-hurdled over a stack of magazines, zigzagging just ahead of the oncoming cars. He cut left, like a football player doubling back against the opposition. He turned it on at the fountain. A full-out sprint to the Croisette.

A gaggle of poodles on one leash waddled into his path. He hurdled them. The dogs' walker shrieked. Brakes screeched and horns blared – the imbecilic bleats of the proletarian cars. He dashed down the side street toward the Croisette.

Ryan spotted a brigade of Cossacks atop their stallions just ahead on the Croisette. He sprinted toward them, slinking down amid the horses. The Cossacks hurled oaths at him and one even spit on him. Ryan pushed his way out the other end. Breathing deeply, he felt invigorated, not afraid. The runner's endorphin fix had kicked in for him. What was happening to him? Sleep-deprived, stinky, and terrified out of his mind with the police on his butt, Ryan had never felt better!

He slowed his pace, tried to blend into the crowd. He angled through the park and headed toward the red carpet. Already, the gate funnels were filled with critics. For once, he was glad to see the horde of his elbow-patched, chain-smoking, opinion-spouting peers. Ryan submerged himself in the pack. He pulled out his *Carte Blanc* ID card and hunkered down amid the herd, moving slowly up the red carpet. A cop's whistle blared, staggered Ryan. The two gendarmes who had been chasing him were at the bottom of the stairs, no more than twenty-five yards away. Ryan pushed his way through the critics, elbowed his way to the front. At the entrance, the security attendants lumbered through their search-drill. One paused to stare at him. Ryan was obviously panting and the attendant said something to his cohort in sharp French. They patted him down. Finally, the guard nodded to Ryan to proceed.

The floor area was jammed with people scurrying to the elevator or hustling to the Film Market in the basement. Ryan hurried up the stairs, scooting as fast as he could without being too obvious. Two guards manned the inner hallway. Ryan flashed his *Carte Blanc*. They waved him through without the usual hassle. He wormed his way into the central area of the Palais, and proceeded to the second floor, up past the espresso cafe. He strode past the Hurrell photos of the stars – Ingrid Bergman, Clark Gable, and Humphrey Bogart – and hustled past the press mailboxes. His heart raced, and his chest tightened. He could hear someone yelling his name but he didn't pause. The low ceiling in this part of the Palais seemed to clamp down on him. Would this be the kind of institutional feeling he would have for the rest of his life? Locked away in a French prison? His endorphin-rush had left, and he felt an awful dread. At that instant, he only knew that he needed to blend in. He avoided eye contact.

He angled into the crowd as he approached the amphitheater at the end of the hallway, the large room where many of the festival press conferences and prestige functions were held. At the entrance, traffic characteristically snagged. The heightened security was making all entrances difficult. He looked back. He couldn't believe it: the two cops were headed his way. Their powder blue shirts stood out amid the patches of dark-clothed crits. They hadn't spotted him yet. Ryan ducked down, kept his feet moving forward. He stepped on the foot of the festival guard at the door. Ryan yanked out his *Carte Blanc* identification card and the guard ushered him through. He stepped inside and it hit him: he was in the auditorium where there was only one entrance and exit. He had no way out. Ryan was trapped.

The auditorium overflowed with journalists. In front of the raised podium, swarms of TV cameramen jostled for position. Ryan scampered down the stairway, looking for an empty spot. Still, he knew he would be a sitting duck. The cops would enter the room and eventually spot him. He stumbled down the stairs, his legs feeling weaker. He paused on a stair. He spotted his colleague Leonard Maltin of Movie Guide fame, delighting a couple of guards by trying on a black beret. Ryan hurried over to him. "Leonard, two cops are chasing me. There's no other exit. I'm trapped," Ryan called out.

"Hello, and the answer is *The 39 Steps*," Maltin replied.

"What?"

"*The 39 Steps*, Hitchcock's 1935 gem with Robert Donat. Not the '59 remake. Surely, you remember the chase scene."

Maltin was right: The best hiding place is right out in the open. "Can I borrow that beret, Leonard?" Maltin handed it to him, and Ryan adjusted it to his head, pulling it down as far as it would go. He took a deep breath and hurried down the stairs to the front. He pushed his way through the cameramen, and skipped up the three steps to the stage. He strode to the microphone. He adjusted the beret, pulling it down over his forehead.

The cameras in the front row pointed straight at him. He felt like he was their prey, in their sights. All around, the print journalists settled down, pulling out their pens and computer notebooks. They hunched forward, ready for his words. He cleared his throat and picked up the microphone. He pretended to inspect it, buying time.

He fussed as long as he could. He glanced toward the back of the auditorium. The two cops had entered. They prowled the rows, methodically inspecting one-by-one.

Ryan tried to appear calm behind the podium. He stared out at hundreds of the world's leading entertainment journalists. He'd have to start soon. But, start what? What was going on here? Why was there such a crowd of eager journalists? Was it an announcement about some new film? Something about the Portuguese New Wave? Was Roman Polanski going to appear? An announcement about Russian financing in the post-hedge-fund age? A lecture on vampires in the old German cinema?

Ryan strained to remember the festival guide, but nothing came to mind. He tapped the microphone. What do you talk about to an auditorium filled with journalists at the Cannes Film Festival? He raised the mic to his lips. "It's hard not to praise the work of the late great French director Francois Truffaut too much," he said. "There has, perhaps, never been a greater man in the cinema than Francois Truffaut. It is especially true in this day and age of the big corporations ruling the cinema," Ryan continued. "We are under the oppressive forces of the American conglomerates, forcing their hamburger tastes and tent-pole movies on the entire world." To Ryan's amazement, everyone began to take notes. The scribes pecked away on their tiny computers and cells. Ryan had played it perfectly: he had figured if you're stuck in front of a whole room full of journalists at the Cannes Film Festival, the one subject you can safely pacify them with is a speech on the beloved wunderkind of the

French cinema, and now the patron saint of contemporary French culture, such as it was. And, the anti-American BS didn't hurt with a group like this.

Ryan squeezed the microphone. He paused as the ink-stained scribes, talking-heads, and cellar-dweller bloggers took in his words. "In this awful cultural void, when films are not made for the love of the cinema but as a product tie-in with a fast-food chain, it is difficult for the humanitarian storyteller to find his or her voice. Yet, it is not only the corporations that are to blame. We are not without guilt. Our entertainment coverage today, with its emphasis on box-office and what is "hot," contributes to bad filmmaking," Ryan said. His enunciation was crisp and clear, free of nervous jitters. He gained momentum. "Film is not about charts. It is not about rankings, or numbers. It is not quantifiable by scales. By our emphasis on money in our media coverage, we only encourage filmmakers and movie studios to chase these false gods."

Every beard and beret in the room smiled and nodded. The room buzzed, as the journalists pointed their digital recorders toward him.

"If all you are obsessed about is box-office charts and numbers, and new technologies advanced by Philistines to take over the cinema, you are no friend of Francois Truffaut." He glanced up to the back of the room. Two more gendarmes had entered. Soon the entire police force would be here, he feared. Once again, he'd be surrounded and dragged through a gaping crowd of his peers by nasty French police. He noticed the first two cops made their way to the exit as the new police surveyed the area.

He spotted Etienne de Viereg, the towering long-haired French journalist and author who often hosted festival programs. De Viereg perched at the edge of the stage, and he did not look pleased. "Thank you for the privilege of addressing you," Ryan concluded. "I now introduce Etienne de Viereg." Ryan strode over to De Viereg and handed him the microphone. The Frenchman thrust him a dismissive eye and proceeded to the podium. Ryan headed up the far aisle toward the exit. He strode calmly, not to draw any attention. Up and up. Only a half dozen rows from the exit.

"Monsieur, Hackbart," a familiar voice rang out. Ryan turned toward it. It was a man in a blue sports coat with a festival seal. Ryan froze. Then, he recognized the public relations representative from the Cannes Police Department, Lt. Savin. The festival's primary spokesperson hurried over to him. Shook his hand. "That was a positively inspirational talk. I too am a big fan of the cinema, the old classic movies, and I couldn't agree with you more," Lt. Savin said. "As you know, I work with the festival and the police, but I am a big fan of your movie critiques."

"Thanks, merci," Ryan said.

"Are you speaking at any other festival events?"

"I'm not sure. Sometimes I sort of stumble into things at the last minute," Ryan said.

Chapter 10

Ryan hailed a white Mercedes taxi across from the McDonald's that now sullied the Palais's perimeter. While its "golden arches" were somewhat camouflaged by municipal-ordered foliage, the fast food franchise stood out among the palms and nearby flower stands. It was a culinary oasis for American festival attendees. The place was packed with festies dying for a meat-and-carb fix.

Ryan ducked into the backseat of the taxi and handed the driver the address he had written down. "You are certain?" the driver asked.

"It's a private residence," Ryan answered.

The cab driver flipped the meter switch and hung a left. He whizzed past the Sofitel Hotel, accelerating as he headed west along the topless-beach roadway. With the fast food places and the jumble of souvenir shops, the area reminded Ryan of Santa Monica on the way to Malibu.

Out on the Mediterranean, sailboats fluttered across the water and their mastheads glistened in the Riviera sun. Still, Ryan saw danger everywhere. He recalled that at a previous festival, hotel guests at the vaunted Eden Roc Hotel were crazed when a speedboat containing black-hooded men carrying assault weapons had descended on the luxury site. It turned out to be a lame-brained stunt for an independent production company that was promoting a low-budget movie on speed-boat pirates.

He wasn't the only one at the festival who now saw menace in what had once been Cannes's singular beauty, a glamorous escape from the hard realities of the world. A harsh, pothole-bounce of the tiny auto jolted him out of his anxious mindset. The driver made an abrupt right at a narrow road and maneuvered the cab inland. The roadway soon turned from blacktop to gravel. The cab zigzagged through the green countryside for nearly two miles before it approached a decrepit pink house. Further down the hillside, a green and tangerine-colored building loomed.

"This is it?" Ryan asked.

"Mais, oui. It is the address you supplied me."

"There will be a nice tip in it for you if you can wait for me for about ten minutes," Ryan said.

"Yes, but I must continue the meter running," the driver said.

Ryan got out of the cab and hurried down the incline toward the old house. No one was around. There was a motorcycle in the driveway. Ryan recognized it as

Henri's cycle, a classic '70s Ducati. He approached the farm house. He knocked. After a moment, he heard rustling inside. The door creaked open, and a tiny woman peeked out. With a red scarf wrapped around her head and a face lined like a wood carving, the woman appeared to be on the sweet side of 120.

"Pardon, je suis Ryan Hackbart. Je suis un film critic de Hollywood," Ryan said. The old woman cleared her throat, started to close the door. "I have come to see Henri," he said.

"Henri?"

"Je suis un ami. Ou est your pool house?" She looked confused. "Your maison du pool," he said.

She pointed down the hillside to the orange shed. "Voici, les poules." Ryan looked more closely. There was no swimming pool, much less a pool house. The old woman pointed toward the greenish shed. Then it hit him. He had the wrong "pool." "Poules" in French meant "chicken." Henri must live in the chicken coop, not a pool house.

Ryan hurried down toward the chicken coop. He could hear squawking. The splintered wooden door was half open. He peered inside. The walls were lined with rows of metal cages, all filled with chickens.

"Henri," Ryan called out. The chickens drowned him out. "Henri, Henri!" Amid straw and dirt, he spotted a woman's powder-blue thong. Ryan also noticed a brown shoe, then, farther down, its mate. The path of clothing led to a thick wooden door. Ryan followed the clothes and rapped on the door. He waited a few more seconds and knocked again. Still nothing. Ryan clicked the latch, and pushed the door open.

They were going at it, fittingly, like a couple of farm animals. Henri was side-saddled against a pale and leggy woman. He glanced up at Ryan. "Merdre, merdre." Henri thrust his right hand into the air. He turned over to his side and patted the girl. She slid off the mattress, and glared at Ryan. It was Giselle, the bottle blonde publicist from BGK.

"Monsieur Hackbart, what are you doing here?" Henri shouted.

"I'm sorry. I'll wait outside," Ryan said.

Ryan retreated past the chicken cages. The stench of the chicken dung, the soggy hay and feathers made him nauseous. He stumbled into a pile of straw and hit his leg against a solid object. He looked down: the straw was covering wine bottles, the same expensive Bordeaux that had been served at *The Ice Princess* party. Henri grabbed a wine bottle and lunged at him. He wielded the Bordeaux like a club. "Monsieur Hackbart, what is the meaning of this intrusion into my privacy?"

"You stole my jump drive," Ryan said.

"What you are talking about?"

"My flash drive that I turned in first day in the office, the one that had my review of *The Ice Princess* on it. I had trouble with the Wi-Fi on the plane, and wasn't sure I successfully transmitted it. So, I brought my flash to the office and left it on Tim's desk with a note."

"That is absurd and insulting," Henri shouted.

"You were the only one who knew it was my jump," Ryan said. "You transferred it into the system. Then, you stole it."

"That is mad, Monsieur."

"Did BGK pay you to get a look at my review early for their clients?" Ryan asked. "Or was it Giselle, trying to get a heads-up and win brownie points?"

"You are going way beyond reason, monsieur," Henri shot back. "My relationship with Giselle has nothing to do with business."

"It doesn't look that way," Ryan said.

"My honor and good name are not disputable, monsieur. I am a veteran professional of this festival. I am friends to many powerful people who work hard throughout the year when you and your Hollywood paper are not even present."

"You're just a guy who lives in a chicken coop who sees a good opportunity on how to get into a young publicist's pants by giving her early access to my review," Ryan answered.

Giselle emerged from the coop. She was nude but texting.

"Monsieur Hackbart thinks I gave you The Ice Princess review early so you would have knowledge of what it was before everyone else," Henri barked.

"That's absurd," she said. "What good would that do?"

"My review and other US trade reviews, would be the first reviews. They would set the tone and would clue you how to use them to your advantage or discredit them if they were negative."

"We would never do that. BGK is professional. Susanne would not allow it."

"I will speak to Susanne about this," Ryan said.

"You must understand the relationship Giselle and I have is a festival relationship," Henri said.

"That's right," Giselle said. "You of all people, Mr. Hackbart, should appreciate festival relationships."

"What?"

"You and your lingerie model, getting it on," Henri said. "And then that other woman with the purple hair and tiny burgundy panties."

"What?"

"It's all over the web," she said. "A friend of mine just hit me with this YouTube of you and her."

"On the web?"

"You didn't know?" she said. "You with the purple-haired black woman in panties on a scooter. It has gone viral," Henri said. "You should check it out. I wouldn't be surprised if you are in all the international tabloids. You are the hot item of the whole festival, Monsieur," Henri said.

"That video is way out of context," Ryan argued.

"Don't be so angry. This is good for you," Henri said. He tossed the wine bottle onto the floor. "I always thought you were rather a boring writer-type, Monsieur Hackbart, but now I can see you having been leading an exciting double life."

Ryan scoffed. "This is all so nuts. Everything is out of context."

"Henri is right," Giselle said. "You are getting more publicity than our stars, clients who pay BGK more than $20,000 a month to create this kind of image. People are calling you 'the action-critic'."

"And the sex-crazed critic," Henri added.

"Now, I know you're messing with me," Ryan said.

"It's true. You've become the star of the festival," Giselle said. "Some are even calling you 'the killer critic.' Susanne said her contact at Jimmy Fallon wanted details on you. I don't know how you have time to review your films." "You are burning the candle at both ends, Monsieur," Henri commented. "It will catch up with you. I can tell you that from experience."

Henri was right: the craziness and lack of sleep had made him loopy. He noticed several boxes and a large heap of blue scarves. Stacks of lingerie were scattered against the far wall. "These look like they're from *The Ice Princess*," Ryan said.

"You are correct, Monsieur Hackbart. Erik Bjorge, created a whole fashion line around the film. As you known he was the costume designer for *The Ice Princess*," Henri said. "He hoped that when everyone saw what Ingrid was wearing on the red carpet at the opening night in Cannes, it would make him into a star designer."

"What's it doing here?" Ryan asked.

"He had some problems with shipment, and I know the area merchants," Henri said.

Ryan picked up a piece of the lingerie. It was silky and smooth with just the right amount of lace. Ryan turned to Henri. "I need you to tell me everything you know about Erik Bjorge and all about his lingerie line. Where is he now and what is he doing?"

"Most of his fashion creations are on a vessel in the harbor. He never bothered to unload it after Ingrid Bjorge was killed," he said.

"What's the name of the ship?"

"The Orgasmo. It is a former military vessel, but it's now a Russian billionaire's yacht."

"Russian?"

"Yes, an old Russian navy ship is now the most fabulous yacht at the festival. It's grander than that other Russian billionaire's, the one where they've had all those crazy parties the last couple years," Henri answered.

"What makes is so special? All these yachts seem basically the same to me. Guys trying to out-dick each other," Ryan said.

"C'est formidable. It is fantastic," Henri said. "It's nearly three-hundred feet and is aluminum and glass. This yacht is like those vacation trailers the Americans drive and live in. You can press the buttons, and it expands on the sides. This one has a beach that sticks out when you push the buttons."

"I think I'll just stick to the real beach," Ryan said.

"I have an acquaintance who works as a steward on this yacht and he has revealed to me that the rich Russian owner is a total pig."

"How so?" Ryan asked.

"He beats the women. They are professionals, but he beats them badly. My friend feels he must call the Cannes police."

"Why doesn't he?"

"He fears for his life. I think he might quit, even though he makes more than $5,000 in tips a week."

"So, most of the missing Ice Princess lingerie is being kept on this crazy Russian billionaire's yacht?" Ryan asked.

"Yes, my friends tell me they are going to destroy all The Ice Princess lingerie when they have a big party at the end of the festival.

"Where can I find Erik?" Ryan asked.

"He went back to Oslo for Ingrid Bjorge's funeral." he said. "He plans to come back. He has to if he wants to rescue his lingerie."

Giselle held her cellphone out for Ryan. "There are all sorts of YouTubes of you and other women," she said. "Here's another one." It showed a video of Delisha's buns, taken that night when they had damaged the James Bond car. But worse, in the background was the Mercedes that they had deserted on the side street. Ryan realized that he was being tailed and videoed. Who was it? The French police? They could connect the dots. Link him to the beating of the tattoed limo driver and Dylko's dead body in the trunk. Ryan felt the noose tighten around his neck, and now for multiple murders.

On a body of water much farther north than the beaches at Cannes, a red and blue bus transported twenty-six teenage accordion players to the Bygdoy Peninsula in Oslo, Norway. They were going to play for the funeral service of Ingrid Bjorge. The Bygdoy Peninsula is the untrammeled part of Norway's capital city, the area with the museums and the Viking burial mounds. With its aggressive environmental and preservation laws, the Norwegian nation had kept it largely off limits to developers. An editorial in that morning's *Dagbladet* had trumpeted the irony of having the oil developer Gunnar Sevareid using it for the site of Ingrid Bjorge's funeral. Despite what the Oslo newspaper had implied, Norwegian billionaire Gunnar Sevareid was a fanatical environmentalist. However, having the press characterize him as a greedy oilman and unprincipled polluter masked his secret plan: Sevareid had laid the groundwork, or, rather, as he once joked, “The deep underwater work,” to rescue the Arctic and save the world.

Ingrid Bjorge’s body would arrive on the ferry in a few minutes. Following her death, she had been transported back to her homeland on Gunnar Sevareid’s personal plane, a Gulfstream G650. She had been cremated, and her ashes placed in an oak coffin. It would be carried by Viking pallbearers to the funeral pyre. The cameras were everywhere, including the Norwegian crews from NRK and TV2, as well as TV3, the all-Scandinavian network. The TV lights strafed the mourners and blazed against the oaken casket.

The costume designer of *The Ice Princess*, and Ingrid’s one-time husband, Erik Bjorge wore a simple brown suit with the bunad shirt of yellow and green. It was the same garment he had worn the day of their wedding. Now, Ingrid was dead and with her, Erik’s dream. With his fashion-line positioned for the entire world to see with the premiere of *The Ice Princess*, Erik had believed he would be a fashion king: He would be the Versace of Norway, the Grand Gucci of the Fjords. The premiere at Cannes of *The Ice Princess* had been his fashion window to fame but now that was gone.

Despite the presence of a Lutheran minister, the funeral was shaping up to be pagan. Erik gazed blankly at the orange flames on the funeral pyre. The white-clad angels, with tall candles held high, circled around the burning wood and the last earthly remains of his ex-wife. All we need now is fucking Elton John, Erik thought. "And our love was like a funeral pyre," he recalled from the old Doors song. As the high orange fire snapped toward the slippery spring sky, Erik cringed and shook: The media was turning the dead actress into a saint. Erik knew that Ingrid was not: You don't get to be the star actress of a prestigious movie that opens the Cannes Film Festival by cavorting only with film-school professors, arts bureaucrats, or other deadbeats. You don't make that big of a leap at such a young age without some sort of lethal accelerator. He knew all too well what she had in her.

The luxury cabin of Gunnar Sevareid's Gulfstream 650 bespoke the super jet's price tag of roughly $60 million. The main cabin was decorated with hand-painted silk wallpaper that was adorned with Viking battleground motifs. The Gulfstream's layout boasted a separate space for lounging or dining. It featured a luxurious bedroom with an en suite bath, and it impressed with a library filled with works of Douglas MacArthur, Sun Yat-sen, William F. Buckley, Jr., as well as two books on animalist existentialism. The seats were equipped with heating capabilities, and included massage. Digital sensors could calculate the groove to each back-and-bottom.

The luxury plane, which seated eight, was not filled. Gunnar Sevareid was sequestered in the main cabin. Among the passengers, Erik recognized the two security men who had been on the Cannes-to-Oslo flight, a multilingual flight attendant, and a physician who always accompanied Sevareid. In addition, Erik spotted an old friend from his Oslo partying days, Asbjorn Magnusson. What was Magnusson doing on Gunnar Sevareid's Gulfstream? Erik sensed he was better off not asking and kept his distance.

Just before take-off, two men who had not been on the Gulfstream's flight from Cannes to Oslo entered. Their faces were weather-beaten and their hair unkempt. They were out of their element, but Erik sensed why they were on board: Gunnar Sevareid had instructed him to create French janitorial uniforms for the two. The specification was that they each have a special tool belt incorporated into the cleaning costume. The tool pouch for the first man, Per Narvesson, a roustabout on one of Gunnar Sevareid's North Sea rigs, included a concealed loop to hold a six-teen inch, four-pound hammer. The get-up also necessitated a holster for a power tool, which could sever a shark's tooth in a mini-second. The second man, Herbrand Ulsvick, required a pouch for a fish scaler with a nine-inch blade. The hardened stainless-steel knife featured a stain-resistant fiberglass handle. The belt included a pouch that could accommodate a gut spoon. Ulsvick was an employee of Gunnar Sevareid's fisheries empire, which was listed on Sevareid's official documents as an "aquaculture industry." For eleven years, Ulsvick had gutted fish from Sevareid's mackerel vessels, which harvested off the western coast of Norway.

Back in his private Gulfstream suite, Gunnar Sevareid nibbled from a container of herring. Despite his notoriety as one of the biggest oil drillers in the world, Sevareid hated polluters. Overall, Sevareid had no faith in governments or environmental entities such as Greenpeace, whom he regarded as hippie dimwits, or any other do-gooder source to solve the climate-change problem. From his days as a young man on the North Sea oil rigs, Sevareid knew that the Russians were intent on plundering the region of its oil, mineral and natural gas. The former Soviet Union had used it as a dumping site for nuclear waste: Sevareid's intelligence team estimated that at least 19,000 massive containers of radioactive waste had been dumped by the Soviets into the region. Putin's Russia continued to use the Arctic as a nuclear-waste toilet.

To combat such evil, Gunnar Sevareid's empire now included a security unit, LOKI. Sevareid had named it after a mythological trickster and adviser to the Norse gods; Loki was the master of deceit and acknowledged as the "prince of lies." Gunnar Sevareid thought it a fitting name for a company that specialized in counter-counter intelligence, misinformation and disinformation. He had established LOKI initially for North Sea oil rig security, but it had evolved to encompass security for sporting, recreational, and global cultural events – such as the Cannes Film Festival.

Gunnar Sevareid gazed out the window as his super-jet descended into a Cannes airport that was off-the-map to the commercial airlines. Moussorgsky's

The Great Gate of Kiev reverberated from the super jet's Bose speakers, and Sevareid smiled. Usually, he had either *Thus Spach Zarathustra* or *Ride of the Valkyries* to set the mood for his landing, but this time he needed the special stimulant of the Ukrainian national anthem.

He speculated that if someone were filming him now gazing out the jet's window as the plane descended over the French Riviera, it should be from the same angle that Leni Riefenstahl had used in making Hitler appear god-like as he descended into Nuremberg. What was the name of that classic propaganda film? Gunnar Sevareid tried to recall. Finally, *Triumph of the Will.*

He thought: *Good title for my autobiography.*

Chapter 11

Considering that he had been up all night, found a corpse, been chased through town by what he thought were cops, delivered an impromptu speech before a packed room of journalists, and confronted a couple having sex in a chicken coop, Ryan wasn't too worse for wear. He recalled a Sean Connery line from the third *Indiana Jones*, where Harrison Ford whizzes along on a motorcycle with his professor father, Connery, clinging for dear life. "This is not archaeology," Connery groused as Indy accelerated away from the bad guys.

"This is not film criticism," Ryan muttered to himself. He dusted off his shirt sleeves, still mucked from his encounter with Henri. He needed a change-of-pace and decided to accept a text invite to a reception that Leonard Maltin was hosting for Matt Damon in the Old Town.

The cab driver dropped Ryan off on the Croisette, between the Carlton and the Palais. He made his way onto the walkway path, savoring the sea breeze and enjoying the colorful mix of festival-goers and tourists. Between the sidewalk and the beach, tall rectangular wooden boxes perched. To Ryan's Wisconsin-raised eye, they looked like the old outhouses at his great grandparent's homestead, but instead they were giant speakers painted in beachfront pastels. The stirring strains of Maurice Jarre's *Lawrence of Arabia* score cascaded from each speaker, creating a sea of sound that played seamlessly all along the beach. As the Middle Eastern tinged movie theme song floated over the sands, Ryan envisioned Peter O'Toole emerging from the desert, head-to-toe in white and his blue eyes sparkling. Best blue eyes ever. Ryan recalled that David Lean conveyed the same blue-eyed majesty with Julie Christie in his next epic *Dr. Zhivago*. Exact same framing: O'Toole's blue eyes and blonde locks topped by a white kufiya, Julie Christie's blue eyes and blonde mane, framed by a white embroidery. Ryan grinned: He was getting his mojo back, loosening his mind with movie associations. A thought: Ingrid Bjorge had those same magical blue eyes.

Further down the teeming walkway, the Palais loomed. The gargantuan cement and glass structure hunched against the little harbor where older sail boats and luxury yachts cohabited. The Palais' spotless glass walls and doors always shimmered in the morning sun, but in this late afternoon, the edifice shoved back the sun's sharp advances. Ryan headed past the municipal police station toward Le Suquet, the picturesque Old Town where the party was being held. The street was crammed with cars, pedestrians, and converging buses. A policeman with oversized plastic white gloves whirled his arms around in a cuckoo-clock frenzy. Ryan hurried up a stone walkway lined with quaint and expensive restaurants. The walk was at a steep angle, and he began to sweat. He wiped his forehead. The sunscreen he had gotten from Nick was sticky as usual.

Ryan recognized the green and gold awnings of La Verna, the restaurant which was the site of the party. La Verna catered to high-rollers: Entrees started at 105 euros, basically the same amount in dollars. Four security guards blocked the entrance to the vaunted restaurant. Ryan approached and held out his festival badge. The guards took less time examining it than it would have taken to listen to a Grateful Dead song. The head guard finally handed Ryan back his *Carte Blanc* card and stood aside. Ryan slid through the guards into the fabled restaurant.

It was dark inside, cavern-like. In his current state of mind, Ryan thought of a sepulcher. He couldn't see much, but the frantic babble told him he was once again entering the domain of the chattering classes.

"Ah, the guy who killed the actress," someone nearby said. The voice sounded familiar. Ryan squinted and detected the grin of a fair-haired gent in a blue windbreaker.

"Don't worry, I won't kill anyone here tonight, as long as they bring me a glass of wine quickly," Ryan said, adjusting his eyes. Then he recognized the man behind the voice – Matt Damon.

"So, you're having an exciting festival Leonard tells me," Damon said.

"He doesn't know the half of it." Ryan felt self-conscious. He knew he looked like a wreck. "Sorry, I just had a fight in a chicken coop," Ryan said. "Plus, I totaled a car last night. An Aston Martin, no less. That's why I'm a little grubby."

"Remind me never to play you in a movie," Damon said. "I'll stick to my more sedate Jason Bourne character."

"Although I know you've heard it before, I think the script you and Ben did for *Good Will Hunting* is the one of the best ever," Ryan said. "I especially love your last line."

"Thanks, I'm always up for praise." Damon smiled, and pulled out a thick cigar from his inner pocket and handed it to Ryan. "George played a joke on me a couple festivals back and told a journalist that I liked this brand of cigar. Now they keep appearing in my suites everywhere I go. I don't even smoke."

"You're lucky he didn't say you loved pork and beans," Ryan joked.

Damon patted Ryan on the shoulder and said, "Sorry, I've got to go and see about a girl." *Great line still.*

As Ryan watched Damon meander back into the party-cluster and dole out more cigars, he spotted Trygve Tecksle, *The Hollywood New Times* Scandinavian correspondent. He approached the short Norwegian who fidgeted with an iPad. "I hope you can help me with this damn contraption," Tecksle said by way of greeting.

"Sorry, I'm a technological idiot myself," Ryan said.

"Your review has become notorious in Oslo," Tecksle said. "You were referenced on the evening news the other night as the 'killer critic'."

"So, am I the most hated man in Norway?"

"Not quite. The most hated man is still the terrorist who shot all those children at the park a few years ago. But, I'd have to say you are second," Tecksle said. "Didn't you read my story?"

"Sorry, I've been a bit crazy lately."

"I was so rushed, I had to transmit it from the flight from Oslo," Tecksle added.

"I had to do the same thing," Ryan said. "Then I get here and all of a sudden I'm a murder suspect."

"But now the focus is off you. People are saying Gunnar Sevareid and Ingrid Bjorge had been having an affair. They say that it is how she got her part. How else would an unknown who had only done some cheap sex films land the biggest movie role in the world?"

"Is Gunnar Sevareid as ruthless as some people here seem to think?" Ryan asked.

"A man does not amass a fortune of nearly $100 billion by being kind and caring," Tecksle answered.

"'Behind every great fortune, there is a crime.' Honoree de Balzac." Ryan turned to see the speaker. It was his friend Dennis Barlowe, who had inveigled his way into the event. Barlowe turned to Tecksle, "How do you think Sevareid can sell his film now that high-powered opinion-makers like Ryan here have trashed it?" he asked. "'Big hair, big guns, big boots, big dud,' what a great opening line," Barlowe noted. "Also, 'the dialogue was dreadful even by the abysmal standards of science fiction.' Do I have that right? And, my favorite line: 'No one has ever accused sci-fi enthusiasts of having people skills, and certainly none of the characters in this movie react in any human way – they are there only to explain the plot'."

"It sounds like you have memorized the review," Tecksle said.

"I know Ryan's writing style," Barlowe noted.

"You managed to score an interview with Ingrid Bjorge before she was killed," Tecksle said. "You were the only one."

"What can I say? It's my charm and professionalism," Barlowe said. "I hate to say it, but her murder was a break for me, I had her exclusively. You wouldn't believe the number of hits I've gotten. By the way, the second part of my interview comes out tomorrow on my site, SinSpin."

"There's a second part?" Ryan asked.

"Yeah, and it's much steamier," Barlowe added. He took Ryan aside. "Speaking of steamy, that chateau after-party the Russians hosted the other night was debauchery at a whole new level. It was even better than that time at MIDEM when Miramax limo-ed all their buyers up to a mountain hotel. They had rented suites with hookers for everyone."

"I never heard about any hookers' party," Ryan said.

"Of course you didn't. That's because you're always reviewing films and missing all the action. This one the other night was a real drug-and-screw fest. It could have won the Harvey Award," Barlowe joked. "The Russians flew in these sexpots from Moscow and Crimea, one for each buyer or producer or whatever these sleazebags were."

"That must have been the event Nick told me he about when he lent me the Aston Martin. He said he was going to a meeting with Russian investors."

Barlowe laughed. "These women were not exactly investment analysts. From what I've heard Nick was pretty coked up during the whole thing."

"This is not official yet and it's not out anywhere, but my sources tell me he bit it at the party," Barlowe said.

"Damn, this festival is getting crazier and crazier," Ryan said.

"Don't let this get out,"

"I still think there's a pattern to all this," Ryan said.

"This is not armchair crime investigation."

"Well, there's just as many suspects here in Ingrid Bjorge's murder as there are in one of those mystery novels," Ryan said. "Although here at Cannes, they are not exactly the butcher, the butler, the baker, the candlestick maker, or even the Indian Chief. Who do you go think killed Ingrid Bjorge?" Ryan asked.

"I'd go with the candlestick maker."

"Not the Indian Chief?"

"Are you kidding? That would be politically incorrect. I'd be drummed out of Hollywood," Barlowe noted. "Seriously, you've got to do what they always tell us at my AA meetings. Don't try to control things you have no power over."

"I didn't know you went to AA."

"It's not for booze. It's for my gambling. Same addiction principles."

"Is it helping?"

"It's a struggle, especially this time of year with the NBA Finals and the Stanley Cup," Barlowe said. "But, the best part is, I'm meeting a lot of babes at the meetings. Lots of coffee and soulful discussions afterwards." Barlowe grinned and patted Ryan on the shoulder. "Great place to meet women."

A tuxedoed waiter approached, and extended a silver tray of dessert temptations: lemon soufflés, crème brulee, and a cornucopia of colorful, sticky, glazed delicacies. Ryan grabbed two shiny strawberry torts for the road. He wrapped them in cocktail napkins and stuffed them in his coat pocket. He realized he had been subsisting the last few days on fruity desserts and coffee. He stood back and watched as Matt Damon circulated, still handing out cigars. Over to the side, he spotted Barlowe chatting up a waiter. Probably scoring some extra desserts for the road, Ryan speculated.

A wave of screams hit Ryan as he emerged from the restaurant. He elbowed his way through the bodyguards at the door. More than fifty autograph hounds, mostly young women and geeky guys, huddled with their digital cameras, cellphones and autograph books. Word had gotten out that Matt Damon was in the restaurant. The crowd quieted when they saw Ryan wasn't the movie star. But, the autograph hounds plunged toward him: if he was *there*, he must be *somebody*.

"Monsieur, s'il vous plait?" A short woman in a Charlie Chaplin hat shoved an autograph book at Ryan. Ryan took the book and signed. The woman gaped at Ryan's scrawl and frowned. "But you are nobody."

"You are right about that," Ryan said. He headed off down the old street, pulling one of the tortes out of his pocket. He ambled toward Mashou, one of the most popular and expensive restaurants in Cannes. He glanced in: Over pink tablecloths and silver cutlery, people supped, smoked, and coiffed. Champagne buckets sparkled, candles flickered, and the sweetest of sea breezes crept up over the ancient walkway. Ryan spotted the gypsy and his little girl. A security guard herded them from the doorway. The little girl's hair was glutted with red-white-and-blue bows, and her eyes were red-rimmed. Ryan approached them and extended the torte to the gypsy girl. She stared at him, frightened.

"Mange," Ryan said. "Mange," hoping she understood. "Eat, eat!

The gypsy reached for the torte, but Ryan pulled away. "No, not for you." Ryan pulled a handful of French coins from his coat pocket. "I will give you money only after she eats," he told the man. The gypsy mumbled a garble of French at the girl, and she lifted the torte to her mouth and nibbled. After a nervous pause, she devoured the torte. Ryan handed her the second one. She dug into it, and began to cry. Ryan finally handed the change to the gypsy. The gypsy counted it, then yanked the little girl away, and they trudged up the old cobblestone walk. Ryan watched them go and took out the big cigar

Damon had given him. He stuck it in his mouth without lighting, then sauntered down the walk, between the ancient buildings. The rain pattered on the old stone and metal signs. It was a hell of a place to be nobody, and, even better, he now believed he knew who Ingrid Bjorge's murderer was. Despite what Barlowe had advised him about not trying to connect all those different players and things, Ryan felt he had a finger on the overall pattern. He had a good idea who the killer was.

The lobby to *The Hollywood New Times* hotel of residence was deserted except for Etienne, the night attendant. Ryan had passed another test. If there had been anything amiss, police chasing him for instance, Etienne's manner would not have been so nonchalant. Ryan reasoned that the coast was finally clear for him: he was no longer a suspect. He believed Erik Bjorge had killed Ingrid in a rage over her not wearing his clothes to the premiere.

Ryan endured no fewer than seven bolts and jolts in the tiny elevator on his way up to his fourth-floor room. His hotel room in past years had been on the first floor, but this year's problem of the Wi-Fi had necessitated a higher berth. It was pitch-dark in the hallway, and Ryan had momentarily forgotten where the French had those tiny switches to light things up. But he had the equilibrium to navigate in the dark. His physical coordination had kicked back in. Finally, Ryan was back to normal, at last ready to start the festival at full speed. Ryan slid his room card into the slot, listened for the click, and opened the door. Inside, he stuck the card in the electrical energizer on the near wall, and flicked on the light.

She sat on the desk chair with her back to him, looking straight out onto the balcony. Her blonde hair shone from the outside lights. She wore a bright blue dress. She turned to him and smiled. And then Ingrid Bjorge got out of the chair and walked straight over to Ryan. "News of my death has been greatly wrong," the reportedly murdered star of the opening night film of the Cannes Film Festival said.

Chapter 12

Ryan was not easily surprised. After all, he had been a writer in Hollywood for nearly a dozen years. Crazy stories abounded in that world; nevertheless, Ingrid Bjorge's resurrection from the dead rattled him. She had been semi-coherent, and revealed she had only slept a couple hours in the last few days. Their discussion was short because she had nodded off. Ryan had insisted she take the bed, while he wadded up some sheets and slept on the floor.

Surprisingly, he had slept well on that night after Ingrid Bjorge had astonished him with her back-from-the-grave appearance. He looked to his bed where Ingrid Bjorge slept face down, her right arm looped over her head. Was he really seeing this? Had he gone nuts? Had last night been a dream? He tried to speak, but his throat tightened.

"Ingrid," he said. "Ingrid, it's morning. Ingrid."

She rolled over, and opened her eyes. Her long blonde hair cascaded over the pillow.

"Did you sleep okay?" he asked.

"I am alive," she said. She smiled and stared at him with her keen blue eyes. "Thank you. It is the first good sleep I have had since this festival began."

"That's great," he said. "I'm glad to hear that. Still, it's so crazy to wake up and find you in my room. I thought when I woke up that you being here would turn out to be only a dream," he said.

"I did not know what to do. So I came here," Ingrid Bjorge said. She stretched her arms above her head. "I trusted you from what I have read about you and seen on the TV."

"Surely you must have someone else," Ryan said. "Someone closer to you."

"I cannot trust the people who are close to me," she said.

"But I'm probably still being watched as a murder suspect," Ryan noted.

"I am sorry," she said. "I do not know anyone at this festival that I now trust. That is why I have come to you. I sense that you are a good person."

"It's funny: I thought I figured out who killed you, and now you're alive and in my room," Ryan said.

"So, who did you think killed me?"

"Your ex-husband, Erik."

"Erik was angry enough to kill me, but he did not kill me, obviously. He took me away. I suppose he saved my life since I wasn't there in the hotel room when that poor other woman was killed," she said.

"If you're alive, who was killed?"

"I do not know," she said. "I feel also like I am in a bad dream."

"Where have you been all this time?"

"At this farm where they grow chickens." "At Henri's?"

"Yes, how did you know?"

"I was there today to see Henri. It was related to you,"

"Erik took me to the chicken farmhouse because it was the only place he knew to go to where no one would expect to find us. He was so angry, and he was not thinking smart."

"Why was he so angry? Because you weren't going to wear his gown on the red carpet?"

"Yes, he said I was killing his dream. I was supposed to wear this dress he had made for me for the opening night premiere, but Mr. Sevareid's people were telling me I had to wear one of the other gowns."

"Prada, Gucci, Armani, probably one of those big-time fashion places," Ryan said. "Fashion is big business. Many people are more interested in what the stars are wearing than the actual event. The top designers fight to get the big stars to wear their wardrobes. When you're on the red carpet, you can be seen by more than one billion people worldwide. It's a great opportunity for advertising."

"But I am not a big movie star."

"Yes, but being the star of the opening night film at Cannes means all the eyes of the world are on you. Only the summer Olympics has more media coverage, and that's only every fourth year. Cannes is every year."

"I had no idea," she said. "We are not so concerned with clothes in Norway. I thought I was just being in a movie. It was not such a good movie either from your review." She tucked her legs under her and quivered.

"What happened on that afternoon just before you were supposedly killed?" Ryan asked.

"I was supposed to do this interview, but Mr. Sevareid had my room changed at the last minute, and that the journalist would meet me in the new room. But that person never came so I went to the movie's reception."

"Who was at the reception?"

"Mr. Sevareid, of course. Erik, Jason Pinelli with a girlfriend. I think she is on MTV. There were also many other people who I did not know."

"Is that when you told Erik you were going to wear another gown?"

"Yes, and at first he thought I was not too serious," Ingrid said. "Near the end of the party, though, he realized I was serious. He said we should go for a walk."

"Where did you go?"

"He took me down to the main floor, and he had someone from the hotel get us a car. He said he was just going to drive around the block."

"Didn't you get suspicious when he suggested a car?"

"No, Miss Clearidge told me there were all kinds of crazy movie-star fans outside the hotel, and I should not go outside on the sidewalk."

"Did he threaten you?"

"No, but he was angry. I said I was just doing what I was being told. Mr. Sevareid had spent a lot of money on experts to make all things go right."

"What did Erik say to that?"

"He kept getting angrier," she said. "Then, he started driving alongside the sea. He told me if I wasn't going to wear his gown to the premiere, he wouldn't let me go."

"Did anyone see you leave the hotel?"

"No, I don't think so. We went down the private stairway instead of taking the elevator because they are so long to wait for. There was only one person on the stairs, some older man."

"Can you describe him?"

"Short man, black hair with some gray spots. He had on a t-shirt, dark sports coat, and American blue jeans. He was yelling into his cellphone in some strange language."

"That describes half the men at this festival," Ryan said.

"I have not seen too much of the festival. I keep reading about it, and I keep reading about me and all these awful stories the writers tell. They say things that are not true and things about me that are crazy to believe. Do they just make them up?"

"Yes, some do. Don't get me started on entertainment journalists, or, even worse, bloggers," Ryan said. "Any idiot with access to the internet can post news these days. To these so-called journalists you're dead. So, they stretch the truth. After all, who is going to complain or contradict them?"

"It must be hard for you. They have the advantage of saying whatever they feel like, but you must stick with the truth," she said.

Ryan smiled. He had never thought of journalism as the "truth." He preferred novels, trusted them more. Novelists could write things journalists could not say without fear of nuisance defamation lawsuits. Plus, readers or viewers in this social-media age did not want the "truth": they wanted "news" that re-enforced their own views and prejudices.

"So, why didn't you try to get out of the car?" he asked.

"I kept thinking Erik would calm down and turn around."

"Weren't you worried about missing your big moment on the red carpet, and what Mr. Sevareid would do?"

"Yes, I was upset. I started to yell at Erik that I was late to put on my movie dress, and everyone would be angry, especially Mr. Sevareid."

"What did he do?"

"He grabbed me and pushed me inside this building. He locked me inside. The air made me cough because of all the smells from the chickens."

"Has Erik ever been violent with you before?"

"He was somewhat wild at the beginning, but we were young. And, I did not do so well at being a girlfriend."

"What did Erik do after he locked you up?"

"I don't know. He stayed out all night and came back early in the morning. He had a French newspaper, which had my photograph. It was an old photo when my hair was much shorter."

"Yes, I saw it," Ryan said. "I like it longer, like you have it now."

"Thank you. Yes, Mr. Sevareid had me grow it for the festival. It was supposed to be a big surprise to everyone," Ingrid said

"What was Erik's reaction to the newspaper story that you were dead?" Ryan asked.

"He seemed to be even more confused than I was."

"How long were you at Henri's?" Ryan asked,

"I was there for two more days," Ingrid said. "Then, an old woman let me out, but she would not talk to me. I had to walk down to the sea where I got a hitchhike."

"Why didn't Erik just go with you to the police that first morning? That would have been the sensible thing to do. It would have saved a lot of people a lot of trouble, me included," Ryan noted.

"Mainly, he was afraid Gunnar Sevareid was behind everything," Ingrid said. "He thought Gunnar Sevareid was dangerous, and a bit mad."

"Why?"

"I don't know. Erik was always fearful of him. He has so much money. Gunnar Sevareid can do anything."

"Do you have any enemies at all among actresses, or people from your dancing days?" Ryan asked.

"Erik is the only one who is ever angry with me, and that is because we were once in love," she said. "He said I must not go to the police because whoever killed that woman would still want to kill me. He told me I should give him a day or two." She sobbed. "I am sorry, I don't mean to cry," Ingrid said.

"It's all right. I could use a good cry myself. Mind if I join in?"

"But, you are an American man," Ingrid said.

"Yes, I know. We can be sensitive when our favorite football team is down on its luck," Ryan said.

She smiled. "I think you can be humoristic too."

"I will let you stay temporarily, but I have to take you to the police this afternoon," Ryan said. "This craziness is getting out of hand, and I don't intend to be the fall-guy."

"Not until after the festival," she said. "I cannot be alive again until this festival is done with."

"That makes no sense," Ryan said. "You've got to go in."

"No!"

"You stay here; I've got to go back to the office."

"When will you come back?"

"It won't be long. I've got to check in with my day job."

"Day job?

"I'm supposed to be reviewing movies," Ryan said. "Instead, I'm stuck in this nightmare."

Ryan glanced at Ingrid – her sparkling blonde hair, her luminous skin, her sexy figure. He knew he needed to take her to the police, but so far she had manipulated him into keeping her existence a secret. Was he being a sucker for a pretty blonde? Was he in the snare of a femme fatale? He didn't think so, but neither did William Hurt in Body Heat or, in the original, Fred Mac Murray in Double Indemnity.

The crowd swarmed toward him. People grabbed at him. A woman tore at his clothes. Ryan tried to turn past them but was bumped in the head with a camera. A crowd of people had engulfed him at the walkway outside The Hollywood New Times hotel. He jostled to make it into the paper's s office, but he was swarmed with paparazzi. Lauren Perrino hurried toward him as he entered the lobby. "Orson came up with something brilliant to compensate for all the bad press the paper's been getting on your account," she barked at him.

"Well, a smart publicist should be able to turn that around, since I'm innocent of the charges," Ryan said.

"That's exactly Orson's idea, that's why he's the publisher. His idea is more thought-out," she said.

"What is it?"

"You're going for a balloon ride," Lauren said. "What?" Ryan exclaimed.

"Orson said the wind spoke to him on his walk on the beach yesterday. It told him that since you're in the news anyway, why not use it to our advantage and have you do something fun and positive for a change. Put it on our website. Stream it. Turn your notoriety into a plus."

"I definitely could use something that's fun and positive," Ryan said. "I didn't know we had a balloon here."

"We're in it with Hands-On. It's some sort of trade-out for the unpaid ad money they owe us."

"So, the wind told Orson W. Woolsey to send me up in a Hands-On promotional balloon?"

"Yes, he can be quite spiritual," Lauren said.

"I understand he has an adobe condo in Palm Springs with Hopi dolls on the fireplace mantel," Ryan answered.

Lauren was impervious to sarcasm. "Hands-On has developed a big movie slate," she said. "They have done extremely well in their international sales here. Plus, they are going to make a major announcement at the end of the festival."

"Well, I'm way behind on my reviews," Ryan said. "But I'll be a team player. When is it?"

"We're not sure of the time yet. It depends on wind conditions or something like that. I'll let you know," Lauren said. She sniffed: "Givenchy?"

"Just my regular cologne," Ryan answered.

"You should cut down on your womanizing," she said.

"It's not like that," Ryan said.

"Whatever," Lauren said. "And be courteous to those people outside the hotel."

"You've got to rip apart the front page. Re-do the web. I've got the banner," Stan Peck bellowed in The Hollywood New Times' office. "Nick Steele has been found dead," he announced.

"What do you mean, dead?" Tim Daniels questioned.

"Dead, dead," Peck said. "He was found in the bathroom of his yacht. His people say it looks like a heart attack. Where's Bernie?"

"He's at an announcement about the new MGM at the Old Palais," Tim answered.

"I've got another exclusive," Peck said. "I found out the producers of The Ice Princess are engaged in a secret auction of the film"

Tim slumped backward, shifting the stories on the screen, making space as Peck peered over his shoulder. "What about the obit for the Hands-On guy, Steele?" Tim asked. "Are you going to write it?"

"His publicist is e-mailing his bio to you," Peck said. "They've become the most successful independent film company of the festival."

"Those guys are just scum-balls from the porn world, trying to go legit," Ryan said.

"You have no appreciation for the underdog," Peck said.

"I just realize the underdog is not always the good party," Ryan said. "I root for people to make it in the movies who didn't go to Beverly Hills High School with producers' daughters, or start out with their father as president of an agency."

"But Hands-On is going into battle against the studios and Netflix and Amazon and everybody," Peck asserted.

"They make sexist, violent, ridiculous movies, and market them to moronic fifteen-year old males," Ryan said.

"Wait till you read my story," Peck said. "It will set you straight."

"I will waste no time in reading it," Ryan said. Peck ignored the jibe, popped his individually selected peanuts into his mouth, and left the room.

"How about you?" Tim asked Ryan. "Everything okay? Back to normal?"

"Not exactly."

"Why? What happened?"

"Something I'd definitely call 'unexpected,'" Ryan said. "I can't figure it out. I might need your help later, though." Ryan lowered his voice. "I might need your advice on something down the line."

"This about the murder?"

"Yes. But it's not just one murder," Ryan said.

"What?"

"Yeah, things are even crazier than people know," Ryan said. "I'm caught up in some international range-war."

"You've got to tell me," Tim said.

"No. "If I do, you'll act on it, and that could jeopardize things for not only me but for others," Ryan continued. "Innocent people could be killed."

"Holy shit! You've got to fill me in here," Tim said.

"Sorry, it's just too crazy," Ryan said.

"Well, suit yourself then. I've been texting Dylko for you, but he hasn't responded," Tim said. "He hasn't filed his Russian film financing story yet either."

"Well, let him know I still want to talk with him," Ryan said in his best pissed-off tone, camouflaging the fact that he knew that Dylko was dead.

As Ryan turned to leave, a copy editor burst from the other room. "You wouldn't believe what Henri has on his jump." He stuck it in one of the computers and began to pull it up. Ryan paused at the door, as everyone from the copy desk hurried over to check out the photos. Like a bunch of school kids, they circled around the screen.

Tim poked his way over and stared at the screen. "Damn, Henri is just the office gofer and he gets to go to all this sexy stuff. How come I never get in on any of this depravity?" The pictures were X-rated shots of the porn actresses. Ryan recognized the setting, the Hands-On yacht. Nick was in nearly every picture, surrounded by scantily clad beauties. The staff was too caught up in the risqué photos to notice as Ryan sorted through a stack of Hollywood New Times t-shirts and caps. He filled his festival bag with the corporate souvenirs and drifted toward the door.

Tim called out to him: "Let's be careful out there."

Three trucks rumbled down a narrow cobbled street. They plowed through a blighted industrial area, a section so run-down it could now be regarded as "hip." The trucks carried 170 cases of empty Bordeaux bottles that had been filled with the cheap wine for The Ice Princess party. Gunnar Sevareid had been billed 1,000 bottles or $100,000 for them. Now, they would be re-filled with more red swill and sold to another Cannes party. Ten-percent alcohol and 1,000 per-cent profit.

The drivers maneuvered the trucks to a backside ramp where Henri stood, flanked by a cadre of day-workers he had culled from among the area's undocumented immigrants. The workers moved large boxes marked "TIP," short for The Ice Princess. The boxes contained the aqua blue lingerie that Erik had designed for his fashion line debut. The workers fitted the boxes between two sections that were crammed with swords, blades and other weaponry that had been used for The Ice Princess opening night party. Henri would also re-use them as decorations for the grand party he was organizing. He would make big money with the party, not only with the door, but the bar, and especially the sale of wine. Post-party he would once again re-cork the bottles, fill them with cheap wine, and then re-sell to a closing-night gala at the Carlton Pier. His years of connections and ingratiation were finally paying off. He would no longer subsist as a tenant on a chicken farm. This year's festival was his great score: With his festival booty, he would buy beachfront property in Golfe-Juan, one short train stop from Cannes' central station.

Chapter 13

The azure gown was cut into a low, sweetheart style, and the fabric, while it reached down nearly to the floor, was slit up the sides. Ice sequins danced up the mesh front, and the back of the dress was open and laced with silver trim.

"That dress was made for you," Ryan said as he closed the hotel-room door and set down the bags that contained Ingrid's new wardrobe.

"It was made for me," Ingrid Bjorge said. "It is the dress Erik designed for me to wear for the opening night premiere." The gown clung to her body in a sexy form-fitting manner. Ryan eyed the dolphin tattoo on her outer ankle.

"You do not like it either?" she asked, acknowledging the tatt.

"No, I think it's kind of cute. Have you got other ones?"

"Not where I could show you," she said. "Mr. Sevareid got upset when he saw it."

"Why?"

"I do not know. It wasn't anything too bold, like some of the girls in Oslo have," Ingrid said.

"Yes, those Oslo girls, very wild," Ryan noted.

"You are being humoristic again," she said. "I am beginning to understand that the words you use are different from what you really feel."

"Yes, it's called dry sarcasm, and it doesn't float well with the literal-minded or the stupid," Ryan said. "I need to be more careful what I say because in person you know that I'm making a point with humor. But when it appears in print, the reader doesn't always get that."

"So, you must be careful with journalists because they use your words, but do not care about your true meaning," Ingrid said.

"Exactly. It's amateur night at the Bronx Zoo," he added.

"That is humoristic again," Ingrid said.

"I brought you some clothes," he said. "I hesitate to give them to you, though. You look so beautiful."

"You said I need to look like every other woman at this festival."

"You could never look like any other woman at this festival. You're way too pretty." Ryan said. "You remind me of Julie Christie in *Dr. Zhivago*."

"I do not know who that is," she said.

"Let me have one last, long look at you before you put on this dreadful film-festival uniform," Ryan said.

She lowered her chin, and then raised it. Her blue eyes latched onto him. Her powder blue dress was nearly a replica for the aqua, chiffon dress Kelly wore in *To Catch a Thief*. Ryan recalled the scene where she stood with Cary Grant at the doorway to her Carlton suite, and she surprised him with a big kiss.

"You remind me so much of Grace Kelly in that gown," he said. "She was a famous American actress from Philadelphia who later became the Princess of Monaco. And, like your character in the movie, she was truly an ice princess. Francois Truffaut once described Grace Kelly as `the paradox between the inner fire and the cool surface,' that is you," he said.

"You are comparing me to another old-time actress again," she said.

"Yes, particularly one who was here at Cannes, and wore a flowing powder blue chiffon gown like the one you are now wearing."

"I used to watch those old movies without the color on the TV in Oslo," Ingrid said. "I loved it when the American actress Lauren Bacall would lower her head and then slowly look up and stare straight into the man's eyes. Then, she would say something in a low sexy voice," Ingrid said. "Or, she would sing something and slowly move her hips. I think I might try that if I ever do any more of this acting."

Ryan was pleasantly surprised that she had even heard of Lauren Bacall. He reached into his festival bag and pulled out one of *The Hollywood New Times* t-shirts and one of the paper's souvenir baseball caps. He also yanked out a pair of blue jeans and a black sports coat that he had purchased at the Monoprix, the pint-sized Target-like store near the train station.

"Having you switch from that gorgeous blue gown to this get-up will be among the great fashion travesties of the year," he said.

She glanced at the festival garb, took it from him, and headed into the bathroom. While Ingrid dressed down, Ryan plugged in his laptop. He needed to type in some program production notes for his film reviews and would need to start cracking on the two movies he had seen that morning. Both had been in foreign languages. Since the subtitles had been in French, Ryan had needed to use the earphones for dialogue translation. Ryan hated the Cannes headsets. Invariably, they never fit right over his ears and the sound level was always erratic. Most films narratives were voiced by the same dispassionate English woman. Her drone-on voice often made Ryan laugh, especially during action or sex scenes. Such dry intonations – "I love you, baby. Your body smell excites me. Show me your rump." It was how Alexa might say it, if Alexa were a snooty Brit. Her monotonic descriptions often sent Ryan into laughing hysterics, not warmly appreciated by his ultra-serious, fellow critics.

Ryan clicked on *The Hollywood New Times* website. He went straight to the fluff: it was his whiff of "Napalm in the morning." He zeroed in on what he considered the paper's most ridiculous column: F. Scottie Young's society column, Biz Buzz with a Twizt. In his latest "scoop," Young bellowed that a new drink, "The Cannes-Tiki," was now the rage at Cannes. It had been concocted by a Majestic Hotel bartender, inspired by the news of Ingrid's funeral and the fire on the Kon-Tiki in Cannes Old Port the opening night of the festival. Ryan read: "a mellifluous elixir of Grand Marnier and Aquavit with a zesty splash of cranberry, topped off with an optimistically pink beach umbrella that is now the "je ne sais crois" among festival-goers." Ryan clicked off the site; that was enough "news" for the day.

Ingrid emerged from the bathroom. Despite the au courant Hollywood wardrobe of jeans and dark sports-coat, Ingrid Bjorge looked fantastic. She twirled around. “Do you think I will deceive people?”

“I don’t think you’re capable of deceiving people, but they might not recognize you.”

“You are making fun of my English again.”

“No, I enjoy your English.”

Ryan pulled out a black *Hollywood New Times* baseball cap from his suitcase. He placed it on her head, pushing it down over her ears. She swirled her blonde mane. “You look beautiful,” Ryan said. “Since everyone here thinks you have short hair because of those old news photos, you won’t be readily recognized.” Ryan handed her a pair of orange plastic sunglasses. She frowned and put them on. “Let me take you out for pizza. It might be one of the last times I can take you out before you realize you are a famous movie star, and then I’ll never get the chance.”

“It all depends on how good the pizza is. We Norwegians are exacting about the pizza, you know,” she joked.

“Afterward, I’m going to take you to the police. You are in deep danger. We can’t do this charade anymore.”

The smile vanished. Her expression froze and her eyes turned steely blue. “No, I cannot do it now,” she said. “You will not take me to the police!” Even among the power players in Hollywood Ryan had encountered - those men and women who really did seem to eat nails for breakfast – Ingrid Bjorge’s eyes were fierce, intimidating.

The Mediterranean Sea whipped and sloshed against the yachts in the Old Port as Ryan and Ingrid passed under the burgundy awning of La Pizza. The host led them through the sidewalk section of the restaurant. The pizzeria was empty, except for a few festival stragglers like Ryan who had never gotten used to the French habit of dining at eight or later. They sat across from each other. Ryan moved the olive oil bottle off to the side and removed the ashtray. He shoved away a glass of crayons, which bored kids could use to draw on the paper tablecloths.

"You have gotten some sun," she said.

"I forgot to bring sunscreen. Someone gave me some packets, but it's so slimy I haven't been using it regularly."

She flicked the front of his hair. "It is blonde now."

"I've been swimming back in LA, and I guess the chlorine got to it."

"I am a terrible swimmer," she said. "The water was too cold where I come from, on the island where my mother worked."

"She worked on an island?"

"Munkholmen Island. She worked at the tourist prison there," she said.

"Norway puts their tourists in prison?" Ryan asked.

"We only put in prison movie critics who come and criticize our movies," she joked. "Munkholmen is an old historical prison that was founded in Viking times by St. Olav. It is in the western part of the country, by the sea. It is also where the Germans had their big guns during the World War II."

"Did you live on the island?"

"No, my mother just worked there in the summer. We lived in Tromso. It is very far north."

"That must have been like living in a picture postcard," he said.

"It was pretty, but not so much like a postcard. It was hard, especially in the winter when it was always dark. My mother was sick much of the time."

"Seasonal Affective Disorder?"

"No, worse. She was often in the hospital."

A boyish-looking waiter, whom Ryan recognized from previous festivals because he looked like Paul McCartney, approached. Paul was getting gray.

"You order what you want, and I will eat what you don't want," she said.

"That will work. The portions are huge here." Ryan ordered the Reine pizza, the Minestrone soup, and a mozzarella-and-tomato salad. He also ordered a bottle of water "avec fiz" to share.

"Have you seen every movie in the world?"

"No, not hardly," Ryan said. "There was a famous movie that was filmed right here in Cannes. It was called To Catch a Thief with Cary Grant and Grace Kelly, who, I think, was the most beautiful actress of the times."

"You were talking about that earlier."

"It's one of my favorites, and it has one of my favorite scenes," Ryan said. "It's a scene where Cary Grant took Grace Kelly back to her hotel room at the Carlton which I still remember as Suite 623 and was going to be a gentleman and say good night, but she leaned into him and kissed him. She wore a beautiful powder blue dress and it flashed with her eyes. He was wearing a tux. Out the window, fireworks erupted all over the bay. It's about the most romantic scene in a movie, ever. He in his black tuxedo; she in her blue dress."

"You have a strange job, but it seems exciting. All the beautiful women who want to be stars must be lining up to meet you, the famous film critic," she said.

"That's right. All my great Hollywood loves -- me and Angelina Jolie. That was between Billy Bob and Brad. Not to mention Catherine Zeta Jones before she settled for Michael. And, Halle Berry is always calling me late at night. Don't get me started about Scarlett Johansson and her sexy texts."

"You are humoristic. Sometimes I do not know when you are teasing me."

"Actually, I'm teasing me," Ryan answered. "I mainly lead an unexciting life. I'm like most modern males who have devolved since the invention of microwave dinners, frozen pizza, and cable TV sports."

"I like that you are modest. That is not so usual with the movie people," she said.

"Have you ever been in a movie before *The Ice Princess*?" he asked.

"No. Well, yes. But not so big of a one. I did a few little ones when I started out, but they were not shown in theaters. No one saw them. I am glad."

"How do your friends in Norway feel about you being the star of the most glamorous film festival in the world?"

"They are very surprised," she said.

"Did you perform in school plays or anything?"

"No, when I was younger I did a lot of sports, gymnastics mainly. I ice-skated much."

"You never did tell me much about how you got into acting."

"I am not supposed to say anything about acting."

"You are the star actress of the opening night film in Cannes, and you're not supposed to say anything about acting?"

"That's what they told me."

"You don't consider that ironistic?"

"You are making fun of my English again. I know the American word is ironic."

"You are the biggest mystery of the festival, and I don't just mean about your murder."

"Why am I so mysterious?"

"Because, most star actresses are vain and self-centered and would love to have their moment in the spotlight, have their picture taken on the red carpet. They would do anything to get there. Yet, you do not care about it. That is ironic."

The Paul McCartney-waiter returned with the Minestrone soup and two bowls. He set it down between them. Another waiter followed with the tomato-mozzarella salad and the pizza. Ingrid took the ladle and dished up a bowl of the minestrone for him.

"When did you know you would become an actress?" he asked.

"I never dreamed of being an actress, certainly not the star in a big movie. Not even when I was a little girl and watched a video of E.T., and I liked Gertie very much."

"The Drew Barrymore character."

"Yes. I guess it was because she reminded me of me with her blonde hair. But even then I did not see myself as an actress. I thought that was only for movie stars' children in Hollywood."

"But you did some acting in Oslo. It said so in the press kit. You got rave reviews for your performance in Hedda Gabler at the Ibsen Theater."

"That is not true at all," she said. "The publicity people at BGK made it all up. They also wrote that I had played in The Wild Duck, and that it ran in Oslo for two seasons."

"It fooled me," Ryan said.

"You Americans think we Norwegians must be doing Ibsen all the time because you read about him at the university. We never do Ibsen in Oslo anymore," she said. "The only thing I did in Oslo was dancing, but that was to pay for the rent."

"You were an exotic dancer?"

"It was four years ago coming up this summer. I was seventeen." She looked down and dug into the gooey pizza, cutting the thick cheese with her knife, slicing the strips of ham.

"What about your father?" Ryan ventured.

"My mother said my father was a big sportsman in Norway, but she never said who he was. She did show me a picture. He was handsome and tall." She reached into her purse and took out a faded, crinkled picture. The man in the photo was imposing, with thick wavy blond hair and dazzling blue eyes. He stood among several fishing boats on a busy wharf.

"I can see where you got your good looks."

"Thank you. I wish I had met him. My mother said he would have become a great man if he had not drowned."

"Boating accident?"

"No, he worked on an oil rig in the North Sea, and that is a very dangerous thing to do," she said. "Many people are killed during their work." She stared off at the sea. Didn't say anything. Didn't blink.

Ryan sipped his water. "I don't mean to intrude. But I've noticed that you seem to have mood swings."

"Yes, it is a condition," she said. "And this festival is making it so much more horrible. It is so odd; I am just someone who was trying to figure out what to do in life," Ingrid said. "Then I get in a movie I didn't even care about. Now I am here and all these people are better off because they think I am dead. By being dead, I am affecting things in a good way, but when I was alive, I didn't really much matter."

"You shouldn't be so hard on yourself," Ryan said.

"I am sometimes sick because of that," she said. "I have a depression."

"Are you taking medication?"

"Yes, Lamictal and a new one I just started, but they do not really help. Cannes is one crazy thing after another, and I cannot tell if it is me having an episode, or if it is simply what is happening at this festival."

"That's understandable. I am so sorry."

Ryan spotted Stan Peck headed down the sidewalk toward the restaurant. Peck was the last person he wanted to see. He certainly did not want him to discover Ingrid. "Put your hand over your mouth and look the other way. And don't say anything," he said.

"Ryan, good to see you out and about," Peck called out from the sidewalk. "Mind if I join you?"

"I've got to get rid of this guy. I'll be right back." He got up and headed toward the host stand before Peck could approach their table.

"I see you've got another beauty," Peck said. "For a journalist, you seem to be getting a lot."

"Appearances are sometimes deceptive," Ryan said.

"I understand you were sitting with Mick Jagger at the Victoria's Secret show," Peck said.

"Guilty on that one."

"I'm on to something big and need to talk to Mick," Peck said.

"How badly do you need to talk to Mick?"

"If I'm talking to Mick, I'm obviously not writing about you," Peck said. Ryan reached into his pocket and handed Peck a business card. It was the business card of the nutty Englishman, the goofball with all the cats in Elizabethan costumes who had pestered Ryan earlier in the festival about doing a story on his cats that performed Shakespeare.

"This card says 'Giles G. Hall, Shakespearean Feline Amusements,'" Peck noted.

"'Giles G. Hall' is Mick's security code name during the festival. Mick is going to produce a version of *Richard III*. Netflix is already interested."

"Okay, that will buy you some time," Peck said.

"Don't tell Mick I gave you his secret cell number," Ryan said.

Peck took the card and headed off toward the Palais. Ryan watched him go and then headed back to the table. He sat down. Ingrid was doodling with the crayons, etching loopy letters on the paper tablecloth. An "I" and a "B" blended in an artsy style.

"What are you doing, practicing autographs?"

"Miss Clearidge and her staff designed a way I should sign for the festival. The "I" and the "B" are mixed together. It is not the way I usually sign my name, so it's kind of strange for me. They said I must sign all things this way because they were going to release jewelry necklaces like that for the movie."

Ryan glanced at the artful signature, the "I" and the "B" looped together. "They certainly have all their marketing bases covered."

"That man you just talked to, is he a powerful writer?"

"He writes for our paper, *The Hollywood New Times*," Ryan said. "He's good at getting stories from people who don't want to talk. If someone avoids him, Peck writes a story about them anyway. Usually, some of his facts are wrong and they call back to complain, and then he gets the real story."

"That is how you journalists work? Make up things?"

"It works for him," Ryan said.

"That must be how that horrible interview with me got to be news," Ingrid said.

"What interview?" Ryan asked.

"I do not remember where it came from," she said. "Erik showed it to me on-line. It was entirely made up."

"It was probably written by some sleazy blogger," he said. "After all, people think you are dead, so they could virtually make up anything about you."

"What about you?" she asked. "You are a journalist and you get paid to look at movies?" Ingrid said.

"Yes, I confess."

"That must be exciting," she said.

"Yes, I've seen 37,078 car crashes and 204,067 fiery explosions and 6.8 million people getting shot or stabbed," Ryan noted.

"You do not like the movies so much anymore?"

"The ones they're making these days are not great," Ryan said. "They've got all this new technology, but the stories are awful. I like the older ones, when movies were about people instead of aliens, explosions, vampires, zombies, comic-book heroes, and slashers."

"You must see many movies that aren't like that here at this festival," she said.

"Well, yes. Festival movies are about people. They're not big screen video games. That's why I like covering festivals. Unfortunately, the films that win the Competition section here at Cannes are not usually all that good."

"You think a bad movie is the one that will win the Cannes big prize?" she asked.

"Yes, you only have to look at who is on this year's festival jury. Roman Polanski is the president. There's also a guy who was a Communist filmmaker and an old actress who used to be the mistress of a famous director," Ryan noted. "And there's a college professor from some university in Ohio who's made a bunch of small angry films about the evils of capitalism. And, there's a woman from Cameroon, who makes movies about birds. The film that wins – no one in the United States will want to see it."

"You should have one of those radio shows where you complain about things," she said.

"Yes, you're right. Here I am in one of the most romantic cities in the world, in the prettiest season and with the most beautiful, mysterious woman on earth. There is no need to complain," Ryan noted.

She lowered her head and covered her face with her hands. "I feel sorry for Erik. His dream is destroyed."

"That's not true. Erik will get great publicity with you rising up from the dead. It will be all over the front pages, on all the TV stations. People all over the world will read and hear about his new fashion line."

"You make it sound so easy," she said.

"Believe me. There will be a press storm when people find out you are alive," Ryan said.

"Oh, no! Are you saying more journalists will be coming to me again for interviews, and following me around wherever I go?"

"Yes, but you can do it for a couple days," Ryan said. "It will help Erik, and I'll guide you through it."

She grimaced, and Ryan saw those blue eyes ignite. He caught himself staring and then looked down at his watch. It was nearly 8 o'clock. He had missed his 7:30 p.m. screening and the security people did not let in latecomers. His chest tightened, and he gasped.

"What is wrong?" she asked.

"Damn! The Matt Damon movie," Ryan exclaimed. "It's nearly quarter to eight. They don't admit latecomers. I've missed the review. Bernie will go nuts."

"But you can see it again, can't you?" Ingrid asked.

"That's not the point. The other papers and websites will all have it before we do," Ryan said. "I've missed the one movie that everybody back in Hollywood is curious about."

Chapter 14

Day 7

Ingrid Bjorge stretched across the tiny bed. Her arms splayed out as she slept. Ryan tiptoed quietly into the room. He had just returned from a 10 p.m. screening of The *Defrocked Assassin*, a hodgepodge of left-wing speeches set amid Fidel Castro's first years in power. It had gotten a standing ovation from the world press. He was still angry at himself for missing the Matt Damon movie and more annoyed for having let Ingrid charm him into not going to the police.

The bed was big enough for one, but two was a tight fit. Ryan found a spot on the floor near the window. He heaped some undershirts and bathroom towels on the thin carpet for bedding. Ryan could hear her breathing, loud and uneven. He plopped down on his makeshift mattress. The next sound he heard was a harsh jingle-jangle. Ryan opened his eyes. The jangle sounded again. Ryan looked around, spotted the phone on the table in front of the window. He grabbed the phone: "Hello. Hello." No one was there.

Ingrid stirred on the bed, opened her eyes. "Good morning. I did not know you were here," she said as she propped herself up.

"You were asleep when I came in last night. I didn't want to wake you."

"You should have woken me." She lifted her head and pulled herself up. She wore one of his t-shirts and the light-blue lace panties from *The Ice Princess*. "I must use the toilet first, if you don't mind."

"Go ahead."

A hard rap on the door startled him. "It's me, Lauren." Ryan jumped into his jeans, yanking on the zipper. He opened the door a crack. Lauren brushed straight in, and, even worse, Stan Peck followed.

"Sorry to barge in, but we tried to call," Lauren said. "Obviously, you don't answer your phone."

"No, I heard it," Ryan said. "By the time I woke up, it stopped ringing." Lauren spotted his French cell on the drawer, picked it up.

"You've got messages," she said as she manipulated the phone. "You've gotten three texts. Didn't you read the instructions?"

"The day I was going to do it, I spent all morning getting grilled by the police," Ryan countered. "Getting dragged in as a murder suspect does tend to frazzle your mind a bit."

"There's been a change of plans," Lauren said. "We've got to do the balloon ride this morning. We need it for the satellite feed, and there's some sort of regulations here during the peak day hours." Lauren handed him an envelope. "This was under your door," she said. Ryan took the cream-colored envelope. It was scripted in an ornate font: "Ryan Hackbart and New Girlfriend." She picked up a roll of toilet paper from his bureau. "Is this Charmin?" she asked.

"Yes, I brought it with me," Ryan said.

"You were smart. French toilet paper sucks," she said. Lauren squeezed the toilet paper.

"Good thing, Mr. Whipple didn't see you do that," Ryan said.

"What?"

"'Don't squeeze the Charmin.' Classic TV commercial," Ryan said. "I saw it in a documentary at the AFI DOCS fest."

"Someone made a documentary about toilet paper?" Lauren asked.

"No, it was a documentary on classic TV commercials," Peck added.

Lauren scowled, which widened to a glare as Ingrid emerged from the bathroom in her blue panties and t-shirt. "I'm sorry, we didn't know you were entertaining again," Lauren said.

"I'm not entertaining," Ryan said. He realized there was no way of explaining Ingrid's presence at that early hour. "Lauren, Stan, I would like you to meet Layla."

"Well, anyway, Ryan, meet us downstairs in fifteen minutes," Lauren said. "Wear something bright, no stripes. You might want to bring your friend here too." She glanced at Ingrid. "Are you an actress?"

"Well, mainly no," Ingrid answered.

"Let me guess," Lauren said. "Judging from your long blonde hair and figure, you're a lingerie model."

"No, I could not be a lingerie model," Ingrid said. "I do not wear underwear. I just have these on for Ryan." That also didn't come out sounding the way she meant it, but Ryan loved it. Still, he knew he couldn't burn all his bridges. He reached for the roll of toilet paper and handed it to Lauren. She took it without saying a word and headed toward the door.

As Lauren opened the door, Delisha nearly hit her as she leaned forward to knock. Delisha was decked out in mustard-yellow silk shorts and a matching ruffled tank top. A silver braid from her hair dangled over her right shoulder. She toted a bottle of Bordeaux. Delisha brushed past Lauren and flashed her happy-girl smile. "Ryan, you didn't tell me there would be this many guests. You are one bad boy."

Delisha's sudden appearance had put Ryan so far up on Lauren's shit-list that he burst out laughing. "Delisha, this is Layla and you know Lauren, of course," he finally said. "Lauren is our paper's publicity person. She has set up a balloon ride for me."

"I'm in charge of worldwide marketing and social-media promotions," Lauren clarified.

"I hope you're doing a lot to promote Ryan," Delisha said. "I think he's your paper's best asset, although I don't think you could promote all his best assets on TV." Delisha turned to Ryan. "I'm sorry to have busted in like this, but I'm just getting back from Naomi's birthday party. I didn't want to go, but you should have been there. It was your kind of strange."

"I've sworn off supermodels' parties," Ryan said.

"You went to Naomi Campbell's birthday party in St. Tropez?" Lauren asked.

"I had some free time, but it would have been more fun with Ryan there making funny comments." She held up the Bordeaux for Ryan. "I took this wine as a souvenir."

Peck gestured toward the bottle. "Can I see that?" he asked. Delisha handed him the bottle, and he examined the label. "This wine costs more than $200 a bottle," Peck said. "This is the also the same expensive red they served at that party up at the chateau." He turned to Delisha. "I don't know what they consider grand theft here in France."

Delisha ignored him, turned to Lauren and the Charmin. "You're so smart, carrying toilet paper with you. The bathrooms are so inconsistent over here," she said.

"I don't carry toilet paper with me," Lauren snapped. She pointed her finger at Ryan. "Well, if we could move to more important matters than wine, how was Matt Damon's movie?" Lauren asked.

"I didn't see it," Ryan answered. "What?"

"It's a long story," Ryan answered.

"I can't believe you didn't see it," Lauren added. "It's the biggest movie of the festival. Everyone is talking about it. And our paper missed it?" Lauren turned away in a huff and headed out.

Delisha shook her finger at Ryan. "Naughty, naughty. Now you've gotten Lauren all upset again. It won't be long before she makes her move on you."

"No way," Ryan said. "She hates me."

"No, it's true. She sees you with gorgeous women like Layla here, and it sparks her interest," Delisha said. "Besides, toilet paper is the way to a woman's heart this week, with these dreadful French tissues."

Ryan pointed at Ingrid. "Does she look familiar to you?"

Delisha inspected Ingrid, gazed at her from a side angle. She pointed to the window. "Look out in that direction with your chin tilted up. Look real serious." Ingrid followed her direction, angling her head and gazing off with a blank expression. Delisha clasped her hands. "It's crazy. Is it true? Is it true?"

"Yes," Ryan answered.

Delisha embraced Ingrid. "You're alive. You're alive. What is going on?"

"That's what we're trying to figure out," Ryan said.

"You have the most exquisite chin," Delisha said. "I love your posters. That huge *Ice Princess* poster of you on the Croisette – that's a great shot. The angle, with your back turned, is off the hook. I wish I had your photographer."

"My photographer is my ex-husband, Erik. He is a fashion designer but he has such a good eye that he is also good with the camera," Ingrid answered.

"Would he do a session with me?" Delisha asked.

"I think he would be happy to," Ingrid said.

"I can't believe this. This is all so incredible, but I've got to run," Delisha said. She pecked Ryan on the cheek. "Can you make it at one o'clock at the Hotel Fleur du Puante today? I have to be there about a cover shoot. It's super-important."

"Okay, but Delisha, you can't tell anyone about Ingrid's being alive. Not a word."

"Don't worry. You know I would never get you into trouble," she said. She smiled and pinched Ryan on the cheek. She turned toward Ingrid. "It was nice meeting you, and I'm so glad you're alive.

"I am also glad I am alive, sometimes."

"You take good care of Ryan now," Delisha said as she left.

"She is wonderful. Is she your girlfriend?" Ingrid asked.

"No, she's a friend, a special friend. We look out for each other," Ryan said.

"Do you want me to wear the movie-people clothes again?" she asked.

"Yes, and no makeup. And don't talk to Stan Peck, the guy who was just here. He's one of our reporters. A real jerk."

"What if he asks me questions?" Ingrid asked.

"Just ask him what college he went to," Ryan said. "He'll go on forever about Boston University and not ask you anything more."

Ingrid hurried into the bathroom to shower, and Ryan opened the envelope. He glanced at the wide-looped lettering on the envelope and wondered who his "New Girlfriend" was. He read: "You and your new blonde girlfriend will both be killed if you reveal her identity or go to the police. We are watching you: every minute, every day and every move."

Ryan noted the use of a colon. Whoever wrote this was not your average person, but someone with writing sophistication. The colon and the solid parallel construction. Here he was getting a death threat, and he was analyzing the writing style. It had worked before, Ryan recalled: The Unabomber was captured after his brother recognized his writing style when the *New York Times* published the killer's "manifesto."

"I saw you on MTV News, Monsieur Hackbart," Henri said. He quashed his cigarette as Ryan and Ingrid emerged from the hotel. Lauren and Peck were already standing next to Henri's dusty green Renault. Peck commandeered the front passenger side, while Lauren got in the back. Ryan squeezed into the middle rear seat. He needed to conceal Ingrid from Lauren's scrutiny. As he hunched in the tiny European car's backseat, Ryan could see Henri flash him a big grin in the rear-view mirror.

"I am disappointed, Monsieur Hackbart, that you could not get me an autograph of the dead actress. I could sell it for a lot of money on eBay."

"Yes, unfortunate," Ryan said. Ingrid ducked her head down further, staring straight down into her knees.

"Aren't you uncomfortable in the middle?" Lauren asked. "We could switch."

"No, that's very kind of you. But I'm in a good position," Ryan lied.

Henri blazed down the side street and hung a sharp left turn at the Monoprix. He made every light and zig-zagged through the congestion. He swung a right onto the Croisette and accelerated past the Palais, honking at festival-goers who wandered between the metal barricades. Lauren slid into Ryan on a hard turn, clenched his knee. Henri turned on the car's CD player. Idiotic French hip-hop shook the car. Peck reached over and turned it off. Peck had his good points, Ryan had to admit.

Henri zoomed past La Pizza and sped along the Old Port toward the Sofitel Hotel. He scooted through double-parked limos. He accelerated into the right turn at the beach. "Have you ever been up in a balloon before, Monsieur Hackbart?" Henri asked.

"No, the closest I've been to a balloon ride was watching *Around the World in 80 Days* in Drew Casper's class at USC."

"What about you, Mademoiselle?" Henri asked as his eyes shifted in the rear-view toward Ingrid. "I am sorry, but I do not know your name."

"Her name is Layla," Lauren said sarcastically. She turned to Ryan with a side-glance, fixating on Ingrid, who still had her head lowered. "Are you okay?" Lauren asked.

"I don't think she's used to the style of Henri's driving," Ryan interjected.

"I think he's doing a great job," Lauren said. "He could make a fortune as an Uber driver in Manhattan."

Ryan diverted his glance to the sea, gazed out on the Mediterranean. The soft morning waves sparkled in a delicate weave, so different from the churning Ryan felt in his stomach. He had to calm himself. He could not let the craziness interfere with his focus on finding the killer. Otherwise, he would rot in a French prison. Or, he would become the new Amanda Knox and endure agonizing years of legal and institutional treachery – his life smeared and distorted by the tabloids, and then further maligned by the biases and agendas of the mainstream media.

He re-shifted his thoughts away from the dour, worst-case-scenario doom that had clogged his mind. He embraced the immediate: it was a gorgeous morning. He was going on a balloon ride with a beautiful woman. You'd have to be a multimillionaire or a billionaire to pull that off during the Cannes Film Festival. He appreciated the irony: their flying adventure would be played out on television all over the world as real news. E! MTV, VH1, and all their pseudo-news cousins, would trumpet it as "up-to-the-minute news," or "the biggest scoop," "in the very latest," or, "we have just learned," "here exclusively" – blah, blah, blah. "Baa-baa-baa," like the sheep they were, Ryan concluded. The real news, of course, would be right under their big, global noses: Ryan was sitting next to a dead woman, the blonde beauty who had starred in the opening night movie at the Cannes Film Festival and who had been reported worldwide as murdered. Among the dead, Ingrid was now more internationally famous than any other woman except Lady Di.

Henri turned onto a narrow secondary road. Potholes did not deter his acceleration. He navigated in his NASCAR style for roughly half a mile, and then slammed to a stop. Lauren let out an expletive and grabbed Ryan's knee.

Ingrid did not move, stared straight ahead. "You okay?" Ryan asked her.

"I hope that this man is not the driver of the balloon too," she said.

A red-white-and-blue hot-air balloon perched amid several trucks. Workers adjusted a Hollywood New Times logo on its mid-section. "I still do not understand why we are going for a balloon ride," Ingrid said.

"Show business," Ryan answered. "Or, as they say nowadays, 'expanding the brand.'"

A canary yellow 1968 Jaguar XKE convertible curled into their midst. The driver wore dark goggles with a red-and-yellow silk scarf draped around his neck. It was Boris. He alighted from the car and talked with the crewmen, gesturing with his hands. After his wind-mill like oration, he headed toward Ryan and Ingrid. A crust of white cream smeared over a scratch on his right cheek. Boris extended his hand to Ryan. "Mr. Hackbart, I am so glad you could come."

"You know me, action-critic," Ryan said.

"You do not have to worry anymore," Boris said. "We found the Aston Martin automobile, and although it is damaged beyond what you told us, I think we will be able to work things out."

"What Aston Martin?" Lauren asked.

"Ryan had a misfortune with an Aston Martin we have leased," Boris said. "It was lucky for him he was not injured nor any harm done to the beautiful lady he was with."

"I nearly got killed," Ryan said. He turned away from Lauren, averting any more discussion of his road escapade. "I am sorry for your loss," he said to Boris.

"Nick was a great spirit. We are buying many ads in The Hollywood New Times as a memorial." Boris paused, giving Ingrid a double-look. "You have a European look. Where are you from?"

"I am from Rotterdam," she lied.

"Maybe we should get a shot of all of you," Lauren said. She signaled to the photographers. Ryan nudged Ingrid away from the cameraman. "She should be in the photo too," Lauren said.

"She can't. There's an exclusivity in her modeling contract," Ryan ad-libbed.

"Come on, we need this beautiful blonde woman in the picture," Boris complained.

"It's the least you could do," Lauren snapped. "We need some positive coverage of you after all the grief you've caused the paper."

"Okay," Ryan said. "But only if I stage it."

"That works for me," Boris said. "But you must work fast because we need to get the balloon back to the rental company in an hour."

"What?" Ryan said. "I thought we were all going up, for a real balloon ride."

"Don't be absurd," Lauren said. "We get the shot with you and the balloon. That's all the TV people need. What does it matter if we go up or not? The point is you're alive and safe and having a great time. That's the news. The balloon is just the hook, setting the visual scene. Besides, since that terrorist thing in Nice and the craziness last year, Cannes is a no-fly zone," Lauren added. "Don't you watch CNN?"

"Only when I'm not on it," Ryan answered. "If we are going to make this look like a real balloon ride, we'll need some action close-ups." He gestured to Ingrid. "Swirl your hair. Shake it." She lowered her head and shook her hair. The blonde locks cascaded over her face, whipped over her shoulders.

"That is brilliant," Boris said. "With her hair going crazy, it looks like she is having great sex."

"Keep shaking your hair, so it hides your face," Ryan whispered to Ingrid. She stepped back and spun it, wildly rotating her head.

"You are a great director," Boris shouted to Ryan. "It's like she is having an orgasm with the excitement of the balloon."

"Chauvinist asshole," Lauren muttered under her breath.

"Now we need a shot of me in the balloon," Ryan said. He climbed over the wicker side and positioned himself in the balloon basket. He gestured to the cameraman. "Shoot it so there is no hillside or trees in the background. Just me and the blue sky. That will look like I am up in the air to the viewer." The cameraman hunched down and shot upward, catching Ryan from a number of angles. Ryan grabbed one of the ropes and pretended to navigate the balloon.

"Cut," Lauren bellowed. Ryan smiled at Ingrid, whose hair hung sheep-dog style over her face. Yet, Henri kept shooting her on the sly.

Damn, has Henri caught on? Ryan thought.

Despite the rampaging craziness, and the phony balloon ride, Ryan was energized. The unpredictability and perils of the last several days gushed through his system. The element of danger in his life, and his role in protecting Ingrid, had juiced his primeval male urges. He had stumbled into the role of a valiant knight. In recent months, Ryan worried that he had unwittingly retreated over the years into a dark psychological cave, viewing pictures on a wall. Cranking out film reviews for a cultural elite does not satisfy man's necessary urges and survival instincts, he realized. Millions of years from now, or whenever, a new life-form would emerge and express its essence and fears in a futuristic hieroglyphic, what kind of mutant entity would be the equivalent of the film critic? Ryan realized he had to back away from that train of thought. He began to hum "Gimme Shelter," his favorite Stones song. Keith and Mick Taylor's eerie guitars swirled in his head and he burst out into his best Jagger: "It's just a shot away, it's just a kiss away...shot away, kiss away..."

"Are you okay?" Ingrid asked.

Chapter 15

The white Mercedes taxi dropped Ryan and Ingrid a block east of the Rue de Republique. Ryan gave a playful tug to Ingrid's baseball cap as he paid the driver with his credit card. He added a very generous tip to keep his expense-account up to par with the excesses of his colleagues. Although less than a half-mile from the Croisette and the film festival, the hotel where they were to meet Delisha was located in an older section. Once desirable, it was now considered a danger-zone in that it had been inhabited by a recent flood of immigrants.

The Hotel Fleur du Puante was a faded pink monstrosity adorned with bougainvillea and primrose, but its sidewalk was snagged by weeds and glutted by litter. The area was clogged with cabs, motorcycles, and limos. Ryan and Ingrid hurried up the winding sidewalk to the face-lifted hotel; it wreaked of the kind of place where, in its glory days, Bette Davis and Joan Crawford might have clawed and tangled.

The cultural incarnation of the adult film festival was in a different but parallel universe from the real Cannes Film Festival. LAID's organizers were intent on carrying on the notoriety and tradition of a previous Cannes Film Festival irritant, the Hot d'Or, which was the adult video world's version of the Oscars. The Hot d'Or had ended in 2009, much to the relief of the Cannes dignitaries.

A pink and purple banner above the walkway proclaimed: "L 'Adult Internationale du Digital" and below it, in a wicked font, LAID.

Ryan stared at the LAID banner and laughed. "Are you maybe not so okay?" Ingrid asked.

He pointed to the banner. "No, I'm okay. I've just got to …" He laughed harder. "Let us linger here awhile in the foolishness of things," he shouted.

"What did you say?" Ingrid asked. "Is this more Rolling Stones?"

"Apollinaire, the guy who wrote 'Let us linger here a while in the foolishness of things.'"

"You do need some sleep," Ingrid said.

Two stick-thin women in yellow, see-through leotards skirted around him. "Let us linger here in the foolishness of things!" Ryan shouted to them.

They didn't linger.

The area outside the faux nouveau monstrosity was crammed with teenage boys, tourists, and paparazzi. On the prowl for the stars of the adult-entertainment world, they surged against the purple velvet ropes at the hotel's entrance. Instead of a red carpet, a metallic pink turf greeted the guests. Silver-sequined statues of two bodies with extreme proportions flanked the entrance-way: a muscular Adonis with a giant penis and a bodacious Venus with heavy booty cheeks.

"They have no tops," Ingrid said.

"Yes, headless monstrosities," Ryan commented. "It's like those two statues at the LA Coliseum for the '84 Olympics. The sculptor is not exactly original."

"You are a critic of everything," she said. "You got me there," Ryan said.

People waved and yelled as they spotted Ryan and Ingrid. "See, they have recognized the famous film critic," Ingrid said.

"Just keep your head down and stick tight on me," Ryan said. They pushed their way through the crowd and onto the pink walkway. A tiny man wearing a purple t-shirt with "LAID" emblazoned across the front shoved a pen and notebook at Ingrid. Ryan clasped Ingrid by the shoulder and guided her away. Onlookers jostled toward them. Two monstrous guys at the door with severe ponytails and ear monitors signaled to Ryan. "Vit, vit," one of the ponytails shouted. An attendant in a tuxedo and top hat opened the door and bowed to Ingrid.

Ryan turned around to see the entire crowd was focused on them: TV cameras, Steadicams, cell-phones, and digital movie cameras. "All these people seem to know you," Ryan said.

"I do not understand it."

Hotel security agents formed a tight barricade at the entrance. They maneuvered Ryan and Ingrid through the throng. A giant arch loomed inside the art deco lobby. It was bordered with metallic gold angel wings. Two women in transparent white gowns flanked the angel decorations. Garish tattoos slid down their breasts, ending in jagged stripes.

The entire entryway was clotted with posters of men and women in various stages of undress and tramped up in outlandish, sexual costumes. Ryan paused to gape at the surroundings.

"Come," she grabbed his hand. "You will start to laugh again, and we cannot be late for your friend Delisha."

The cocktail lounge was authentic-antiseptic. Ryan led Ingrid to a diamond-shaped table in the far corner. They sat down in purple upholstered chairs. "I knew we should not have come out in public. I knew I should have stayed in that chicken house where I would be safe from all these crazy festival people," Ingrid said.

"You're right. People seem to recognize you," Ryan said.

"I still think that someone will try to kill me again once they find out that I am alive, if they don't know that already."

An older couple wandered over to them. The woman wore a Green Bay Packers t-shirt, while the man was similarly sophisticated in a checkered sports coat. "We just love your work," the woman said to Ingrid. "It's revitalized our marriage."

"Thank you, I guess," Ingrid said.

"We were wondering about your facials," the woman said.

"I do not do much with my face, just plain water and a lotion," Ingrid answered.

The couple laughed. “That’s so sweet of you to say it that way,” the woman responded. They squeezed each other’s hands and left.

“I do not understand,” Ingrid said. “I never did any cosmetic commercials.” A spiky-hair guy in neo-hipster, John Lennon glasses approached Ingrid.

“What was it like to screw Sir Rico Bronco? You seem too small for a guy with such a big dick.”

Ryan sprung up, and the man backed off. “Don’t hurt me.” He back-pedaled away. “Keep up the good work,” he called back to Ingrid. “I love the way you scream when you climax.”

“These people seem to know you as a porn star rather than as *The Ice Princess.”*

“I do not understand what they are talking about.” She reached out and rubbed his forehead. “You are still sticky with sunscreen,” Ingrid said. “And you are red. Everyone will think you have been at the beach, sipping movie-people mineral water and looking at the girls without the tops.”

“That certainly sounds more credible than the real story,” Ryan said.

Two men in hotel blazers approached. “We are with hotel security,” one said. “Would you like some assistance?”

“That would be great,” Ryan said. “Could you keep people away from her? I’ve got to find a friend in the lobby.”

“Certainement.”

"Excuse me, but I need to see some identification first," Ryan said. The two men nodded and both produced hotel badges and photo IDs.

"Merci, thanks," Ryan said. He turned to Ingrid. "Stay here. Try and keep your head down." He glanced at the security men, who nodded back. "I'll be just over there in the lobby and gift-shop area looking for Delisha," he told Ingrid. "Put your phone on speed dial for me. If anything happens, hit me."

Ryan hurried from the lounge, looking for Delisha. She had been so insistent that they meet here at 1 p.m. And, it was nearly 1:15. He hoped that Delisha was on her standard "model's time." He did not want to leave Ingrid alone too long. He spotted a hotel gift shop and grabbed a *Nice-Matin* from the newspaper stack. He also picked up three weekly tabloids – *The National Enquirer*, *The Star*, and a German one, *Das Scheistab*. The German magazine featured a page-one picture of Ingrid's corpse being wheeled out of the Carlton Hotel. A blanket covered her head, and her feet dangled from the gurney. The body had no leg tattoo, Ryan noticed.

Someone jerked Ryan by the elbow. "He raped my girlfriend, Goldie. He gave her a Bill Cosby-cocktail, then he beat her up, and raped her," Delisha blurted out. Her hair was puffed out in a green Afro and her eyes were red. "That guy from the party. The little guy who lent us the car, I knew I recognized him from somewhere. He raped Goldie, and he got off!"

"Delisha, what are you talking about?"

"In LA when she started out in acting, Goldie did some adult videos for this slime-bag and his brother out in Chatsworth. He kept harassing her, always grabbing her ass. Then, he raped her."

"Did she press charges?" Ryan asked.

"Yes, but he got off. This was before all the Harvey Weinstein stuff came out. Before #Me Too started. It was basically his word against hers, and the cops didn't have any evidence that stuck."

"No DNA tests?"

"Yes, but the DNA had to be screwed up. It didn't match," she said.

"Was Goldie ever on drugs?" Ryan asked.

"She was in Promises once, but she's completely clean now," Delisha answered, referencing the famous rehab center. "I've got to go. I've got some painting to do."

"What?" Ryan exclaimed. "That's the information you had for me?"

Delisha ignored him and dashed off through the clogged lobby. Ryan watched her as she maneuvered her way through the throngs of admiring men. He hurried back to the cocktail lounge. His heart jumped: Had it been stupid to leave her with two virtual strangers, although they were "security?" He was clearly off his game. He gasped, then calmed: things were okay. The two security men had bracketed Ingrid, keeping onlookers at bay. Ryan showed the head-shot of Ingrid from *The National Enquirer* to the security men. In the

Enquirer photo, her hair was pixie-short. "Have you seen this woman in the hotel?" he asked.

"Mais, oui," the first guard exclaimed. He pointed to Ingrid. "It is her, Mademoiselle Goldie Jolie. She is the star actress here. She will get three Golden Thongs."

"Thank you very much," he said. As the guards left, Ryan sat next to Ingrid. "You look upset," Ingrid said.

"Delisha has come up with something about Nick Steele," Ryan said. "About his history as a sexual predator."

Ryan handed Ingrid the German paper. The blonde corpse photo took up nearly half the front page. It was from a lower side angle. The woman in the photo was mostly covered, but it showed the very top of the woman's blonde head. Also, her right foot dangled uncovered over the end of the gurney.

"Isn't your tattoo on your right leg?" Ryan asked.

"Yes, just above my ankle." She lifted her leg for him to see.

"Didn't you say Gunnar Sevareid was upset about your tattoo?" Ryan asked. "Yes, he was angry I got it just before the festival. He said it would ruin the red carpet for him. He is a very old man sometimes in his thinking."

"Well, I'm sure he would have noticed that this girl, who is identified as you, does not have one."

"Well, he maybe didn't see this photo."

"These photos, or ones like it, are all over the world. Gunnar Sevareid knows you are not dead."

"But why would he not say I was not dead?" she asked.

"I don't know the answer to that, but whatever it is, it's not good," he said. Behind them, more people crowded around. The hotel security guards held the onlookers back. "These people here have you mixed up with someone else," Ryan said. "Someone who is a porn star here looks a lot like you. That's why these people keep coming over to speak with you and crowding around you like this. That's why you're getting these disgusting sexual comments and questions."

"It does not make good sense. I don't look the way I used to look. Those photos you see of me on TV and in the papers, they are old. Without my long hair."

"I've been told your *Ice Princess* director Jason Pinelli was into porn big-time," Ryan said.

"Who would know such a thing?" Ingrid asked.

"A friend of mine, Dennis Barlowe. He's one of those guys who tends to find out these sorts of things. He's got a nose for the kinky stuff. It's possible my friend Dennis knew your movie director Jason Pinelli. He said Pinelli was into blondes. I'm beginning to think that the woman who is the big winner at this porn festival is the woman who was killed. The woman who everyone thinks you are."

"That sounds even crazier," Ingrid said.

"We've got to involve the French police," he said.

"I cannot go to the police. I cannot be at this awful festival anymore."

"No, we must go to the police." She buried her head in her hands. The sleeve on her arm slid up, and Ryan spotted a bandage. "What happened to your arm?" She slid her sleeve down. Ryan reached forward and rolled it up to reveal cut marks. "Seriously, you have a big problem, and we need to fix it," he said.

"It is nothing. It is over with. I am fine!" She jerked away and got up from her chair. "We must go," she said. She stopped suddenly, turned to Ryan. "So, you are really serious that Jason Pinelli murdered this blonde woman who looked like me?"

"Well, it's possible. He's an angry guy," Ryan said. Ryan's phone blared out the "Notre Dame Victory March." He answered, listened and didn't say a word. He jammed the cell into his pocket. "We've got to go."

"Where?"

"To smell the roses."

Chapter 16

Red, yellow, white, orange, and pink – they were the most beautiful roses Ryan had ever seen. Separated in rectangular blocks, they blossomed around a stone memorial to France's World War I veterans on the eastern edge of the Croisette. Ryan and Ingrid moved through the rose garden, passing the folks who were strolling and sniffing the roses. At this mid-afternoon moment, the rose garden was caressed by the sun's rays and massaged by the sea breeze, but Ryan and Ingrid hardly glanced at the flowers. They sat down on a park bench. Ryan fixated on his cellphone, punching at the screen with his right index finger.

"You are very upset," Ingrid said.

"I still can't figure out this French cell," he said. "My friend Dennis Barlowe tried to get it working for me, but the only thing he seems to have done has been to annoy me with that 'Notre Dame Victory March' as my ring-tone." Ryan jammed the cell into his sports-coat pocket. He inhaled: four seconds in; four seconds out. The scent of the garden filled his nostrils. He had finally stopped to smell the roses only because someone was framing him for murder.

"This policeman we are meeting, you think he is a good guy because he likes old movies," Ingrid said.

"Well, it's a start," Ryan said.

"I am glad you are meeting him here. All these roses, it's so beautiful," she said.

"Damn, I didn't think of that," Ryan said. "Its beauty now worries me."

"What do you mean?" she asked.

"Alfred Hitchcock. He was a movie director. Horror and thriller movies."

"I do not understand," Ingrid said. "You are not making good sense."

"Hitchcock always staged his scariest scenes in public places where it seemed nothing bad could happen, like in a field or at the United Nations or on Mt. Rushmore," Ryan explained. "The most frightening scenes don't occur on a rainy night with creaky noises."

"When you get nervous and confused, you go to the old movies to find an answer," Ingrid said. "You think Jason killed the pornography actress?"

"I think it might be true," Ryan answered.

"You think it is him because you do not like him because he beat you up at the party?" she asked.

"He didn't beat me up," Ryan emphasized. "He sucker-punched me." Ryan took her by the hand. "You must not be seen by Lt. Savin," Ryan said. "Go sit over by that war monument and keep your head turned away." Ryan watched as she circled past the war memorial and sat on a bench. Less than a minute later, Lt. Savin approached. "I know who your killer is," Ryan said by way of a hello.

"I hope it is the same man we are bringing in for questioning," Lt. Savin said.

"Jason Pinelli, right?"

Savin nodded, lit a cigarette. "You would make a good detective," he said.

"I have another scoop for you," Ryan said.

"I know. Where is she?" Lt. Savin asked.

"How long have you known Ingrid Bjorge was not murdered? Ryan asked.

"We suspected it all along," Lt. Savin said. "The department still isn't certain who the dead woman is. And now she has been cremated and buried in a foreign country."

"I have a good idea who the murdered woman was," Ryan said.

"Who?"

"I'll let you know when I need a bargaining chip with your police department, if they start harassing me again," Ryan said. "It's still surprising no one has reported the dead woman was missing."

"It is a film festival. People come and go all the time," Lt. Savin said. "Take day trips to Saint Tropez. Go to parties up in the hills. Get in accidents with James Bond's car."

"You know about that?"

"There are still many unanswered questions, but we are getting a bit of the picture," Savin said. "We have been in meetings all night about Gunnar Sevareid."

"Good," Ryan answered. "He's definitely a big factor and a potentially very dangerous guy. But what I can't understand is why would Gunnar Sevareid claim the dead woman was Ingrid when he knew it was not her all the time?"

"We do not know, but we are working on some theories," Lt. Savin said.

"Since it seems that she is alive, Ingrid Bjorge could be in danger like Eve Kendall in North by Northwest," Ryan said.

"You have seen too many movies, especially Hitchcock," Lt. Savin said. He reached in his wallet and took out a plastic card. He handed it to Ryan. "Here is the card for the gate to my apartment. It is in part of an old villa on the Rue de Claude Raines just across the main roadway. It is not far from here. The gate code is 3609."

"So, what are you saying?"

"I know you have Ingrid Bjorge or know where she is," Savin said. "Get her and meet me there later. I will help you, bring you in from out of the cold," Lt. Savin said. "You and I are on the same side." He looked in the direction where Ingrid sat. He then patted Ryan on the shoulder.

"What are you going to do with Pinelli?" Ryan asked.

"Same as what we did with Erik Bjorge, whom we haven't ruled out yet. We will ask Pinelli to give a sample for a DNA test," Savin said. "When you get to my place, lock the door, and don't do anything stupid."

"Don't worry. I'm too tired," Ryan said.

"I sensed that," Lt. Savin said. "Otherwise you would not be going to my apartment. You would be citing Alfred Hitchcock's

Frenzy, where the unjustly accused killer let the man who had framed him use his flat."

Ryan's stomach dropped. "Dammit!" he exclaimed.

"Don't worry," Lt. Savin said. He patted Ryan on the back. "I am just going to prove to you that life is not so much like the movies. And, of course, your Jon Finch character in Frenzy was cleared."

"Yes, you're right," Ryan said, his mind tracing back to the movie's last scene where Finch got the killer to incriminate himself just as the police arrived.

Ryan and Ingrid hurried past the Miramar Hotel, crossed the crowded street and turned right at the Anaconda Room. A block up, they turned onto the Rue d' Antibes. Ryan paused in front of the Ma Mie lingerie store. Its white windowsills and clean glass sparkled in the afternoon sun. He pointed to an azure one-piece bathing suit in the window display. The swimsuit enticed as a series of strings that cupped a tiny bottom. "Pretend you are engrossed in the lingerie," he said to Ingrid. "I've got to check if we're being followed." He turned toward the busy street.

"No one will believe it if a man is standing in front of this lingerie store and not looking in," Ingrid said.

"You're right." He smiled and peered back into the window. The display was back-dropped by a poster for The Ice Princess. Ryan pointed to the fashion centerpiece swim suit. "It's got your aqua blue, The Ice Princess color."

"Oh, yes. That is Erik's design."

Ryan peered at the skimpy azure swimsuit. "How could that ever stay on someone?"

"He fit it on me. Erik had me stand without any clothes on, and he began to tie me up with all this string and fabric."

"Designers have all the fun."

"Oh, yes. We had fun," Ingrid said with big twinkle in her eyes. She pointed to the left side of the window - a blue teddy and a silky blue mini-skirt. "These are all Erik's. They were all specially designed for the movie and Erik's new fashion line."

"He's definitely an inspired guy," Ryan said.

"Yes, ever since I first met him he was always talking about Vera Wang, and how she started out as someone who tried out for the Olympics in ice skating and did not make it. But she turned her dream of ice skating to fashion. She designed her own wedding dress, and she created her own line. Erik was once a promising figure skater but did not make professional."

"Well, he still can make it as a designer. Your death, and the news that you are alive, is going to bring huge publicity for Erik and his fashion line. He will get even more notoriety now."

Ryan noticed a poster of Ingrid half obscured behind an azure bra. Her back was turned, and the image barely showed the right side of her face. She was bedecked in only aqua blue ribbons. Over her body, darker blue letters proclaimed: "Scrumptious lingerie, Ryan Hackbart, Hollywood New Times."

"Look, it's you on that poster, and they've quoted me on the lingerie," Ryan said.

"You are now a woman's lingerie critic."

"The only problem with this ad is that I didn't write the line. I would never use a fey word like 'scrumptious,' unless I was being facetious."

Ingrid admired the poster. "C'est tres jolie," she said. "I am using my French."

"Jolie?" Ryan exclaimed.

"What?"

"I just remembered - Goldie Jolie is the name of the blonde who was supposed to come to Nick's yacht for a T & A shoot the day I was there," Ryan said.

"I don't understand. What are you thinking about?" Ingrid asked.

"I was on the Hands-On yacht earlier in the festival, and Nick was making a big deal about this blonde named Goldie Jolie who hadn't showed. This Goldie Jolie was supposed to be in his porno movie," Ryan said.

"You have maybe come up with a good idea," Ingrid said.

"I get that way in front of lingerie stores."

"It is not the kind of apartment I would expect for a police man," Ingrid said.

"He's not exactly a policeman. He's the public-relations guy for the Cannes police department," Ryan noted.

Lt. Savin's apartment was ample by French standards, roughly thirty by thirty. It boasted a high ceiling and a brick fireplace. A multicolored abstract painting hung above the mantel. Simple off-white molding framed the ceiling, separating it from light yellow walls. Three large windows, their shutters open, overlooked the busy street below. On the wall opposite the fireplace, a birdcage extended outward. Wooden birds in bright shades of red, green, yellow and blue perched in primary array. A copy of Dag Aftenblad, a Norwegian newspaper, topped a slew of other publications on the room's coffee table. Ingrid picked it up and glanced at the front-page story. "I can't believe what they write in newspapers. They say Mr. Sevareid forced me to have sex with him. That is not true at all."

"Can I see the article?"

"But you do not read Norwegian."

"Maybe I can recognize names or something." Ryan scanned. Four paragraphs into the story, he noticed Stan Peck's name amid the Norwegian. "It's Peck," he said. "He made all this up, and now this Norwegian newspaper is repeating his lies."

"Journalism is like a cancer. Untrue news stories just keep growing and growing." Ingrid said. "And, they are killing me."

Ryan pulled out his cell. He clicked the speed-dial: "Tim, it's Ryan. Give me a call, or text me as soon as you can. I've run into some complications." Before Ryan could put his cell back in his pocket, it blasted out the 'Notre Dame Victory March' again. He picked up. The voice on the other end was so loud even Ingrid could hear it.

"Sweetie, you've got to come right now."

"Come where?"

"Jail," Delisha answered.

"What?"

"I'm in jail," she exclaimed. "This is my one call, so don't screw it up. If you don't get here immediately, they're going to haul me off to Nice."

"Why are you in jail?"

"It's those slimy producers. I went to their boat, and I painted over their insignia."

"You painted on the Hands-On yacht??"

"I just painted "La Rapist" over the boat's name."

"I'll be right there," Ryan said. He clicked off the phone.

"That was Delisha. She's in jail because she painted 'rapist' on the Steele brothers' yacht."

Ingrid smiled. "I do like her."

"Don't go anywhere, and don't open the door for anyone!"

"Where do I post bail?" Ryan asked. The Clouseau detective pointed inside the glass window, gestured toward a clerk seated at a metal desk. The door buzzed and Ryan stepped into the hallway of the detective offices. Once again, Ryan felt his chest tighten, and he gasped for breath. “I’m here for Delisha Blair,” he told the clerk.

“She is upstairs in custody. You cannot see her,” he said.

“I’m not here to see her. I’m here to post bail.”

“I do not see the paperwork for her bail,” the clerk said.

“Please, get the forms. I will sign them, and I will do exactly as you require.”

“You must come with us, Monsieur,” Clouseau-Man said.

Clouseau-Man whisked Ryan into an interrogation room. Six men hovered around him. They perched around a table with enough notebooks, digital cameras, recorders, and pens to start their own Office Depot franchise. They asked him the same questions over and over. After an hour they gave up. Clouseau-Man opened the door and Delisha dashed in. She rushed over to him. She wrapped her arms around him.

“I need you for a couple of hours,” Ryan said.

“Ingrid, hello. Hello? Bonjour. Ingrid!”

No response. Ryan hurried across Lt. Savin’s living room. No one was there. “I can’t believe it,” Ryan said. “I specifically told her not to go anywhere or do anything until I got back.” He peered out the window, looking for Ingrid. He spotted two gendarmes gazing up at him. Ryan closed the shutters.

"You've got to chill," Delisha said. "I'm sure there's an explanation." She stretched, bent down, and touched her toes. She straightened up and glanced at the wall paintings. "This cop has good taste in art. These are from Picasso's early cubist period."

Ryan jolted. "Gunnar Sevareid travels with Picassos!"

"What?"

"He is a Picasso buff," Ryan said.

"Look, you've got to relax, Sweetie," Delisha said. "Your mind is too overactive. You're out of balance."

"If Sevareid travels with Picassos, he evidently knows of the Picasso Museum near here in Antibes. And, if he was there a couple of years ago, he would know Lt. Savin."

"Sweetie, you've got to calm down!"

"I'm such an idiot. I led him right to her," Ryan said.

"You think Gunnar Sevareid is behind all this?" Delisha asked.

"We've got to go to the Carlton. I've got to save her!"

"I am sorry, Jean-Robie, but I need your help. I can't go to the police," Ryan said.

"When you can't go to the police, then it is truly a matter for a man in my position," Jean-Robie said with a twinkle. He made his way from behind the Carlton's reception counter and shook Ryan's hand.

"This will blow your mind, Jean-Robie," Ryan said. "It's about Ingrid Bjorge."

"The dead actress?"

"She's not dead," Ryan answered.

"Qu-est ce que c'est? What?" Jean-Robie stammered.

"She's been with me. At least, she was with me until an hour ago," Ryan said.

Jean-Robie gestured toward the black leather chairs on the left side of the lobby. "We must sit down. You are breathing too fast."

"She's alive, Jean-Robie. But she soon might be dead. Gunnar Sevareid might be going to kill her."

"C'est incredible...Not possible!" Jean-Robie exclaimed.

"This whole thing is so crazy, but I'm now sure Gunnar Sevareid has been behind everything since the get-go," Ryan said.

"I don't follow," Jean-Robie said.

"Gunnar Sevareid knows she is alive. He has to have seen a German news article," Ryan explained. "It had a picture of her on the gurney with her foot dangling out. But there was no tattoo. Ingrid Bjorge has a small tattoo on her ankle. Gunnar Sevareid knows that."

"This is a police matter. Not something for a humble hotelier like myself," Jean-Robie said.

"Ingrid Bjorge is alive. Gunnar Sevareid has her. And there is no telling what he will do with her."

"Mr. Sevareid is our most important guest. He is paying a large sum of money for the privilege of not being disturbed," Jean-Robie stressed.

"Jean-Robie, if you don't do something, she could be killed. She is in great danger!"

Jean-Robie sighed, and got up from the chair. Ryan turned to Delisha. "Wait for me here in the lobby. If I'm not back in half an hour, call the police. But not Lt. Savin."

The thick cream-colored door to the Imperial Suite opened on the third ring. The butler, uniformed in a burgundy sports coat and earphone, peered out. "Claude, would you tell Mr. Gunnar Sevareid that I wish to see him. It is a security matter of the most urgency," Jean-Robie said. He rattled off something else to the butler in rapid French. The butler ushered them inside.

The entrance way reflected the suite's price tag of $32,000 per night. Its oak floor was edged with a dark cherry border. Jean-Robie and Ryan followed the butler into the main sitting room. The suite was adorned with period furniture – Louis XVI and Directory. Thin praline curtains shimmered in the sunlight. The walls were a soft cream with caramel-colored sofas. The chairs were garnished with light-colored pillows: powder blue, light pink and lime green.

Gunnar Sevareid appeared from an inner room. He proceeded to the window, and closed both doors to the balcony. At the same moment, two men in black suits emerged from the side bedroom. One proceeded to stand by the entrance-way, while the other stood behind Sevareid.

"What is it?" Sevareid finally said.

"It's about Ingrid Bjorge. She is alive," Ryan said. "You already know that."

"No, Ingrid Bjorge is dead and buried at the Rikskvaller cemetery in Oslo," Sevareid said.

"You likely have her here or stowed away somewhere," Ryan exclaimed.

Gunnar Sevareid glared at Jean-Robie. "What is this?"

"Jean-Robie is not involved," Ryan said. "I forced him to let me in here. I know you are responsible for Ingrid Bjorge's disappearance. You had her taken from Lt. Savin's apartment just a little while ago. He alerted you as to where she was. He is your inside man in the French police force."

"This is an incredible fiction," Gunnar Sevareid said. "Haven't you done me enough harm with your horrible review of my film?"

"This isn't about my review."

"What gives you the right to come here to question me with this fiction?"

Ryan pointed to the near wall, toward a riveting, colorful abstract painting. "I have come because of your Picassos."

"I am not in the frame of mind, Mr. Hackbart, for American humor," Sevareid exclaimed.

"I know you would have been at the Picasso Museum in Antibes, and I know Lt. Savin worked there," Ryan said.

"You are not making any sense!"

"The woman who was murdered was a blonde porn star named Goldie Jolie, a woman who looked like Ingrid."

"This is beyond the preposterous, beyond even the fiction a crazy Hollywood writer would come up with," Sevareid pronounced.

The door buzzed. The butler opened the door, and three members of the French National Police entered. Gunnar Sevareid barked at them in French. Sevareid glared at Ryan. His silver-blue eyes seared, brutally cold. "This is the man who is responsible," Gunnar Sevareid said. He pointed to Ryan.

The head policeman advanced toward Ryan. "Your passport, s'il vous plait."

"I never got it back. The police still have it."

"You must come with us, Monsieur," the officer said.

Ryan tried to move his feet, but he was glued to the carpet. His body sagged. His cell phone rang: once again it blasted out the "Notre Dame Victory March." Ryan reached down into his pocket and pulled out his cell.

"Hello…what? … Hello, hello?" Ryan dropped the phone to his side. It fell on the thick, creamy carpet. He looked up to Gunnar Sevareid. Ryan tried to speak. Nothing came out. He took a deep breath. "That was Ingrid Bjorge," he finally said. "I am so sorry. You don't have her here. My mistake."

"You are a crazy person!" Gunnar Sevareid shouted.

Ryan's hands shook. He gulped. He took deep breaths: four seconds in, four out. He looked directly at the Norwegian billionaire. "Mr. Sevareid, you alone identified the body for the police. But, you knew it was not her," Ryan said.

"That is preposterous. How would I know?"

"Because the woman who was killed, the woman you identified, had no tattoo on her ankle," Ryan said. "You knew Ingrid had a tattoo on her ankle, and you often criticized her for it. You certainly knew this woman was not her, yet you led the police to believe it was her." Ryan looked at the head gendarmes and then back at Sevareid. "Now, I believe, you are planning to kill her so there are no further complications with this whole crazy thing," Ryan said.

"I would never kill her! I would never kill her," Gunnar Sevareid raged. His blue eyes ignited, like lightning bolts from Thor.

Ryan endured the Norwegian billionaire's icy glare. Then he heard his own voice say, "I believe you. You would never kill her, Mr. Sevareid. I can see that by your eyes."

The world's fourth richest man did not answer. He sat down in one of the caramel-colored chairs. For a long minute he did not utter a word. Finally, Gunnar Sevareid looked directly at Ryan. "My daughter, where is she? Is she unharmed? Where was she calling from?"

Ryan and Jean-Robie emerged from the private elevator of Gunnar Sevareid's suite and entered the Carlton lobby. Jean-Robie was dazed, but smiling. He put his arm around Ryan's shoulder. "Monsieur, you are amazing," Jean-Robie said. "C'est formidable. That was brilliant."

"I can't believe I said that," Ryan said. "It just came out. I'd never had any suspicion before. But his blue eyes, they were Ingrid's."

Jean-Robie slapped him on the back. "'Only the most daring cavalry officers fall from their horses.' That's what Napoleon said."

"Sounds more like a Kevin Costner line to me," Ryan noted.

"Again, thank you Monsieur Hackbart. You have invigorated the life of a humble hotel employee. Every day I dream of doing heroic things. Usually my only task is to listen to Americans complain that the hotel has no organic beefsteak. Or answer all day long their bourgeois questions: 'Where is the Starbucks? Where can I get a kosher pickle?'"

As Jean-Robie returned to the Carlton's concierge desk, a pair of arms clasped Ryan from behind. "Sweetie, you look scary. Are you okay?" Delisha asked.

"I'm better than okay," Ryan answered. "I just discovered something unbelievable. I've got to call Tim at the office." He reached into his pocket for his cell. As he pulled it out, a red sunscreen packet fell to the floor. Delisha picked it up.

"Is this the sunscreen you were telling me about?" she asked.

"Yes."

"You don't mind if I take this, do you? The rays have been killing me." Delisha scrunched up the packet and sliced into it with her fingernail. She squeezed the contents into her left palm. She rubbed her index finger into the substance. "This is whacked!" Delisha exclaimed.

"What?"

"I don't know what it is, but this is not sunscreen," Delisha said. She waved her hands in the air, away from her body. "I need a bathroom."

"What's wrong?"

"This isn't sunscreen. It's cum," Delisha shouted. Hotel patrons stopped in their tracks.

"What are you talking about?"

She held up her palm to Ryan. "Look at this texture. Feel how slimy it is."

"It's probably European-style sunscreen," Ryan said.

"Well, look at you. You're red all over your face," she said. "One thing is for sure, this is not sunscreen. Where did you get this stuff?"

"You're not going to believe it," Ryan answered.

"Yes, I am too going to believe it," Delisha said. "I know exactly where you got it. You got it from that sick bastard Nick Steele, didn't you?"

"Yes, I got it from his medicine cabinet," Ryan said.

"That's his technique. He rapes women and then he plants the stuff from these packets on them. This is not sunscreen. It's semen!" Delisha snapped. "That's how he got off with raping Goldie. He planted some other guy's sperm on her. That's why the DNA didn't match his."

"But, where's he going to get another guy's sperm?" Ryan questioned.

"He could have gotten the sperm from his male porn actors. Collected their 'jizz'. I mean the honey girl would do it."

"Honey girl?"

"In the adult film world, the honey girls jerk off the actors before the sex scenes, so their jizz doesn't seep out."

Ryan examined her hand. The goo was certainly thinner than any sunscreen Ryan had ever seen. "But who would package this stuff for him?" he asked.

"He would have no problem with that. Those adult-film companies in the Valley have packaging plants on Rinaldi for their sex DVDs," Delisha said. Onlookers no longer pretended not to eavesdrop. Delisha reached into her purse and pulled out hand wipes.

Across the lobby, Ryan spotted Stan Peck. "Damn, just what I don't need," he said. "I need you to get rid of Peck."

Delisha spotted the scribe. "Oh, that horn dog. I'll do my thing." She flipped back her hair and sashayed straight toward Peck. Within seconds, Delisha maneuvered the journalist into one of the lounge chairs. She perched on the arm of the chair, leaning into Peck.

Ryan turned to exit, but he was hemmed in by the crowd that had gathered around him. Their cell phones snapped at him.

Chapter 17

The Victoria's Secret suite at the Carlton Hotel was stacked with boxes and posters. Remnants of parties – random pieces of lingerie, half-filled wine glasses, and empty Evian bottles – littered the room. Tall stacks of catalogs, left over from the fashion show, were scattered about.

"Nicole? Ro? Shan? Rita? Anyone here?" Delisha called out as she ushered Stan Peck into the suite. No models, only the furniture and the tracings of the lingerie goddesses. Delisha sauntered across the room, flipping her hair back and swinging her butt in the tightest, most provocative fashion.

"So, does Tyra Banks ever come here?" Peck asked.

"No, but some of the girls use it as a pit stop between parties."

"Did I tell you I did a phoner with Mick Jagger," Peck said.

"Cool, he's a singer, right?"

"Mick's going to produce Shakespeare, starting with Richard III."

"Is he going to put songs in it?" Delisha asked.

"I don't know. When I talked to him on my cell, he was a bit crazed," Peck said. "He kept trying to mimic blues lingo, kept saying 'cats' when talking about the actors. I know the Stones go way back in their musical roots to Muddy Waters and those old blues guys, but Mick seems like a bit of a nutcase."

"This festival makes everyone crazy," Delisha said.

"You've got to tell me what you know about this murder case," Peck said. "I have solid information that Ingrid Bjorge got her part by sleeping with Gunnar Sevareid. Not surprising, since she was once a stripper."

"What do you have against strippers?"

"Nothing," Peck answered.

"That's good," Delisha said. "Because if you had something against stripping, that would sure mess up my plans." Delisha opened a cupboard door, and grabbed two highball glasses and a fifth of Johnnie Walker Black.

"If that's real liquor, I'm in," Peck said. "I'm so sick of all this Bordeaux and mineral water. People here at the festival pay 10 euros for a six-ounce bottle of Coca-Cola. That's roughly 10 bucks!"

Delisha uncapped the scotch bottle and poured a generous four fingers into the glass. "Would you like a splash?" She stumbled and the glass flew out of her hand, straight at Peck. The liquor sprayed on his pants.

"Damn, look what you've done," Peck complained.

"Oh, I'm sorry. I didn't mean that kind of splash, I meant a splash of water in your drink." She placed her right hand on Peck's upper thigh, rubbing the wet spot.

"Luckily, I can expense these," he said.

"You are ripped for a press person," Delisha said. "Most writers are flabby, but you're cut."

"I work out," Peck said. "And I have the same personal trainer as Oprah's executives at OWN."

"Get these wet pants off," Delisha demanded.

Peck pulled them down, wiggling out and revealing Transformers boxer shorts. "You've got to tell me what Ryan has been doing."

"He's been mainly doing it doggy-style," Delisha answered. "Plus, he's into spanking. He loves my butt."

"Not sexually," Peck said. "I mean what has he been doing professionally? Is he on to something?"

"Well, sex is the main thing he has been doing at this festival. The man is a sex-machine. None of the pro athletes I've been with comes close to Ryan in the sack. The man's a total freak, but right now I'm more interested in what you are going to do with your pants down," Delisha said. She poured Peck another glass of scotch. She pulled her blue scarf out of her purse. "Drink up. You seem stressed. I want you chill."

"I can get wild, with someone as sexy as you," he said. "When my story breaks, I'll be famous. I'll have a book deal and my own talk show. I could do a lot for you."

"I'll bet you could, but first I'm going to ravish you, Mr. Pecker."

"Peck. Stan Peck."

Delisha reached for his hand, fondled it, and slipped the blue scarf around his left wrist.

"Hey, what's this?"

"A little game I've got in mind for us. You'll like it." She tied his wrists together, yanked the knot tight. She picked up a pair of red mesh stockings from a nearby table. "Put this sexy thing on your ripe muscles." She reached down and began to knead the inside of his leg, just above the knee. Peck lifted his right leg, and she slipped the lingerie on his right foot, pulling it over the ankle. Delisha snuggled against him, pushed him farther out onto the balcony. As she positioned him against the rail, Delisha kissed him on the neck. She slid her hands down his arms, past his elbows, and curdled her fingers around his forearms. She wiggled into him, caressing his member with her left hand. With her right hand, she flipped the scarf over the balcony and looped a pretty knot. West Philly quality.

"Hey, you tied me to the railing!" Peck yanked, but the scarf did not give.

"I'll be right back." She dashed back into the hotel room, and returned with the bottle of Johnnie Walker. She splashed him again, sloshing liquor all over his body.

"Hey! Stop it! Enough is enough!"

"Oh, but you look so cute out here. I'll bet the neighbors upstairs think so too." Delisha pointed to a balcony where an older couple peered down. "Besides, I get off doing it in front of an audience."

"Come on. You've had your fun. Let me loose," Peck pleaded.

"You're right, but I tied such a good knot I'll need some scissors. Excuse me, while I go look for some, Mr. Peckerhead." She scooted back into the suite.

"Hey, hey, you can't leave me here! I'll get sunburned," Peck yelled. She came out to the porch with a tube of real sunscreen. "I've got just the thing for you.' She squeezed the cream onto her index finger. "Let me rub it on your forehead." He leaned back, and she reached over and began to spread the lotion: her index finger teased his forehead as she spelled out the word "SEX."

That should stand out nicely when the rest of his face turns red.

Delisha headed back into the suite, slid the glass door shut. Clicked the lock. Peck yanked at the scarf. Tried to free himself from the railing. "Hey, let me go! Untie me, you bitch!"

But Delisha did not hear Stan Peck's pleas. Inside the Victoria's Secret suite, she straightened her clothing, placed the scotch bottle back inside the cabinet. She rinsed the glasses and washed her hands again, still obsessed with the cum she had touched. As she left the Victoria's Secret suite, Delisha secured the door, placed the "Ne pas entrer" sign on the outer handle.

When the elevator door opened, and the handsome man held it for her, she smiled. In the tiny elevator, a beneficent spirit came over Delisha. She wouldn't leave Peck out there too long. He'd burn in the strong Mediterranean sun. Just long enough to get his face red, so the sun lotion could spell out "SEX." Then, she'd call the police and tell them a pervert was on the loose in the Victoria's Secret hotel suite. From her personal experience with the French police, Delisha estimated it would take Peck at least a day to get out of jail. And who knows, maybe he would soon be in a police van to Nice with a big friendly fellow-traveler.

She strode through the Carlton's luxurious lobby and out into the sunlight. Behind the barricades, a crowd of fans strained to get a glimpse of emerging celebrities. Several onlookers pointed their cells at Delisha, snapping away. She rewarded them with her glowing smile.

"You are one of the models, yes?" a man with a thick German accent called out.

"Yes, I am," she said. He thrust a pen and notebook at her. Delisha signed: "Naomi Campbell. Let's get naked!" Feeling even more artistic, she drew three big hearts around the signature. Always willing to help Naomi spread her brand. Delisha crossed to the center divider of the Croisette, barely glancing down at the purple and yellow pansies. It had been a stimulating afternoon, and, for the first time in days, Delisha felt relaxed. Keeping up with Ryan was more than she had bargained for. She had underestimated him. That was new: she usually overestimated men. Maybe she had scratched Ryan off too early. No, he was a rebound; she was pumped on the hormonal stimulants of the south of France and the glamour of the film festival. She had gone down that road before, too many times. Taken in by the splendor and the ceremony, and the man of the hour. Perhaps now she could finally get in some shopping on the Rue d'Antibes. Get her grandma back in Philadelphia something nice. Maybe even some cologne for Purvis. No scratch that – he was over. She'd find a nice guy for a change. Not just yet, though, after the festival.

The reflections of the flames from the stone fireplace flickered across the pink tablecloth, jabbing at the cutlery. Ryan and Ingrid sat side by side at Mashou, the venerable restaurant in the Old Town section of Cannes. On this rainy eve, the tables had been re-arranged to accommodate a large party, although it could hardly be called a party in terms of the solemnity of the gathering. The dinner was to celebrate Ingrid's return from the dead, but it was less lively than a wake. Talk was muffled. Gunnar Sevareid seemed distracted. Ryan counted ten chairs and nine people. The chair to the left of Gunnar Sevareid was empty.

As the fire crackled, a waiter placed a silver pail of vegetables in front of Gunnar Sevareid. Other waiters worked their way around the table, setting a bucket in front of every third guest.

"I still can't believe how you figured it out that Mr. Sevareid is my father," Ingrid whispered to Ryan.

"I surprised myself," Ryan said. "But when I saw his eyes, and I saw that same blue, the words shot out of me," he said. "I never even knew it until I heard myself say it."

"I have been making some phone calls to Norway, some of my mother's old friends," Ingrid said. "They tell me Gunnar Sevareid was frequently in Munkholmen on business and that he was often in Tromso. He obviously met my mother there."

"And your mother was beautiful," Ryan said.

"Yes, my mother was beautiful but suffered from emotional illness, and I fear my father has great-man disease – he is ruthless and loves only himself."

A woman with a lavender Hermes scarf draped over her head entered the restaurant and sat down in the empty chair next to Gunnar Sevareid. It was the BGK publicist, Susanne Clearidge. She spoke to Sevareid in hushed tones. A wine steward marched out from the kitchen, stopped next to Sevareid. When the Norwegian billionaire finally noticed him, he nodded a perfunctory acceptance without sniffing the cork. Throughout the five course dinner, a dead unease dampened the conversations. Even the overattentive waiters stayed away as much as possible.

Before the dessert, Gunnar Sevareid rose. He held up his wine glass, and Ryan noticed that his hand shook. "This is the best day of my life," Sevareid said. "It is the most joyous occasion because I can finally acknowledge and embrace the wonderful daughter I learned about too late in her young life."

The guests in turn, toasted with the Norwegian "skall."

Gunnar Sevareid continued to hold his glass aloft, but he could not go on. The billionaire slumped down in his seat. Ingrid gulped, and a tear trickled down her cheeks.

The call came mid-way through the dessert, twixt the lemon torte, the raspberry soufflé and the crème de menthe delicacies that no one was eating. The sharp beep, like a military order, unnerved everyone. Gunnar Sevareid picked up. He pressed the cell to his ear, and then the Norwegian billionaire dropped the phone onto the table. No one spoke.

"It is most troubling," he said. "Erik's DNA was on her body. Nothing from Jason Pinelli, but there was also another DNA in her private area," he said. Gunnar Sevareid cleared his throat.

He took a sip of water. He leaned forward and picked up his pink napkin, set it down, reached for the mustard container, and moved it.

He stood, pushing himself up to his full six-foot-five-inch dimension. "I have something to reveal tonight," he said. "It is something that has tormented me my entire life. The reporter at the press conference was correct. I do have Nazi blood in me. My father was an SS soldier stationed in Norway during the World War II occupation. At the time, Heinrich Himmler had implemented the Nazis' 'Aryan Supremacy' program." Sevareid paused and looked directly at Ingrid. "In propagating the Master Race, the Third Reich encouraged German SS officers to have sexual relations with blonde-haired, blue-eyed Norwegian women."

Ingrid clasped onto Ryan's hand. A waiter emerged, "Would anyone care for..." Ryan shot him a glance, waved him off.

Gunnar Sevareid continued. "From what I have learned it is most likely I was born in 1944, the offspring of a sexual coupling between an SS officer and a Norwegian secretary. But at birth I was, basically, a child of the Third Reich. I was baptized underneath a Nazi dagger. This dagger has hovered over me my entire life, like the Sword of, the Sword of... I can't remember the name." He looked to Ryan.

"Damocles," Ryan said.

"Yes, thank you. My entire childhood was very harsh. I will spare you the horror. I was moved from a Lebensborn home – that's what they were called. They were in no way a real home, but, were a barracks for children born to SS officers and Norwegian women. I had many problems when I was young. I was called a Nazi bastard. His voice trailed off. "Finally, I was taken to an institution in the north of Norway, in Tromso. You could say I was abandoned."

Gunnar Sevareid took a long sip of water; his hands no longer shook. "In my midlife when I had attained more success than I deserved, I learned that I had fathered a daughter. It was with someone I had met during my younger years, my oil rig days." He looked directly at Ingrid. "When I found you just a few short years ago, and I learned of your hard life and your mother's illness, I wanted to make it up to you. I discovered you had dreamed of being an actress." He trailed off. "As is my blood curse, I overdid it. I thought that by making you a big movie star it would somehow overcome the years of..."

His voice trailed off. "Also, I adapted a son, Erik. No one outside of Erik and I know that we are not blood related," he said looking directly at Ryan. "That is why I could grant that he marry Ingrid. I knew they were not blood brother and sister." He slumped in his chair. Ingrid rose from her chair and approached her father. She took him by the hand and led him from the restaurant.

Susanne Clearidge dropped her cigarette on the cobblestone pavement outside the restaurant, and watched as rain droplets soaked it. The film critic and the publicist did not speak for a long minute. "Did you know anything about this?" Ryan finally asked.

"I sensed there was something in his background, but nothing to compare to what he just told us," she said. "My god, you never really know what people carry inside them."

"I read something about the Lebensborn program back when I was an undergrad at the University of Wisconsin," Ryan said. "There were roughly 12,000 of these children born in Norway during the War years that had been fathered by German SS. Now that they are older, some, like Gunnar Sevareid, have been coming out and talking about it. One of the ABBA singers did that. They had been persecuted and harassed all their lives by the other Norwegians. Their childhoods were awful."

"It certainly gives you perspective on all the daily irritations that we here at film festivals call crises," she said. "Trivialities, at most."

Ryan nodded his agreement. "Did you have to scrap your whole Ice Princess PR campaign?"

"No, ironically, all this madness made it easier. It sounds sick to admit it, but this murder, from a publicity vantage, was a gold mine," Clearidge said.

"If I were a conspiracy theorist, I would say the filmmakers staged Ingrid's death to salvage a bad movie by getting sympathetic publicity on the internet."

"You have an overactive imagination, "she said.

"I'm quite certain that Erik did not murder anyone," Ryan said. "After all, there was other sperm DNA on Goldie Jolie."

"She was a porn star. What do you expect?"

"Also, I still think someone from your office was privy to my review of The Ice Princess."

"I doubt that," she said. Clearidge lit a cigarette and coughed. "I never touch these things. The last time I had one was three Cannes ago."

"People from our office who don't smoke are smoking here too," Ryan said.

"Is this Henri a temporary employee of your paper?" she asked.

"Yes, he works for us just here at Cannes. I think it's his fourth festival for us," Ryan answered. "He paves the way through the French, cuts the red tape, runs the errands, and calls the right people. He's our fixer. Everyone in our office loves him."

"It's amazing how at a festival like Cannes, it's always the interns, the temporary help or the new people who seem to run things," Clearidge said. "People who know the least about what they're doing – have never been to this festival, or any festival – are running the show."

"Tail wagging the dog," Ryan said. "How will you handle announcing Ingrid's being alive to the press?"

"I haven't figured that one out yet. Thank god this festival is nearly over."

"You could put her atop a donkey and have her ride down the Croisette," Ryan said. "You could plant the crowd, have people wave palm leaves at her and cry out in rapture."

"That's been done before," Clearidge said.

"And very successfully," Ryan said. "It certainly would make a great photo-op."

"It's a sick suggestion, which is why I like it," she said. "But, no thanks. I'm not about to procure a donkey at this time."

"You wouldn't have to get an actual donkey," Ryan noted. "You could get one of those Cossack horses and put big ears on him."

"You have a sick sense of humor," Clearidge said. "I knew there was a reason that I liked you."

They laughed and the rain picked up. The power publicist and the film critic ducked back under the awning. "I still think Nick Steele could have done it," Ryan said.

"You should let this thing go." Clearidge squashed her cigarette further into the pavement. "Besides, the police already ruled Nick Steele out."

"What? Since when?"

"The police also checked the sperm DNA against Nick Steele's DNA they got during his autopsy. Mr. Sevareid insisted that they do that, but there was no match."

"I have another theory," Ryan said. "Nick Steele has a history of rape. He got off back in Chatsworth with a rape when he was an adult video producer. A friend of mine told me he raped one of her friends."

"So?"

"I think Nick Steele, as well as his brother Boris, deposits other guys' sperm on his rape victims," Ryan explained.

"You're serious?"

"Yes. I dropped off a packet with Lt. Savin on my way to the dinner."

"A packet?"

"Yes, he stores the stuff in little packets that look like those ketchup/mustard things," Ryan noted.

"Now I know you've been watching too much CSI and have reviewed way too many mystery movies," Clearidge said. She poked her hand out from under the awning. The rain trickled on her fingers. She brush-kissed Ryan. "I should be going. And get some rest. You are sleep-deprived. It's affecting your mind."

Ryan watched as Hollywood's most powerful celebrity publicist disappeared down the wet cobblestone walk. Raindrops pattered against the old hard stone. A tiny woman huddled outside a souvenir shop. She shielded her head with that day's copy of *The Hollywood New Times.*

Chapter 18

High on a hillside on the eastern edge of Cannes, not far from the huge cross at the top, Asbjorn Magnusson emerged from a dusty blue Renault, its license plate caked with mud. Magnusson popped the trunk and removed a portable contraption. He found an open spot in the grass and assembled the object. It opened into an easel. It was a decoy in case any passersby wondered what he was doing, or a Google-in-the-sky spotted him.

The luxury area was awash with spring flowers, which lined impregnable walls and forbidding gates already camouflaged with bougainvillea. The foliage glistened in the late Mediterranean morning, cleansed by the prior evening's rain. The neighborhood was called Croix des Gardes hill – "hill of the cross" in honor of the giant cross that loomed above the city.

Magnusson peered down from the hilltop perch. He gazed out at a panoramic view of Cannes and the Mediterranean. In the opposite direction, snow-capped Alps glistened in the morning sunlight. All around him, the hazel green landscape was adorned with sculpted cypress trees and dwarf palms, garnished by a smear of mimosa, lavender, cactus, roses, and bougainvillea. It was a polar different setting for the prior assignment Asbjorn Magnusson had carried out for Gunnar Sevareid; on that day of howling wind and -40F temperature on the Norway/Russia border Magnusson had shot powerful tranquilizer into a sleigh-team of reindeer. With the animals unable to deliver transport them through the white-out hell, the sleigh of Russian soldiers surely did not survive.

Magnusson squinted in the sunlight and retrieved a canister from the trunk. He knelt down, opened the receptacle and pulled out the parts for a high-tech rifle used in the eastern Ukraine, the SGM 12.7. It had worked well against the Russians during Putin's assault on the country. With its many wooden parts, the weapon looked like a gentleman's collectible. But it was deadly and practical: the gun's muzzle brake reduced recoil. Magnusson appreciated the professionalism of his employer, Gunnar Sevareid, in supplying him with the perfect tools of his trade.

Magnusson assembled the weapon's components, ever wary of his surroundings. He studied the multicolored villa where his subjects were ensconced. It was painted in bright hues: purples, red, greens, and yellows. The garish paint job was out of character with the Mediterranean serenity of the luxurious Belle Epoque neighborhood. Not surprisingly, the villa perched just up the bend from a property owned by Papa Doc Duvalier's son, "Baby Doc," who had bought it after fleeing Haiti. Now, the luxury villa was serving as a dormitory for eight of the Cossacks.

Magnusson dabbed a globule on the easel: a sinister orange. He slashed away with his brush, inspired by the soft breeze and the glowing azure sea below. The hours passed, and he continued to paint. Finally, in early afternoon the Cossacks emerged from their dwelling. Eight of them. Just as he'd been told. They formed a semi-circle of pool chairs with one leader facing the group.

Magnusson raised the rifle. He pulled the trigger: One, Two, Three, Four, Five, Six, Seven, Eight. All dead, ensured by the hollow-point Ukrainian bullets. Magnusson fired one last bullet, straight into the pool.

They should find that.

Six minutes later on that splendid hillside, a cleaning truck arrived at the domicile where Magnusson had splattered his subjects. The truck proceeded through a security gate. Once inside the compound, two men in janitorial uniforms emerged from the vehicle. The two fish-gutters that Gunnar Sevareid had flown in from Norway did not waste any time. They assembled a party tent over the pool area, covering the bodies. When the bodies were out of view, they sloshed cleaning fluids over the kill-areas. Next, they removed tool boxes from their truck and embraced their task.

"Gimme dat!"

Ryan jolted. A green-haired woman with a ponytail hovered above him. She leaned into him and pulled off her top. She swirled her breasts, whipped them over his face and smeared her nipples on him. She pressed her right nipple against his mouth. She yanked off his shorts. Pushed his shoulders down, and groped between his legs.

She pawed at his member and rolled over. She heaved her body into the mattress, spread her arms out.

"Gimme dat!" Delisha screamed.

"What?"

"I be rollin'!"

Ryan opened his eyes. He was twisted and naked in the bed. Delisha stretched out, nude and splayed in a gymnastic form, grasping a pretzel-sized pillow. A pair of green panties lay in the corner. A shiny orange mini-skirt protruded from under the bed. Ryan spread his fingers. Stretched them. Clenched a fist. Sharp pain. His hands were tight and sore. He had kneaded, rubbed, tickled, pinched and massaged Delisha's back for over an hour. Ryan looked for his watch. It was on the floor. He picked it up. Nearly 7 a.m. Still early. He lay down next to Delisha, spooned her. Her hair was matted against her neck. The ponytail, laced with silver streaks, jutted out against the head board.

Ryan stretched in the narrow shower. His hand ached as he gripped the shower holder. The cold water pelted the top of his crown. He shivered, turned the shower off. He stepped out of the tiny compartment and reached for the towel rack, empty. The last towel was crumpled on the floor, amid a stack of others. A good sign: the end of the festival was near.

Delisha coiled in a sitting position on the bed and painted her toenails. "Sorry about popping in so unexpectedly," she said.

"I always love to see you, especially when you're ravenous."

"I just went crazy. It's been building up in me."

"You were great!"

"Thanks, Sweetie. You have really strong fingers, you know."

"It's all that typing." He raised his hands, and clenched them. "Where did you come from last night? It must have been some party."

"I took a Tesla."

"Okay, but from where?"

She laughed and shook, her hand jutting out from her toes. She examined the polish. "Now look what you made me do. It's all smeared."

"Sorry, but you said you came from somewhere in a Tesla."

"Not the car, baby. The pill. I came in on the pill."

"The pill? I'm not following you."

"Ecstasy, Sweetie. The pills now are branded. Everything is marketing. Some are Tesla, some are other corporate names."

"You're messing with me."

"When is the last time you've been in a club?"

"Not since my Glock has been in the shop," he answered.

She giggled and pulled her hands away from her toes. "You've got to stop making me laugh. Doing toenails is a very serious business. I'm all smeared again."

"So, you came directly from some club where you took an Ecstasy pill that is branded Tesla."

"You're just lucky I didn't take a Boeing. You'd still be doing my back. And then you'd have to be 24-hour man. Maybe longer."

"I wonder what Elon Musk thinks about this," Ryan said.

"Since you insist on speaking of cars, that big goon who was driving the Mercedes whom we messed up on the road – the Neanderthal with the three tatts that look like those nipples on the top of the Carlton – he was there too."

"Oh damn, did he see you?"

"No, it was too crowded. Besides, I wasn't wearing my green hair the night he gave us a lift."

"I'm just not crazy about the idea that he's up and around." Ryan said. "And, I don't have any green wigs to disguise me."

"Sweetie, I don't even think he looked at you that night. Remember that tiny silver outfit I wore? He was too focused on my boobs and my ass to even see you."

"Well, that's certainly believable," Ryan said. "I still don't know if I believe that Ecstasy pills now go by corporate names."

"You can Google it if you don't believe me. Or easier, you could just ask your office assistant, that French guy."

"Henri? He was there last night?"

"Yes, and this party was in that old warehouse that we ended up parking near that night in the Mercedes. Not only that, your guy Henri was dishing," Delisha added. "He was all over the place. He was charging 100 Euros a pill."

"And he was getting that?"

"Of course, it was that kind of crowd. Where are we? We're at Cannes, Sweetie. Who comes to Cannes? People with tons of money and who want to let loose. If it was me, I'd charge $200 a pill."

"You could get $300."

"You always say the sweetest things," she said. "Your writer friend, the old hippie one, was there too."

"What hippie, writer friend?"

"The older, gray-haired guy. He seems to know Henri."

"Oh, you mean Dennis Barlowe," Ryan said. "That would be his type of scene."

She pulled out a hand mirror and examined her eyes. "Do my pupils seem dilated to you."

"Yeah, they do."

"Darn, I've got a thing today, and some of these girls would definitely notice that I did some E. You don't have any sunglasses I could borrow for a while?"

"Yeah, I've actually got a bunch of them. He reached in the night drawer and pulled out a red plastic-rimmed pair."

"These are great! Did you get them on the Rue d'Antibes?"

"No, at a Thrifty Dollar back in L.A.," he said. "I always take a bunch of cheap pairs to Cannes because I'm always losing them or sitting on them. I lost a pair of really great Tom Cruise-type Ray Bans the first year I was here, so I've never worn expensive shades since."

She popped up from the bed and stretched her feet over the edge. "Well, on to more important matters. What do you think of my toes?" she asked.

Ryan glanced down at her shiny aqua toenails. "I'd like to suck them the rest of the festival," he said.

"Hey, no fair! I'm already super horny from that E. You can't be saying stuff that makes me even wetter!"

"What is the French word for 'bullshit?" Ryan asked.

"Bullshit," Henri answered.

"Well, then, bullshit." "No, it is true," Henri said.

"Don't lie to me, Henri," Ryan said. "You've been involved in pirating my review." Ryan leaned against a box in the reception area to The Hollywood New Times' hotel suite office.

"I must tell you, I am a good guy," Henri said. "I told everything to Bernie, and he has spoken with Mr. Woolsey."

"All these photos you take; do you have an assistant or someone else who takes the photos if you can't be in two places at once?" Ryan asked.

"No, I take them all. I would never submit someone else's photo for mine. Would you let someone else see a movie for you, and write up the review and put your name on it?"

"I see your point," Ryan said. "You seem to have become tight with both Boris and Nick when he was alive," Ryan said.

"I do some work for their company," he said. "I've got to make a living too. The last couple years I have been helping out here with certain things."

"Nick and Boris Steele paid you to be a spy inside The Hollywood New Times, find out things, steal things, get their pictures in the paper, didn't they?"

"I would not say it like that," Henri protested.

"You peddle reviews before they are printed. Nick hired you to steal my Ice Princess jump drive, didn't he?"

"You have no proof of that. Who would believe you? Nick is not around to stand up for his good name."

"And you just gave it to Giselle later as an afterthought, to get into her pants," Ryan said.

"I do not need to do deceitful things to get women," Henri answered.

Ryan glanced around, confirmed that no one else was around. "If I don't get some answers from you, the police will," Ryan said. "Your ecstasy-pushing career will be over."

"This I can tell you. Mr. Woolsey was very afraid that Dragan Dylko was working on an important story that would ruin his chances to get a job with the rich Russian."

"The 'Russian', meaning the billionaire, Nikita Besova."

"Yes, Mr Woolsey hopes to get a high position with the new studio Besova is building in Moscow. I heard him talk about it one night at the Eden Roc where he stays. I deliver packages and gifts and things he gets from studios and publicists and big movie producers. Very nice gifts that he does not want the rest of the paper to know about."

"And you found this out by overhearing him when you make deliveries?"

"He looks down on all people," Henri said. "He sees me as a little man, an office messenger. Also, he does not like you. He thinks you look good on the TV. He wants to be the big star on the TV."

"Okay, that is helpful. We can work together. Tit for tat," Ryan said.

"Tits, tatts? What are you talking about?"

"It's an expression meaning 'you do something for me, I do something for you'," Ryan said.

"So, it does not mean anything about tattoos on breasts?" Henri asked.

"What doesn't have anything to do with tattoos on breasts? What am I missing out on?" Tim Daniels asked as he entered the office.

"You didn't miss anything," Ryan said. "We were just kidding around." Tim handed him a pink slip of paper. "What's this? Am I being fired?" Ryan asked. He glanced at it and then realized it was one of the office's pink message pads.

"This message came for you earlier here. The French temp took it," Tim said. Ryan squinted at the little slip. It read: "No match. La Jal."

"That make any sense to you?" Tim asked.

"It means Nick Steele's DNA does not match the sperm that was found on the corpse. It, basically, rules him out as the killer."

"DNA? What's this all about?"

"The French police contacted the Comprehensive DNA Information Systems back in the states to get them to run through the crime scene DNA. That's the national database for DNA that the cops use back home. I don't know what "La Jal" means, though, if it's a person or a thing."

"Might be one of those rapper-type names," Tim said.

Pipes rattled. Water flushed. The bathroom door swung open. "Ryan, will you come into my office?"

It was Bernie. He did not look pleased. Ryan followed him into the little office.

"Close the door," Bernie said as Ryan entered his back office. "First off, I am glad to hear you are all right. I know you've been under a lot of pressure here."

"Thanks," Ryan said. "It's been a nightmare, still is."

"I'm going to get right to the point, because this isn't going to be pleasant for either of us. So let's get it over with."

"Shoot."

"I've been taking a lot of heat from Woolsey that you missed the Matt Damon movie review," Bernie said.

"I got my schedule mixed up with all the police and murder craziness."

Bernie waved him off. "Let me finish," he said. "Between you and me, you've stolen Woolsey's stage."

"What?"

"Everywhere he goes, Woolsey has people come up to him, and all they want to talk about is you," Bernie said. "Off the record, you know how Woolsey likes to be the center of attention, and with all the social media coverage you've been getting, there's no room for him. You've become something of a celebrity."

"Come on. Being a celebrity is nothing that I'm interested in."

"Another thing, people keep telling him what a great speech you gave on Truffaut at the Palais and how everyone is tweeting about it."

"The Truffaut speech was something I was forced into by circumstance," Ryan said. "Look, it's not my fault the police mistakenly hauled me in as a murder suspect. I didn't ask for this, and I've endured a lot of crap because of it. My life has been hell this whole festival."

"I know, but Woolsey's also steamed because you didn't do a story on this English producer who does Shakespeare."

"That's ridiculous. It's this nutty guy who dresses up cats in Shakespearean costumes."

"Nutcase or not, this guy has been giving Woolsey grief all week," Bernie added. "Look, I understand your position, but you've got to understand mine too. Woolsey has asked someone else to take over the reviews for the rest of the festival."

"What? I'm the head film critic."

"This isn't my decision. When we get back to LA, Woolsey wants to sit down with both of us and discuss the review situation."

"The review situation?"

"Look, I know you're a terrific reviewer. Personally, I think you're the best. As not just your boss but as a friend, it's in your interest to keep a low profile," Bernie said.

"So, you don't want me to review the closing night film?"

"No, the new guy has got it."

"Who is this new guy?"

"He's someone Woolsey met at on a media-law panel in Brussels," Bernie said. "Woolsey said, and I quote, 'he's really into film.'"

"Damn, this is outrageous. He's hired some 'film buff'?"

"Look, I hear you," Bernie added. "You're not hung over, are you?"

"No, why?"

"You keep wiping your forehead like you've got a headache."

"I think I am getting a headache. But it's not from any alcohol or drugs," Ryan answered.

"And clear out your mailbox. The temp has been complaining that it's overstuffed."

Ryan headed for the outer office, where the makeshift mailbox was located. His box was crammed and overflowing. One classy envelope stood out. Ryan's name was carefully scripted in a flowing grand-style. He slit it open. Inside, a stiff vanilla card read: "Mr. Hackbart, I must talk with you. I did not alter your review. Do not reply electronically. Select a time and place for us to meet. You are in very much danger. Sincerely, Dragan Dylko."

Ryan read it again. How long had that note been in his box? Ryan hadn't checked his mailbox since the beginning of the festival. Had Dylko been reaching out to him from the beginning? Perhaps Ryan had it all wrong about Dylko.

Ryan's cell phone blared the "Notre Dame Victory March." He picked up. "Did you get my message?" Lt. Savin asked.

"Yes, I'm surprised it wasn't a match with Nick."

"You did not get the second part?"

"What second part?"

"About the convict who is in prison in California now. His sperm DNA matched," Lt. Savin said. "The match comes from a man who is now in jail in Los Angeles." The message the temporary, French receptionist had written down now made sense to Ryan: "La Jal" was not her spelling of someone's name, but rather, was meant to be "L.A. Jail."

"That's incredible. The sperm is from a guy who wasn't even at Cannes," Ryan concluded.

"Yes, he wasn't here at the festival, but his sperm was," Lt. Savin said.

"Please tell me this guy was once a porn actor in L.A.," Ryan said.

We're checking into his background, but you've got to realize it is early morning in California."

"This means the sperm could have come from one of the packets," Ryan exclaimed. "Those sperm packets the Steele brothers used to cover their rapes."

"Yes, but this sperm did not have the same DNA we took from Nick Steele when we did the autopsy. The California prisoner and the dead producer's yellow packet do not match," Lt. Savin answered.

"I've got one more packet for you," Ryan said. "A red one."

"I don't understand," Lt. Savin.

"Nick used yellow, and Boris used red," Ryan said.

"I am not following you," Lt. Savin said.

"For some reason, they both had different ones, probably because of the fact that they were both active sexual predators," Ryan said. "I've a red one still in my room at the hotel, in the inside pocket of my blue sports coat. I'll call you in a couple hours."

"What?

"In addition, I found some torn cotton women's underpants in their medicine area. I suspect for good measure the murderer might have planted the panties at the scene. The cotton panties would have served the same purpose as a cotton swab," Ryan explained. "The Steele brothers smeared someone else's semen on the panties in case a vaginal examination didn't work."

"Yes, there were cotton panties at the murder scene," Lt. Savin said. "We need to talk."

"Sorry, I have to be at a party," Ryan said.

"What? You are going to a party when this investigation is at its peak?"

"A working party," Ryan said.

Chapter 19

Ryan ducked down to avoid the spray and bent his knees to cushion the boat's bouncing. Five other passengers, including three women in de rigueur black miniskirts. They huddled in the front of a tender, one of the rubber transport boats that whisked partygoers to the super-yachts anchored offshore. They bounced along the water toward the reconfigured Russian freighter that had been reincarnated as a luxury yacht. The high-tech monstrosity christened as the "Orgasmo" was docked about a quarter-mile off the Palais, just east of the promontory lighthouse. It was the setting for a festival finale party thrown by Hands-On and their Russian investor, Nikita Besova, who was reportedly worth upwards of $18 billion.

To say that the Russian billionaire had been drunk since the vessel had embarked for Cannes was an exaggeration: he had been sober for three days out of port. The last few days in Cannes were another story: some of the Cossacks had remarked that he was blasted enough to take command of a Russian nuclear submarine. Guests on the vessel rarely saw Besova since he had been holed up in his suite with prostitutes for most of the week.

The imposing vessel was intended to be the mother of all watercraft. The "Orgasmo" dwarfed all previous yachts that had sprouted up in the past several years. The looming super-yacht was outfitted with extended projections: it looked like a giant biblical ark.

To Ryan's film-critic eye, it resembled a shinier version of the ark in John Huston's dopey movie, The Bible.

The bow of the vessel was overrun with people outfitted in Old Testament regalia: shepherds with staffs, Romans with shields and swords, and exotic belly dancers in colorful neon-glow bikinis. Amid this religious splendor, the available Cossacks stood at attention, forming a phalanx for the arriving guests.

The deck was covered with a red carpet. A seven-piece band played famous movie themes. Amid a blaring rendition of The Guns of Navarone, a platoon of waiters in Roman Legion attire scurried about the deck, while multitudes of voluptuous women promenaded in seductive party clothes. A woman in a tight-fitting tunic grabbed Ryan. She sparkled with large gold-colored bracelets. "You don't recognize me with my clothes on, Mr. Hackbart," she said.

"Sorry, it's been a crazy week," Ryan responded.

"Veronica, from the Hands-on yacht shoot. Remember that day when you were doing the story on those two dirtbags?"

"How could I forget?"

"And remember I asked you about doing a sex video to launch my career. I was doing a raunchy cop shoot."

"How did the cop thing go?"

"I'll never work for those dirtbags again," she said. "They made us stay there all day, and only paid us half of what they said they would."

"The Steele brothers have a reputation for stiffing people," Ryan answered. She jangled the bracelets in front of him. "But I got even and took a bunch of stuff. These used to be handcuffs, but I had them separated by a fisherman. I thought they'd be the perfect bracelets for this party."

"What did you do for your cop video?"

"It was an S&M thing. I wore a cop's uniform and arrested this Asian girl, and then we went at it. Then a couple of other cop-actors arrested me, and I did blow jobs."

"And they were all wearing cop's uniforms?" Ryan asked.

"Right, but a lot edgier than the standard police uniform."

"Did they have gold and red trim on them?"

"Yes, how did you know?" she responded.

Ryan hugged her. "Thank you! Thank you!"

"For what?" she asked

"You just solved something important for me," he said.

"I'm glad, now don't forget about me when you get back to L.A." She hugged Ryan again, and sashayed off, her bracelet-cuffs jangling from her wrists.

Leonard Maltin had been right: actors in cop's uniforms. It was now obvious to Ryan that Nick and Boris had planned for their phony cops to kill him. They would have dragged him off somewhere, dumped his body. Made it look like a suicide, which would have been supported by the bogus note Ryan had found in his hotel bathroom. Case closed: Film critic killed star actress.

Ryan peered out at the great rubber, air-filled monstrosity that bobbed in the bay. It was a 30-foot bearded man in a toga. It was attached to a buoy. The toga-man hoisted a tablet in one hand and pointed a saber in the other.

Lauren Perrino huffed up next to Ryan, leaned out over the rail and pointed out to the inflated toga-man. “It’s impressive, isn’t it?”

“Well, impressive in the sense that the giant Pillsbury Dough Boy was impressive in Ghostbusters,” Ryan said. “But this guy out on the buoy reminds me more of John Belushi in his Animal House toga.”

“John Belushi would never play Moses, even if he were still alive,” Stan Peck called out as he approached. Peck was bedecked in a white tuxedo with his obligatory Hunter S. Thompson shades. A paisley bandanna covered his forehead. “If you hadn’t noticed, I got the Hands-On Bible story exclusively.”

“I can’t believe Robert Downey, Jr., would do a Hands-On movie,” Ryan said.

“Well, so far it’s just an agreement in principle, but Hands-On is prepared to come up with $35 million for him,” Peck added. “Besides, the project’s a sequel to The Ten Commandments, although they haven’t settled on a title yet.”

“That’s easy, The Eleven Commandments? Or, how about Mo’ Moses?” Ryan joked.

“Not even slightly funny,” Peck said.

“They’re doing it with their new classics division,” Lauren said.

“Hands-On Classics? That’s an oxymoron,” Ryan said.

"No, it's called Future Classics," Peck said. "By the way, Ryan, Boris confronted Woolsey yesterday about you. He said he's canceling all their ads with us."

"What's the difference? They never pay for them anyway," Ryan countered. "By the way, Stan, I like your new look. The bandanna works."

"Tell that black girlfriend of yours there will be payback," Peck snapped.

A woman in yellow veil and belly dancer costume swirled in front of Ryan. Her hips dipped. Her hair swirled, and her eye-slit gleamed. "Guess who I am?" she asked.

"You're the VHl version of Jezebel."

"I'm not sure what that means," Delisha answered, "but I'll take it as one of your odd compliments."

"They might be odd, but they're heartfelt," Ryan said.

Delisha pointed to the revelers: a menagerie of Cossacks, hipsters, Old Testament harlots, and, at the far end of the deck, a horse. "This is like that old movie you made me watch at the Nuart after we first met," she said.

"Yes, Fellini Week," Ryan answered. "The one we saw was Satyricon."

She pulled down her veil and escorted him to the railing. "So, back in L.A., we're still friends, right? What has happened between us was just a festival thing, right?"

"You know I'm always there for you," Ryan said.

"Just like a man," she said. "Who's been saving whose butt over here, anyway?" She kissed him on the cheek. "I've got to admit, you've tired me out, action-critic. The last few days with you have been whack."

"Delisha, I never would have made it through this festival without you," Ryan said. "We went viral, you know, on that microscooter chase. You in that burgundy lingerie."

"I've been getting some heat on that," she said. "The Victoria's Secret people are all upset. They are complaining about how it damages their brand."

"Some people just can't take a joke," Ryan quipped.

"I'd like to apologize for jumping you that night," she said. "I know I should have never taken a Molly. I'm not ever taking anything like that again. E is scary."

Ryan noticed a knife jutted out from her belt. "Is that the blade you took from the driver who tried to kill us?" Ryan asked.

"Yes, and it's great, pure titanium. I wish I had this back in the day in Philly," she said.

"Girl, you're not going to do anything rash here."

"No, I am going to have a good time, especially when I meet that shitbag rapist's brother Boris Steele." She patted the knife. "By the way, I looked it up. This is a Russian-made knife. Those three spire tatts on the dead guy, that's Russian mob for number of years in prison."

Ryan reached over and grabbed the knife. "If you want to get back at the Steele brothers, this is not the way to do it."

"He'll get off otherwise," she insisted. "Give that back to me."

"No, he won't get off. I promise," Ryan exclaimed. "I'm going to get him, and what I am going to do to him will be much worse than anything you could do with a knife."

"You promise? You'll give him what he deserves?"

"I promise," he said.

"I'm coming with you when you see him, though. That's not negotiable." She hugged him just as Peck and Lauren Perrino approached Ryan. "After this festival, I want my blade back," she said. Delisha flipped back her veil and slithered away. She blew Peck a kiss.

With a blast of Bill Conti's classic Rocky theme to propel him, a man in a tuxedo appeared at a microphone. "Please, please we will now have a twenty-one-gun salute, honoring this great man, Nicholas Steele," the announcer intoned. Cossacks marched in precision to the end of the ship. They pointed their rifles out to sea. Their firearms had been retrofitted by a special effects lab to only produce a shooting sound, but not to discharge ammo. Still, the "crack" of their guns shuddered like a snare drum, accenting the "thud, thud, thud" of the fireworks. From the sandy beaches, the cannon-like electronic gear on the music boxes shot blue laser darts across the early-evening bay. The band blasted into an upbeat tempo on the theme from Das

Boot, the haunting refrain about young German submariners sailing to their certain death in World War II.

The Cossacks plundered wooden crates on the deck that contained blue lingerie. The teddies, bras, panties, leggings and assorted delicacies fluttered around the deck. The Cossacks danced around with the goodies, swirling them aloft. The Cossacks romped with the porn stars, a la an end-of-world Saturnalia. Amid the revelry, drunken guests huddled against the far side of the ship, clutching wine glasses and teetering from the vessel's movement. Ryan savored the scene of drunken Cossacks, biblical figures and Roman soldiers, and belly dancers: The Bible as costumed by Frederick's of Hollywood.

Ryan needed to find Boris, and suspected he would be tucked away below in the bowels of the yacht. Ryan surveyed the deck, spotted the main stairwell to the downstairs area. He signaled to Delisha.

The gray metal stairway was narrow, steep, and low. Ryan ducked his head beneath the piping and lights. Delisha followed on his heels. They crept through a passageway that seemed more like an underground tunnel than a portion of a luxury yacht. Ryan hunched like a submarine commando. They inched toward a narrow door. It was flecked with chipped paint and long Russian words. Ryan pushed open the door. The room was jammed with electronic sound equipment and crammed with high-tech gear. Photos of naked women littered a glass desk.

The door slammed behind them. “What are you doing here?” It was Boris.

“I’ve found out some interesting things about you and your brother back in Chatsworth, and your porn videos,” Ryan said.

“We are into many creative endeavors,” Boris said. “We are a media conglomerate.”

“You’re a couple of sleazy guys who made a lot of money shooting porn. Now you are unlawfully distributing Ingrid Bjorge’s early movies,” Ryan countered.

“We own them,” Boris said. “We have her husband’s signature. Erik Bjorge has signed with us.”

“Ex-husband’s,” Ryan said. “But you don’t have hers. She owns half the rights. Your contract is no good without her signature.”

“We have her signature.” Boris removed an envelope from his coat pocket. “Here is a copy.”

“That’s not her real signature,” Ryan said.

“You are insane,” Boris yelled.

“I know it is not her real signature,” Ryan said. “That is the way she has learned to sign for autographs. It’s designed to be easy to write fast. Look at the way the “I” and “B” hook together. Her publicist, Susanne Clearidge, had her staff design that stylized signature for Ingrid to use here at the festival. This document you’re waving around is dated months ago, before she used her new signature.”

Boris glanced down at the contract copy. "You are a very mixed-up person."

"You tried to get her signature early on when you had Henri ask me to get her autograph for him. You needed to have a model for your forgery, Ryan said.

"If you ever say this again, I will sue you for slander, and I will sue your whole newspaper. I will bring all the forces of my legal department at you," Boris ranted.

"You just better pray you land in a dark awful prison somewhere before Gunnar Sevareid comes after you. He does not take kindly to people messing with his daughter," Ryan countered.

Boris froze. "What?"

"Gunnar Sevareid will go medieval on you," Ryan said, uttering one of his favorite Tarantino lines. "Not to mention what the Russians will do to you when they find out you have lied to them about the video rights."

"You are insane," Boris said. "I will get public opinion on my side with my Robert Downey, Jr./Bible movie, and I will stream her videos in all these foreign countries. With all these different legal systems, it will be impossible for the courts to decide anything."

"At this moment, the Cannes police are having those red and yellow packets of sperm you plant on your rape victims analyzed."

"What is this insanity you accuse me of?"

Delisha shoved Boris. "You had the male actors shoot their wads with the honey girls before they did their scenes," she said. "You collected their semen and planted it on the women after you raped them!"

"That is as preposterous as Gunnar Sevareid being the blonde slut's father,"

Boris shouted.

"The sperm you planted on the dead woman's body will match with a prisoner in the L.A. County Jail," Ryan said. "He is one of your former porn actors, isn't he? The name Sir Rico Bronco Rogers ring a bell?"

"This is too far-fetched for even one of those CSI shows," Boris said.

"You raped and killed a blonde woman who you thought was Ingrid Bjorge when she wouldn't sign your contract. You went to her room at the Carlton, but you did not know she had changed rooms because her father, Gunnar Sevareid, feared for her life," Ryan added. "You saw a blonde who was wasted, and you raped her."

"Why would I kill a blonde who isn't even the right one?"

"Because you said it yourself that day on the yacht, 'all blondes look alike.'"

"She was a good lay. But that's all I did," Boris said. "You'll never work in this town again."

Ryan laughed. "People don't say that anymore – 'you'll never work in this town again'." It's a cliché, like you."

"We have evidence that you killed Nick. You made him OD."

"What?"

"We have your fingerprints on his medication bottles. That day I caught you in our medicine cabinet on the yacht."

"Nick sent me there for sunscreen," Ryan said.

"When you went into our yacht bathroom, you loaded his prescription bottles with deadly pills. We have your fingerprints on the pain-killer bottle."

"That is such bullshit," Ryan yelled. Yet, he recalled touching one of the bottles and picking it up. He also remembered that he had pilfered a Vicodin for the headache he had from Jason Pinelli's sucker punch at the opening night party.

"And now you will have another murder on your hands," Boris ranted. "We have evidence of how you killed the Russian journalist Dragan Dylko because you claimed he changed your movie review. You left his body in the black Mercedes, but you accidentally dropped your purple bowtie in the trunk." Boris sneered at Ryan. "Vladimir!" Boris yelled. "Vladdy!"

A side door sprang open, and a monstrous Russian burst into the room. It was the Mercedes driver that Ryan and Delisha had beaten on the road. The brute glared at Delisha, lumbered forward, and hurled her against the wall.

"You will both be guillotined," Boris yelled. He pulled out a .38, and waved it.

He pointed the gun at Delisha. Ryan pulled out the titanium knife, and slashed it across Boris's neck. Boris staggered, lurched sideways, and the gun went off. Straight into the Russian's face. Flesh and bone particles scattered. Boris stumbled over the Russian, blood gushing from his neck. He grabbed his throat, staggered and fell to the floor. He coughed, gagging on his own blood. He convulsed, died.

Ryan and Delisha peered down at the two dead men. Finally, Delisha leaned over Boris, blood still seeping from his neck. "You got his carotid," she said to Ryan. "Nice work."

"Damn, I didn't mean to kill him," Ryan said. He looked down at the bloody knife in his hand.

"You had no choice. It was self-defense, and it was the right thing to do. You saved my life, Sweetie." Delisha took the knife from Ryan, wiped it down with her Ice Princess scarf, and positioned it in the Russian's hand. "Damn, that's an awesome sauce blade." She stepped back to assess the scene, took one last glance at the knife. "Hate to leave such a beauty, but the cops will now think they killed each other. We're off the hook."

"That works for me."

Ryan and Delisha scurried through the cramped hallway leading from Boris' office. Footsteps clanked above them. Stan Peck's voice reverberated against the steel walls.

"Oh, shit!" Ryan muttered. "Peck will tie us to the murders!"

Delisha pulled off her top, and slid out of her pants. "We've got to make it seem like we've been sexing," she said. She grabbed Ryan's zipper, yanked down his pants and wrapped herself around him.

Peck and two other men approached. They gaped as Ryan and Delisha dug into each other. "You two are disgusting," Peck said. "Have you seen Boris Steele?"

"Buzz off," Delisha yelled, "We're sexing here."

Peck's jaw dropped. He pulled himself back and hurried toward Boris's galley. Ryan watched him go and started to re-adjust his pants. "We're not done," Delisha whispered. "We've got to do this right. No one will suspect anyone involved with a murder would be having sex right outside the crime scene. We've got to keep going."

"That works for me," Ryan said. She pulled Ryan's pants down further, ripped off his shirt, and jerked her Jezebel costume completely off, revealing only her lacy Victoria's Secret bikini.

Seconds later Peck dashed back from the chamber. "Boris Steele has been killed," he shouted. "Did you two hear me? He's dead, some goon just killed him!"

"I told you to get lost! We're busy here," Delisha yelled.

"While you two have been out here rutting, Boris Steele has been murdered," Peck shouted. He snatched one last look at Delisha, and hurried away.

Delisha hugged Ryan, but he pulled away. "Girl, the police will be here any minute!"

"Even better!" she exclaimed.

Ryan and Delisha scampered up the narrow stairs. “I really had you there. You thought I wanted to put on a sex show for the cops,” she teased.

“I was up for it,” he countered.

“Liar,” she said.

They emerged from the stairwell. A shaft of blue light knifed across the water. The slashing strains of the guitar intro to “Layla” resounded on the yacht’s speaker system. Ryan and Delisha made their way through the party-goers.

The Cossacks, drunk out of their minds on the free booze, careened around the deck. Security officers hurried toward them, trying to break things up before they got completely out of hand. In the bay, the Robert Downey, Jr.-as-Moses balloon wobbled, and then wiggled free from its buoy. In one flatulent whoosh, the rubber figure popped up into the air.

“Robert Downey, Jr., is flying,” Delisha yelled.

The entire mass of revelers looked up to the sky. High above, Robert/Moses floated face-down, his arms spread out and his mouth agape. With a gold tablet extending from his left arm and his right arm with the saber pointed upward, Rubber Robert/Moses ascended languidly over the bay of Cannes. He fluttered, crisscrossed by the electric-blue laser lights.

The fireworks lit up the sky; it harkened to a military bombardment. An army of French National Police swarmed toward the stairway, rushing toward Boris’ office. Stan Peck sauntered over to them. "What happened down there?" Ryan asked. "You said something about Boris."

"You two just missed the crime of the festival, and I got all the details," Peck bragged. "There was this brute with tattoos who had a big knife in his hand. Boris's throat was slashed. He evidently shot the guy in self-defense. My story is exclusive."

"I can't wait to read it," Delisha said.

Chapter 20

The Palais windows sparkled with the flashes of cameras and cellphones. The red carpet sizzled in the glare of the klieg lights. The kettle drums of "Thus Spach Zarathustra" thundered across the spectacle. The crowd buzzed, eager for the arriving stars who would ascend the red carpet and enter the Palais. The final film of the Cannes Film Festival would soon screen. High above the entrance, a LED screen flashed a montage of the glories of Cannes red-carpets past – Cary Grant, Sophia Loren, Francis Ford Coppola, Francois Truffaut, George Clooney, Maurice Chevalier, Catherine Deneuve, Louis Malle – in tuxes and gowns.

Ryan ducked around the temporary, iron-bar fences that held back the crowd that had gathered. A squadron of dark blue vans lined up just east of the Palais. French national guardsmen smoked cigarettes and chatted, waiting for the real show to begin. With the French National Police, the Cannes Police, and private security contingents, that military-like presence had to be discouraging to anyone who would try to bolt onto the red carpet.

Some festival fans had been encamped on the sidewalk since the previous evening. They all hoped to get the best video of the major stars who would ascend the red carpet for the closing-night film. Others had arrived in the early morning, and had positioned lawn chairs behind the barred metal gates that served as human conduits, as well as protective shields, for the stars.

Ryan ducked under the iron bars, side-stepped, and jostled away from the hordes. The closing-night film was titled The Courtesan and the Monk. The film was co-financed by a number of European partnerships, an aspect Ryan suspected appealed to the festival selection committee: it would not detonate any nationalistic range-wars over its selection. The Courtesan and the Monk was directed by a young Mexican director "in the Dali-Bunuel tradition," and featured an international cast. Robert Downey, Jr., and Halle Berry had roles, but were not listed as the stars. "In the Dali-Bunuel tradition," clued Ryan to the fact the film was gory and bizarre. Another negative for Ryan, its running time was two hours and forty-eight minutes. More in the Terence Malick tradition, Ryan thought. He gazed out across the azure water and spotted darker hues of blue. Further out, purple ripples warned of coming winds.

Across from the Majestic Hotel, he angled toward the sea. He struggled against the waves of people who plowed toward the Palais. Ryan's cell pinged, a text that Ingrid had arrived for the event. He spotted a cavalcade of festival luxury vehicles, the Cannes insignia of the Golden Palm highlighting their windshields. He knew that Gunnar Sevareid would be in the first vehicle. He also figured that Ingrid would be further back in another vehicle. She would not exit until Sevareid, Erik and the entourage drew the paparazzi away. They would create a diversion; after all, no one knew yet that Ingrid was "alive."

Ryan watched as Gunnar Sevareid's security phalanx parted the paparazzi. All cameras and cellphones were pointed at them. As the sea of serpents departed, the door to the last security car opened and a man hunched out, followed by Ingrid draped in a blue towel. Her long, blonde hair sparkled. Ryan elbowed his way through the crowd, approached Ingrid. "Did you have a good time on the yacht?" she asked.

"It was a killer party," Ryan answered.

Ryan and Ingrid nudged past onlookers and jostled their way to the red carpet. Ryan displayed his Carte Blanc and Ingrid presented her Special Guest pass. The guard inspected Ryan's badge closely. He slid back the iron-barred gate and smiled. "It is a pleasure, Monsieur, to see you all dressed up," the guard said. "I have been watching you on the internet all week."

The guard gestured for them to proceed up the red carpet. Ryan squeezed her hand. "One, two, three, go," he said. They took their first steps in unison, landing on the red carpet in perfect sync. "We were lucky that he concentrated on me. He would have been in for a surprise if he saw who you were."

"Yes, I am lucky tonight," she said. "I won't have to be famous again until tomorrow."

They began the regal ascent up the red-carpeted stairs. The carpet was lined by photographers and TV news people. The camera flashes sparkled on Ingrid's azure gown. A diamond necklace glinted around her neck. Her blonde hair glowed, and the blue gown sparkled. White gloves covered her forearms. In her festival finery, Ingrid exuded a regal grace, like a true princess. She filled out the alluring strapless dress Erik Bjorge had designed for her to wear to the opening night premiere of The Ice Princess. Ryan pulled out a blue Ice Princess scarf from his tux pocket. He wrapped it around her shoulders.

"We must stop now," Ryan said. "Turn around and wave to everyone." They paused midway up the red carpet, and waved to the crowd of photographers and the screaming fans. The camera lenses pointed at them resembled gun barrels.

Ingrid clasped his hand, tighter. Ryan could feel her fingers through her glove, wet.

"You are as beautiful as the actress in The Ice Princess," a photographer called out. Ryan put his arm around her shoulders.

'I am so relieved," she said. "No one seems to recognize me with my long hair."

Down below, the crowd erupted into ear-splitting cheers and shrieks. A flurry of gendarmes surrounded a black Prius. The crowd roared, screaming and whistling. Robert Downey, Jr., stepped from the vehicle. The star was outfitted in a maroon tuxedo with an orange bowtie. Ryan and Ingrid paused to gape at the flurry below. A guard motioned to them. "Entrer, s'il vous plait, Madame and Monsieur. You must not block the entrance."

Ryan and Ingrid stepped into the theater lobby with its high ceilings, gorgeous chandeliers, and splendid windows. Ryan shuddered, recalling the morning he had been dragged through this same lobby and hauled unceremoniously down the red carpet. His festival had come full circle: dragged in shame down the red carpet at the start of the festival, and now, at its culmination, he had ascended it with the beautiful woman he was alleged to have murdered.

Someone reached out from behind and tapped Ryan on his right shoulder. Ryan whirled, still in survival mode. It was Halle Berry. "I'm sorry for intruding, but I couldn't help but notice your date's beautiful complexion," Berry said. She turned to Ingrid. "You have such beautiful skin."

"Thank you," Ingrid said.

"Another nosy question, what do you use?" Berry asked.

"Nothing really. I ate a lot of mackerel when I was growing up in Tromso," she said.

Berry nodded and glanced at Ryan. "I've seen you somewhere."

"That's possible," Ryan said. "I write for The Hollywood New Times."

Berry's jaw dropped. "Oh, my god, you're that guy," she said. "You're the critic. I keep seeing you on the internet."

"I confess," Ryan said.

"You're the guy with all these gorgeous women, but she's the same one," Berry exclaimed. "It's the same African-American woman but with different wigs and weaves."

Ryan put his finger to his lips. The star actress smiled and drifted back to her partner.

"So far, she's the only person who has recognized Delisha through all those wigs," Ryan said.

"Women look more closely at other women than men do," Ingrid said.

"Well, maybe at their faces," Ryan added.

The Courtesan and the Monk dragged through its nearly three hours. Ingrid dozed intermittently. The film's long-anticipated ending inspired the predictable standing ovation. "I guess I would not be good at your job," Ingrid said. "You cannot fall asleep if you're a famous film critic."

"The trick is learning to sleep with your eyes open."

Roughly 100 National Guard stood erect as Robert Downey, Jr., emerged from the Palais. Hundreds of fans had waited in place through the grueling duration of the movie for the opportunity to see the star one more time. Downey's maroon tux gleamed in the flood of lights. He waved to the crowd. In perfect synchronicity, as if planned, the giant rubberized Robert Downey, Jr., wobbled over the Palais. Rubber-inflated Downey, Jr., in biblical garb, fluttered straight up into the evening blue of the Mediterranean sky, and hovered in a truly star-like turn. The gigantic figure trembled in the night breeze. Rubber Robert glided over the red carpet, his arms outstretched. The movie fan multitudes pointed their latest digital gizmos to the sky and snapped photos of the wobbling inflated Moses.

The crowd roared: “Ro-bairt, Ro-bairt, Ro-bairt!”

Ryan focused on the Trinitron screen, transfixed as light blue lingerie fluttered down toward the red carpet, onto the men in tuxedos and the women in their designer gowns. The crowd gasped. “C’est les terrorists!” one guard yelled. Everyone ducked for cover as the blue objects fluttered above.

“C’est lingerie,” a movie fan yelled. “Voici, lingerie. Le lingerie.” Revelers grabbed the lacy blue delicacies and waved them aloft, as if in triumph. Rubber-Robert dropped more lingerie on the throng. It was the missing Ice Princess fashion line that was to have been introduced at the festival. Still wary, the National Police scurried to pick up the slinky droppings. Finally, real Robert Downey, Jr., reached out and snapped up a light blue bra that wafted down from the sky. He waved it to the crowd. People scampered to pick up the blue booty. All around, hysterical movie fans elbowed and pushed each other, grabbing for the pieces of lingerie.

Ryan pulled out his cellphone and began to shoot, scoping for the full magnitude of the sexy manna dropping from heaven. He laughed and took Ingrid’s hand; it was limp. Sweat lined her forehead. “I am so glad this red carpet craziness is getting over,” Ingrid said. “I am not feeling so well.”

“Don’t worry, I see your security van and your father’s people.” He put his arm around her. Three Viking security guards from Gunnar Sevareid’s detachment appeared, formed a blocking wedge for them. They ushered Ingrid through the crowd, separating the masses of onlookers.

Ingrid wobbled as the Vikings guided her toward the Majestic Hotel. Gunnar Sevareid's security van waited out front. Before she got into the vehicle, she turned around, pulled back toward Ryan. She kissed him squarely on the lips. "Thank you! Thank you for saving me!"

Ryan lingered as Duane Allman's guitar wept "Layla" from the festival speakers, curdling under the stirring piano chords. He paused to savor the magic. Fireworks rained over the bay. The masts of the yachts glowed, like holiday decorations. The electric blue laser lights danced along the shore. Klieg bursts drenched the trees in shades of pastel. The treetops dazzled with kaleidoscopic swirls of pink, orange, and blue. In this magical moment of color, sea breeze and festival spectacle, Ryan peered up toward Le Suquet, the Old Town. High up over the stone twelfth-century castle, the full moon shone down on its medieval clock tower; the clock's arms now pointing straight skyward in a dramatic midnight position.

Ryan gazed further up at the dark blue sky. What was left of Rubber Robert/Moses leaned inland and popped toward the Hotel Splendid. Atop the hotel, as Rubber Robert/Moses floated inland, the neon blue lettering spelled out "S-P-L-E-N-D-I-D."

Ryan hurried toward the park that bordered the Palais. He had arranged to meet Delisha after the screening. He spotted her near the calliope. She too wore a light-blue gown, and had topped off her beauty with a blonde wig. "I would say you look like a movie star, but movie stars today do not have that Grace Kelly regal beauty that you have," he said.

"Thank you, Sweetie. I will have to Google this Grace Kelly woman you keep comparing me to," Delisha said.

"She was from Philadelphia, like you," Ryan said.

"Probably not West Philly, though."

"No, Main Line," Ryan answered. "Main Line and West Philadelphia, together at last."

"You're so sweet."

"She became the Princess of Monaco," Ryan said. "Tonight, you are the Princess of Cannes."

Ryan and Delisha hurried through the little park and past the giant calliope, heading toward the Croisette. Ryan cupped her waist. Energetic festival-goers hurried past them. From the park's winding pathway, Ryan and Delisha bounded onto the Croisette. A banner of colored lights extended high above – "Bienvenue, Festival du Film."

Ryan and Delisha ambled past the luxury shops: Givenchy, Prada, and Cartier. Reflections of people smeared the windows as they ran down the Croisette Boulevard, away from the Palais and the premiere. "I do not understand where this big rubber thing got The Ice Princess fashion-line," Delisha said.

"I can only guess some of it could have been stashed there by Nick and Boris, holding Erik's fashion line hostage by hiding it inside the rubber Robert Downey, Jr."

"That sounds completely whack, so it must be true.

As they dashed along the sidewalk lining the main hotels, the National Police and the white-shirted municipal police held the onlookers back. At festival's end, Ryan felt triumphant and, finally, safe. From nightmare to fantasy, Cannes had given Ryan the full festival E-ride.

Black luxury automobiles clogged the arched entrance-way to the Carlton Intercontinental Hotel. Security men and attendants blockaded the entrance as Ryan and Delisha bounded up the semi-circular drive. Jean-Robie Ginibre emerged. "Once again, I suspect you have had an eventful evening, Monsieur Hackbart," he called out as he embraced Ryan. In his best Maurice Chevalier, he kissed Delisha's hand.

"I know it's the grand finale night of the festival, but I need a room, if you've got one," Ryan said.

"Follow me," Jean-Robie said. "Once again, I am coming to the rescue for one of your impossible requests."

Delisha clung to Ryan as flashbulbs sizzled. With her arm tightly around his waist, they passed the reception desk. Delisha's azure dress clung to her in all the right places. Ryan strode with the dignified command of a gent born to wear a tux. The entire lobby gawked at them.

"I have a special corner suite for you, Monsieur Hackbart," Jean-Robie said. "I am bestowing on you Suite 623, the room you once told me was the site of your all-time favorite movie moment in To Catch A Thief." He ushered Ryan and Delisha to a private elevator as in-house security parted in their wake.

"I can't thank you enough Jean-Robie, for everything," Ryan said. "You must fill me in tomorrow on all that has transpired," Jean-Robie responded. "I have heard that Mr. Boris Steele was murdered."

"I heard that too," Ryan said.

"Well, it may be unkind of me to say, but I feel this festival is better off without him. Whoever did it has my thanks," he said.

"That's very kind of you to say," Delisha said as she squeezed Ryan's hand.

"How was he killed?" Ryan asked.

"They say he was stabbed to death by a Russian gangster," Jean-Robie answered.

"That sounds about right," Ryan said.

"I hope you tell your newspaper about my heroic participation for your paper's final festival coverage," Jean-Robie said.

"And not only will I make sure that they mention you, but I'll be sure they include the superfluous hyphen in your name," Ryan answered. Jean-Robie grinned and handed Ryan the signature Carlton room card.

Ryan wrapped his arm around Delisha's shoulders. She nuzzled against him as they exited the elevator and headed toward their suite. At the gold-handled door, Ryan snapped in the entry card. He pushed the door open. Delisha turned, facing him. As the evening breeze snuggled in across the room, Delisha wrapped her arms around him. Behind her, Ryan could see that the windows had been left open. The curtains fluttered in the evening breeze. Through the open windows, he could see the brightly lit yachts, and the blue-silver streams of lights. A grand eruption of pinks, blues, silvers, and greens sparkled across the sky.

The kaleidoscope of colors exploded as the fireworks shimmered down, and formed an aurora of magical brilliance. Ryan envisioned Cary Grant and Grace Kelly in To Catch a Thief at her doorway at the Carlton. In that incandescent flash of his mind's eye, that gloriously romantic movie moment was no longer an unattainable reflection for Ryan. Through the crazed magic of the Cannes Film Festival, Ryan and Delisha had morphed into the forms of Cary Grant and Grace Kelly. Ryan's all-time favorite movie moment from To Catch a Thief had entered into the frame of his own life – he in his black tux, and she in her light blue gown.

Chapter 21

The Last Day

"I am nervous."

"You're nervous? I'm nervous," Ryan answered.

"But I still am not used to the fact that he is my father," Ingrid replied. She had come to the luxury suite at the Carlton where Ryan and Delisha had celebrated the festival's grand finale. Ingrid had asked him to accompany her to a meeting with her father.

"I am so happy that you said you would come with me," she said. "He frightens me, and I don't know what is going to happen."

"Well, I usually don't have coffee this early in the morning with a woman that the press says I killed," Ryan said. "Not only with her father, but with her ex-husband, as well."

"Where is your beautiful friend?"

"I think she's loading her handbag with all the soaps and conditioners from the bathroom," Ryan said. "She's going to give them to her grandmother back in Philadelphia."

"I do like her," Ingrid said.

Ryan and Ingrid continued down the Carlton hallway toward Gunnar Sevareid's suite. Ingrid stopped at one of the doors, the entrance to the suite where the murder had been committed. She reached in her purse and retrieved a room card. She slipped it into the door slot and opened. "This is the room where I stayed when I first came to the festival, before Mr. Sevareid moved me." Ryan peered into the room.

"You cannot come in," a workman from inside called out.

"This is Ingrid Bjorge. She is the star of the opening night film and this was her suite," Ryan explained. The workman shouted excited French toward the bathroom. Ryan headed in that direction.

In the lavish bathroom, another worker hunched over. He extricated a tiny camera from the wall. It had been camouflaged, inserted into the center of a sunflower that was part of the wallpaper décor. Ryan bent over to examine where the micro-cameras had been hidden. He turned to Ingrid. "Your father clearly suspected something. He installed these cameras, even in the bathroom. If you were in danger, he would see. He did not trust just the usual Carlton security, however great that probably is."

"The cameras recorded me going to the toilet?"

"That wasn't their purpose. If someone would have wanted to kill you, the bathroom would be the place least likely to have cameras." He continued, "I found out that's where the murder took place of that woman who the killer thought was you."

Ryan's cellphone erupted again with the "Notre Dame Victory March." "Oh, my god," he said. "Oh, my god!"

"What?"

"Eureka!"

"What is wrong?" Ingrid asked.

"Nothing at all is wrong, something is finally right. I just figured it all out, who tried to kill you. And, I've got to say, 'Cheer, cheer for old Notre Dame.'"

"Hey, I guess you've come to appreciate your new ringtone." Dennis Barlowe called out to Ryan as he hurried toward him in the Carlton hallway. Barlowe's hair was mussed and his black sports coat was unbuttoned.

"Yes, very funny inputting the 'Notre Dame Victory March' as my ring-tone," Ryan said.

Barlowe grinned. "You must have had a really good night. You look especially dapper this morning."

"Even without my purple bowtie?" Ryan shot back.

Barlowe ignored the comment. "I need some coffee. I hear these Norwegians have strong stuff."

Ryan pushed the buzzer to the door of Gunnar Sevareid's Imperial Suite. Barlowe stood behind him. The same butler in the dark-blue suit opened the door. Ingrid approached from the side. "My father has brewed his most special coffee."

Ryan and Ingrid, followed by Barlowe, entered the main suite. Gunnar Sevareid rose from a caramel-colored chair. He sported tan slacks, dark-brown loafers, and a yellow knit shirt. "I hope you were able to rest well, Mr. Hackbart," Sevareid said.

"Yes, thanks."

"You have a very beautiful girlfriend," Sevareid noted.

"I can't say she's my girlfriend," Ryan answered.

"You should solve that problem, make her your girlfriend," Sevareid said. He glanced at Barlowe.

"I asked my old friend Dennis Barlowe to come here with me for this meeting," Ryan explained. "He's a journalistic colleague, and he always brings perspective."

"I see the fireworks must have kept you up all night," Sevareid observed.

"By the end of the festival, I always run out of clothes," Barlowe said.

"Would you like coffee?" Sevareid asked Ryan. "It is, perhaps, stronger than you are used to."

"No, thanks," Ryan said. "My friend will have some, though."

Sevareid nodded to a servant, then fixed his gaze on Ryan. "You have returned my daughter safely to me, and now you have saved Erik, who has been like a true son to me, from a murder charge," Sevareid said.

"Need anything else?" Ryan asked.

The Norwegian billionaire's stern countenance broke out into a smile. "I am coming to appreciate your American humor," he said. He pointed to the morning's Cannes edition of The Hollywood New Times. He picked up the paper, and read out loud: "Hands-On Cruises to Holy Land." Sevareid smiled and held the paper aloft. "Do you know this writer Stan Peck?"

"He's the poster boy for bad journalism," Ryan said.

"Through his lack of professionalism, your paper has bought into this whole phony narrative, that Hands-On is a thriving company, and that the Russians' attempts to get into the movie business are entirely honorable. At least, I hope you got right the fact that Boris Steele is, indeed, dead."

"Good riddance," Barlowe noted. "Plus, it's very likely that he killed the porn star Goldie Jolie."

"The murder of Goldie Jolie was the one crime he did not commit," Ryan said.

"What? You said yourself that he did it," Ingrid said.

"Yes, he did rape her. But that does not necessarily mean he killed her," Ryan said. He turned to Gunnar Sevareid. "You asked us all here this morning for a reason, other than to convey your muted congratulations to our paper, didn't you?"

"You have something important to say, I sense," Sevareid said to Ryan.

"I do have something to say, but it is difficult," Ryan said. "The fact is, Boris Steele is not guilty of the murder of the actress Goldie Jolie, who he thought was Ingrid. He is not guilty of murder."

"What?" Barlowe said.

"He didn't do it. Someone else murdered the porn star, Goldie Jolie. True, Boris Steele raped her and left. Later, someone else came in," Ryan said. "Someone who found the girl had been beaten and knocked unconscious. And the opportunity presented itself."

"I still don't understand," Ingrid said.

"Someone who knew she wasn't you, although she was in the room where everyone thought you were. By killing her, he would set up Boris for murder, and get rid of this woman who was going to fill in for Ingrid on those video tapes that Nick would sell to the world. He saw a golden opportunity to kill several birds with one stone."

"You are making everything so overly complex. It was a rape and murder," Barlowe said.

"Yes," Ryan said. "But not by the same person. And that other person also knew the room number that Ingrid had at the beginning of the film festival. Before Mr. Sevareid had her moved to another room for her safety."

"I am not sure I am following all this," Ingrid said.

"The killer had to know her room number or, at least, have access to it. And someone could have found out that information if he had access to Susanne Clearidge's public relations office. For instance, someone who had written the press kit for The Ice Princess," Ryan noted. "Also, the person who murdered Goldie Jolie had a huge financial motivation. He owed the Russian mob more than $500,000 for a bad sports bet on an NBA game. He had procured that betting money from Nick and Boris, who, of course, had gotten it from the Russians."

"You're really stretching something here," Barlowe interjected.

"I'm thinking of someone who needed the money desperately. The Russian mob is not a forgiving organization." He turned to Barlowe. "Someone who saw a golden opportunity to kill several birds with one stone: solve his debt problem, sell global rights to the story of the year. And, it was someone who had access to my Ice Princess review," Ryan said.

"That would have been Henri, and that Russian guy, Dylko," Barlowe said.

"True, but someone who had access to the original review. Someone who knew my password and could hack in as I was writing it on the plane to Cannes. I don't know of anyone other than you who has those cyber skills, my man."

"Hey, this is way too far-fetched," Barlowe said. "I think you're way stressed out."

"I checked it out," Ryan said. "It is possible to hack into a laptop computer even when it is on an airplane."

"I think I need some more coffee," Barlowe said. "I'm beginning to get lost in your brilliant but overwrought scenario."

"It's not overwrought at all," Ryan said. "In fact, it's rather simple. The motive was money. Money for someone who had just lost a huge sports gambling debt. Someone who bet the house on the Lakers to lose in the NBA semi-finals. Someone who thought it was a slam-dunk to bet against them because he had information that LeBron James could not play because of an injury. Someone who owed more than $500,000 on a gambling debt that was now held by the Russian mob."

"You're way out of bounds here, man," Barlowe countered. "Get some rest."

"I also have written proof." Ryan reached into his coat pocket and pulled out a piece of paper. "This is a print-out of my original review, as it was in my laptop. You will notice the word scrumptious is not in the original review, but it is in the published and internet version of my review."

Ryan reached down and picked up an Ice Princess press kit from the coffee table. He flipped to the costume design section. "'The scrumptious light blue lingerie is'...need I read more?" He turned to Barlowe. "You wrote the press kit for BGK. You never mentioned that Susanne Clearidge had hired you to write for them. You used that word and then you used it again when you altered my review."

"Hey, man. I can't believe what you're saying. So what if I used the word scrumptious. It's a fitting word. I'm not the only one who would use it to describe lingerie. Half the men in the world would."

"You have found the writing fingerprint, the DNA of the writing style," Sevareid said.

"Yes, every writer has one," Ryan said. "We fall in love with a word and overuse it. I am guilty of that, and my friend here, even though he is an excellent writer, committed the same stylistic crime. Fell in love with a word. His writing DNA matches."

"Come on, man," Barlowe said. "This is so crazy. Your brain is fried."

"And that night when I was so stressed out and called you, and we went back to your apartment, you lifted my purple bowtie. You then gave it to Boris to plant in the trunk of the car with Dragan Dylko's body. And that's where the police found it. You were setting me up for another murder. You knew that Dylko was going to come to me and explain that he didn't alter my review. That it was printed exactly as it had been transmitted from the plane. With your alterations, of course."

"That is ridiculous conjecture," Barlowe said. "You think a jury will believe that?"

"A jury does not have to believe it," Sevareid said. "It might never reach that far."

"Hey, come on," Barlowe pleaded. "You make these crazy accusations, and you threaten me with vigilante justice?"

"Call it what you like. Or, I could let my old friends the Russians handle it," Sevareid deadpanned. "For your information, we have the killer on camera."

"Well, I am sure your cameras have revealed someone who does not look like me," Barlowe said. "No way is my face on some security tape."

Ryan turned to Sevareid. "Did the killer have a mustache?"

"How did you know?" Sevareid asked.

"I know because I saw disguises in my so-called friend's apartment that night. After he had stolen my bow tie and loaded me up with some kind of medication, I came to. I looked for my bow tie and came upon all sorts of mustaches and make-up, and a couple of movie disguises. Did the killer also wear an Elmer Fudd-type cap?"

"Elmer Fudd cap? I do not understand," Sevareid said.

"A winter cap that covers the forehead and has ear flaps. It looks quite ridiculous."

"Yes, that is exactly the kind of cap he wore!"

Ryan turned to Barlowe and then back to Sevareid. "If you check out my ex-friend's apartment, you will find them."

Sevareid addressed Barlowe. "I will give you twenty-four hours as a gesture of compassion. We don't have to make the announcement for another day that Ingrid is alive," Sevareid said.

"This is such bullshit," Barlowe claimed.

"Bon voyage, Monsieur," Sevareid added.

Barlowe scrambled to the door. He called back to Ryan. "Call me when you get back to LA. We'll go to Starbucks on Montana. I hope I'm in a frame of mind by then to laugh this off. This is so bogus! Total bullshit." He slammed the door and left.

Gunnar Sevareid folded his hands together. He sat back and gazed out the window. No one said a word. Ryan could feel Ingrid go limp at his side. He reached out for her hand, clasping it. Gunnar Sevareid rose and walked over to the coffee urn, and poured another cup.

"Well, the question is, do we tell this to the police, or do we keep it in the family," the fourth richest man in the world said. Gunnar Sevareid took a sip of the strong Norwegian coffee. He savored the contents. "What will we say at our upcoming press conference?" he said to no one in particular. He strode over to the window and pressed a button.

A morning sea breeze fluttered in. Gunnar Sevareid turned and looked at Ryan. "Could I talk to you in private for a moment?" Ryan got up from the couch and followed the tall Norwegian into a sitting room. Sevareid closed the door and drifted to the far wall. He paused in front of one of the Picasso paintings, a jagged mélange of triangles and primary colors. "This film festival has been an eye-opening experience for an old man, who thought he had seen it all in his lifetime."

"It's been an eye-opener for me, as well," Ryan said.

"I realize from the little you know about me you must think that I am a despicable and heartless monster."

"I don't think of you that way," Ryan said.

The Norwegian smiled. "Well, I have been thinking of you since the other day. That was pure madness coming to my room like you did."

"I know," Ryan said. "I surprised myself."

"Crazy behavior is often what is needed. I applaud you for it," Sevareid said. "You are correct about me. I have done many ruthless things in my life. Everything you have heard is probably true. But there is one thing you must believe: I wish only the best for my daughter."

"I do believe that," Ryan said. "But, I still do not understand why you subjected her to this monstrous charade? Taking her from her life and making her a star?" Ryan asked. "You threw her loose into this crazy pit. Turned her over to media hyenas and fake-news wolves."

"I did not think of it way," Sevareid said. "I thought of the Cannes Film Festival as the greatest opportunity she could have. In a short time, she could catapult to heights my years of neglect had not allowed her to do." He turned and faced the Picasso, staring straight into a jumble of Cubist colors. "The hubris of an old man. I handle the darkest forces in the political and business world, so I had the vanity to think I could seize my personal life, as well. Clearly, I don't have many years left. I thought I could jump-start Ingrid's life by making her a famous actress, leaving her with some personal momentum."

"Your daughter is world-famous," Ryan said. "But that is not for her. Movies and celebrity are the worst thing she could have. Frankly, I think it would be a death sentence for her."

Sevareid nodded and turned to look at the Picasso once more, its bright, jagged lines erupting in a frightening chaos. "I have been looking for a successor for my movies."

"You're not staying in movies?" Ryan exclaimed.

"Only till I master them," Sevareid answered. "If I don't do something like movies, I might get bored and annihilate too many powerful Russians," he said. "Or, throw the political world into chaos. Start a war. In fact, I have already found a cause that I am willing to go to war for."

"What? You've got to be kidding!"

Sevareid set down his coffee cup, approached Ryan. "I have an offer for you. A generous offer," Gunnar Sevareid said. "I have come to know you well in the last few days. I have seen you under pressure, and I have seen the way my daughter has responded to you. You could do a lot for yourself, make an old man happy, and with your knowledge and love for the movies, well…"

Ryan laughed. 'Sorry, I don't mean to be disrespectful, but you are crazy."

"My being crazy is not exactly a 'scoop,' as you journalists would say it," Sevareid continued. "I am offering you the chance to change Hollywood, or whatever it is called now. To return it to the glory days. With my backing, you would have the resources, the power, and the machinery to make the kinds of movies that once delighted the world. Not the explosion and special effects monstrosities your country foists upon mankind today."

Ryan's imagination fast-forwarded: he was being offered a chance to play Walt Disney, Steven Spielberg. Move over James Cameron, he would be "king of the world." With Gunnar Sevareid's billions, Ryan could restore a town and the magic of once-proud studios that had been ravaged by foreign criminals, second-and-third generation screw-ups, piracy, the internet, iPhones, package-distribution companies, and MBA's.

"I appreciate the offer. I'm overwhelmed," Ryan said. "But my friend is right, my brain is fried. I need to soak my head in something."

"It's time to check-out, and you want to take a bath?" Delisha exclaimed.

"I've got some deep thinking to do, and a bath is the best place to do it," Ryan said. "Even though I've already had my Eureka moment for the day."

"Great, I'll help you, Mr. Archimedes," Delisha said. "See, I can quote smart stuff too."

Delisha pulled down her sweat pants and headed to the hotel suite's bathroom. Ryan followed and stripped down along the way. She turned on the faucet. "How did your meeting with the Norwegian producer go?"

"Well, the good news is we discovered who the killer is, and the bad news is we discovered who the killer is. It turned out to be my longtime friend Dennis Barlowe."

"Oh, Sweetie, I'm sorry. Are you sure it was him? He seemed so helpful all the time."

"That was just a clever ploy, pretending to help me find the killer. I now think he might have been responsible for other things as well."

"Really?"

"I think the other murders might be tied in," Ryan said. "The surprising thing is that his motivation really had nothing to do with the festival. He had a huge sports gambling debt, and had borrowed a ton of money to bet against the Lakers in the semi-finals. Someone he knew at UCLA Medical Center had told him that LeBron would likely not play for the rest of the series."

"So what did the Russians have to do with this?"

"Barlowe used his relationship with Nick and Boris Steele to get the money, which they had procured from the Russians. My buddy Barlowe was scared the Russian mob was going to kill him when he couldn't deliver on his bad bet."

"That's still no reason for him setting you up for murder," she said.

"I agree. In the end, he was willing to let me rot in a French prison or be executed for what he did."

Delisha tested the water. "Perfect," she said. They climbed in. The water churned and gurgled as they eased into the middle.

"I'm sorry there's no soap or bath oils. I already packed them for my grandma," she said.

"Who needs soap when I've got you to rub on?"

She splashed him. "You are always so bad."

"And you always lead me into temptation."

"I'm pumped about flying back to New York with you," she said. "How did you manage to switch your flight and get my ticket?"

"I'm going to be on Jimmy Fallon."

"No way," she exclaimed. "That's fantastic."

"It's true. Susanne Clearidge, the BGK publicist, set it up. Fallon probably owes her for all the celebrity clients she sends his way."

"My grandma says she saw you on TV in that balloon ride. She thinks you're very handsome. It was on E! or Inside Edition or one of those other celebrity shows."

"Well, at least now I guess it's better to be mistaken as a balloon adventurer than a murder suspect," Ryan said. "It's crazy, I've never been up in a balloon, and I obviously didn't kill anybody but those are the two things for which I'm now recognized."

"Well, my grandma thinks you're great."

"Just based on that balloon ride?"

"Well, I suppose she's read other things?"

"Well, the things written about me lately have all been crazy, making me out to be a murderer," he said. "Delisha, what have you been telling your grandma about me?"

"Nothing much, just things about the festival. Little things. We did a lot of stuff together."

"Delisha, you haven't been telling her everything?"

"No, of course not." She caressed him.

"Quit trying to change the subject," Ryan said. He whispered into her ear, "Delisha, what have you been telling your grandma about me?"

"Just the facts," she laughed. "I told her you're a really good writer."

"She likes me because you told her that I'm a really good writer?"

"Well, I told her some other things. That you know a lot about really old movies."

"And that's why she likes me, because I'm a good writer and know a lot about really old movies," he said. "Tell me what you really told her."

"Well, I can't remember them all. Little day-to-day things," she said.

"So, your grandma really likes me because I'm a good writer, know a lot about old movies, and she was fascinated by all our little day-to-day things?" He moved in closer, caressed her waist.

"You can't hold me like this and ask me all these questions," she said.

"Well, I'd like to meet your grandma someday."

"That's great because when we are in New York we could take the train to Philly. It's really easy."

"Oh, that was quick. You've been thinking about this before? Haven't you?"

"Well..."

"Now, let me get this straight, this is the same grandma who is always telling you to find a nice guy and settle down?"

"Umm..."

"And now she wants to meet me?"

"Well..."

"And is it safe for me to assume that your grandma might be kind of a matchmaker?"

"Yeah..."

"And she's the same grandma you said can be really bossy and always gets her way?"

"But..."

He kissed her and wrapped his arms around her shoulders. "This is beginning to sound like your grandma is hearing wedding bells, or rather, starting to ring wedding bells."

"Well...

"Delisha, did you also tell her that I'm in love with you?"

Delisha's jaw dropped. "Sweetie..." She nuzzled closer. "Well, do you want to take the train to Philadelphia or not?"

"All aboard!"

Chapter 22

Late Breaking Update

Stan Peck's story about the Cannes murders appeared the day after the festival ended in The Hollywood New Times. It concluded that producer Boris Steele had died while defending himself against a Russian criminal who had raped one of his actresses. It was picked up by CNN and MSNBC, who both trumpeted that it smacked of longtime "Russian collusion." It was subsequently picked up by BuzzFeed.

Based on information from a French waiter, The Globe ran a story that was headlined: "Incest at Cannes: Ingrid and Erik." The tabloid retracted the story after the Norwegian billionaire slammed them with a multimillion-dollar libel suit. In the following edition, the tabloid ran a six-page insert on the beauty of the Norwegian fjords and the fortitude of the Norwegian people, which perplexed its supermarket readership.

The reviews for Cannes' closing-night film, The Courtesan and the Monk, were scathing. The representatives of the US studios in attendance had no enthusiasm for it. "A foreign film with Halle Berry in it, and she's not even nude, how unprofessional can you get?" groused the acquisitions head of a package-delivery-carrier-turned-entertainment entity. Even France's Le Monde, a staunch defender of the festival, expressed disappointment, damning it with the faint praise of a "daring and courageous failure."

Delisha was courted by the Creative Artists Agency in Los Angeles, and signed a promotions contract. In a related matter, Victoria's Secret was deluged with orders of the burgundy lingerie that Delisha had worn during the street-chase that had gone viral; their website had temporarily crashed with the onslaught of orders.

The Defrocked Assassin, the Competition film celebrating the late Cuban dictator Fidel Castro, was presented with the Cannes Film Festival's highest honor, the Palme d'Or, by jury president Roman Polanski.

Stan Peck's exclusive about Mick Jagger producing Richard III ran on the front page of The Hollywood New Times. Jagger ridiculed Peck's story in London's Evening Standard. One day later, Keith Richards responded to a Rolling Stone query that Jagger wanted him to play King Richard. Richards surmised that Jagger must have meant he would play Little Richard and "not any guy from Shakespeare."

Robert Downey, Jr.'s lawyers filed a complaint in Los Angeles Superior Court against Hands-On Productions for, well, just about everything. Since Nick and Boris were dead and the company's books were indiscernible to government accountants, Downey received only positive publicity.

The photos of Ryan and Ingrid on the red carpet that the publicist Susanne Clearidge had orchestrated by leaking to a handful of favored journalists created a sensation. Ingrid was beautiful in the aqua blue gown, and with the added notoriety of her "rising from the dead," it catapulted The Ice Princess' fashion line into the sales stratosphere.

As a condition from Gunnar Sevareid, Dennis Barlowe gave up journalism and retired to Santa Fe, New Mexico, where he formed friendships with several retired TV comedy writers. Forty days after his arrival, Barlowe died of a heart attack, and his ashes were spread near Taos. Barlowe had written a pre-obituary for himself that appeared on his website, SinSpin. Ryan grinned when he noted that Barlowe had inserted the by-line of Joe Gillis, the failed screenwriter in Sunset Boulevard, on the obit. Prior to his demise, Barlowe had released one last shot, "a blog from the earth," as he deemed it. Ryan was pleased because it castigated The Hollywood New Times and Stan Peck for reporting "fake news" and Orson W. Woolsey for publishing it.

Gunnar Sevareid did not return to Norway after the festival but was rumored to have jetted to Astana, Kazakhstan, for a meeting with a Russian oil ministry executive. Tensions between the Russians and the Norwegians had escalated, and they were growing increasingly adversarial over Barents Sea mineral rights and the Russians dumping radioactive waste into the Arctic.

Ryan's flight back to Los Angeles was re-booked by The Hollywood New Times to stop off in New York so Ryan could do the The Tonight Show with Jimmy Fallon. The appearance had been arranged by Susanne Clearidge of BGK. Ryan was complemented with a luxury suite at Trump Tower, and Delisha accompanied him. The talk show host's banter with Ryan focused entirely on The Ice Princess lingerie line and Ryan's hot-air balloon adventure.

The day after Ryan's appearance on Jimmy Fallon, the New York Times Arts & Leisure Weekend section published a front page photo of Ryan and Ingrid ascending the red carpet and an accompanying story that was very accurate. The same day the New York Post ran a photo of Ryan and Delisha in her burgundy lingerie dodging pedestrians and an accompanying story that was less accurate but more true. Upon spotting the Post's sexy photo while shopping on Fifth Avenue for a gift for her grandma, Delisha howled with glee. She texted Ryan: "Sweetie, we did a lot of things in Cannes, but they don't have photos of the best ones."

While packing for his train trip to Philadelphia with Delisha, Ryan received a text from Gunnar Sevareid. It read that an important visitor was about to knock on the door of Ryan's luxury suite at Trump Tower. Simultaneous with Ryan's reading the text, the doorbell buzzed. Ryan hurried across the expensive Persian carpet and opened the door.

A tall man in a blue suit, starched white shirt and red silk tie stood before him. "Mr. Hackbart, I apologize for the abrupt intrusion, but we have some very, very important matters to discuss." The man thrust out his handshake and entered the room. He strode past Ryan to a mahogany table and moved a piece of Walpole china. He stood back, moved it again. He surveyed the room. He glanced at the ten-foot, floor-to-ceiling windows that looked down on Central Park and revealed the Manhattan skyline. "I'm glad they gave you this one," he said. He turned to Ryan: "Mr. Hackbart, your country needs your help."

Dammit! Now what?